TERANESIA

ALSO BY GREG EGAN

Quarantine
Permutation City
Axiomatic
Distress
Diaspora

Published by HarperPrism

TERANESIA

A NOVEL BY

GREG EGAN

HarperPrism

HarperCollins books may be purchased for educational, business, or sales promotional use. For information please write: Special Markets Department, HarperCollins Publishers Inc., 10 East 53rd Street, New York, NY 10022-5299.

FIRST EDITION

Designed by Jackie McKee

Library of Congress Cataloging-in-Publication Data

Egan, Greg, 1961–
  Teranesia / Greg Egan. — 1st U.S. ed.
     p. cm.
   ISBN 0-06-105092-X
   I. Title
  PR9619.3.E35T4 1999
  823—dc21   99-10583

99 00 01 02 03 ❖/RRD 10 9 8 7 6 5 4 3 2 1

Thanks to Caroline Oakley, Anthony Cheetham,
Juliet Ewers, John Douglas, Peter Robinson,
Kate Messenger, Diana Mackay, Philip Patterson, Ben Hall,
Russell Galen, David Pringle, Lee Montgomerie,
Gardner Dozois, Sheila Williams, Francis Lustman,
Ellen Herzfeld, Dominique Martel, Wolfgang Jeschke,
Bernhard Kempen, Pedro Jorge Romero,
Ivan Adamovic, and Carlos Pavón.

Chapter 1

The island was too small for human habitation, and too far from the commonly traveled sea routes to serve as a navigation point, so the people of the Kai and Tanimbar Islands had never had reason to name it. The Javanese and Sumatran rulers who'd claimed tributes from the Spice Islands would have been oblivious to its existence, and Prabir had been unable to locate it on any Dutch or Portuguese chart that had been scanned and placed on the net. To the current Indonesian authorities it was a speck on the map of Maluku *propinsi*, included for the sake of completeness along with a thousand other uninhabited rocks. Prabir had realized the opportunity he was facing even before they'd left Calcutta, and he'd begun compiling a list of possibilities immediately, but it wasn't a decision he could make lightly. He'd been on the island for more than a year before he finally settled on a name for it.

He tried out the word on his classmates and friends before slipping it into a conversation with his parents. His father had smiled approvingly, but then had second thoughts.

"Why Greek? If you're not going to use a local language . . . why not Bengali?"

Prabir had gazed back at him, puzzled. Names sounded dull if you understood them too easily. Why make do with a lame Big

River, when you could have a majestic Rio Grande? But surely his father knew that. It was his example Prabir was following.

"The same reason you named the butterfly in Latin."

His mother had laughed. "He's got you there!" And his father had relented, hoisting Prabir up into the air to be spun and tickled. "All right, all right! Teranesia!"

But that had been before Madhusree was born, when she hadn't been named herself (except as the much-too-literal Accidental Bulge). So Prabir stood on the beach, holding his sister up to the sky, spinning around slowly as he chanted, "Teranesia! Teranesia!" Madhusree stared down at him, more interested in watching him pronounce the strange word than in taking in the panorama he was trying to present to her. Was it normal to be near-sighted at fifteen months? Prabir resolved to look it up. He lowered her to his face and kissed her noisily, then staggered, almost losing his balance. She was growing heavier much faster than he was growing stronger. His parents claimed not to be growing stronger at all, and both now refused to lift him over their heads.

"Come the revolution," Prabir told Madhusree, checking for shells and coral before putting her down on the dazzling white sand.

"What?"

"We'll redesign our bodies. Then I'll always be able to lift you up. Even when I'm ninety-one and you're eighty-three."

She laughed at this talk of the metaphysically distant future. Prabir was fairly sure that Madhusree understood eighty-three at least as well as he understood, say, ten to the hundredth power. Looming over her, he counted out eight hand flashes, then three fingers. She watched, uncertain but mesmerized. Prabir gazed into her jet black eyes. His parents didn't understand Madhusree: they couldn't tell the difference between the way she made them feel and the way she was. Prabir only understood, himself, because he dimly remembered what it was like from the inside.

"Oh, you pretty thing," he crooned.

Madhusree smiled conspiratorially.

Prabir glanced away from her, across the beach, out into the calm turquoise waters of the Banda Sea. The waves breaking on the reef looked tame from here, though he'd been on enough queasy ferry rides to Tual and Ambon to know what a steady monsoon wind, let alone a storm, could whip up. But if Teranesia was spared the force of the open ocean, the large islands that shielded it—Timor, Sulawesi, Ceram, New Guinea—were invisibly remote. Even the nearest equally obscure rock was too far away to be seen from the beach.

"For small altitudes, the distance to the horizon is approximately the square root of twice the product of your height above sea level and the radius of the Earth." Prabir pictured a right triangle, with vertices at the center of the Earth, a point on the horizon, and his own eyes. He'd plotted the distance function on his notepad, and knew many points on the curve by heart. The beach sloped steeply, so his eyes were probably two full meters above sea level. That meant he could see for five kilometers. If he climbed Teranesia's volcanic cone until the nearest of the outlying Tanimbar Islands came into sight, the altitude of that point—which his notepad's satellite navigation system could tell him—would enable him to calculate exactly how far away they were.

But he knew the distance already, from maps: almost eighty kilometers. So he could reverse the whole calculation, and use it to verify his altitude: the lowest point from which he could see land would be five hundred meters. He'd drive a stake into the ground to mark the spot. He turned toward the center of the island, the black peak just visible above the coconut palms that rimmed the beach. It sounded like a long climb, especially if he had to carry Madhusree most of the way.

"Do you want to go see Ma?"

Madhusree pulled a face. "No!" She could never have too much of Ma, but she knew when he was trying to dump her.

Prabir shrugged. He could do the experiment later; nothing was worth a tantrum. "Do you want to go swimming, then?" Madhusree nodded enthusiastically and clambered to her feet, then ran unsteadily toward the water's edge. Prabir gave her a head start, then pounded across the sand after her, bellowing. She glanced at him disdainfully over her shoulder, fell down, stood up, continued. Prabir ran rings around her as she waded into the shallows, the soles of his feet slapping up water, but he made sure he didn't get too close; it wasn't fair to splash her in the face. When she reached little more than waist height, she dropped into the water and started swimming, her chubby arms working methodically.

Prabir froze and watched her admiringly. There was no getting away from it: sometimes he felt the Madhusree-thing himself. The same sweet thrill, the same tenderness, the same unearned pride he saw on his father's and mother's faces.

He sighed heavily and swooned backward into the water, touching bottom, opening his eyes to feel the sting of salt and watch the blurred sunlight for a moment before rising to his feet, satisfyingly wet all over. He shook his hair out of his eyes and then waded after Madhusree. The water reached his own ribs before he caught up with her; he eased himself down and started swimming beside her.

"Are you all right?"

She didn't deign to reply, merely frowning at the implied insult.

"Don't go too far." When they were alone, the rule was that Prabir had to be able to stand in the water. This was slightly galling, but the prospect of trying to tow a struggling, screaming Madhusree back to safety was something he could live without.

Prabir had left his face mask behind, but he could still see through the water quite clearly with his head above the surface. When he paused to let the froth and turbulence he was making subside, he could almost count grains of sand on the bottom. The reef was still a hundred meters ahead, but there were dark purple starfish beneath him, sponges, lone anemones clinging to fragments of coral. He spotted a conical yellow-and-brown shell as big as his fist, and dived for a closer look. In the water everything blurred again, and he almost had to touch bottom with his face to see that the shell was inhabited. He blew bubbles at the pale mollusk inside; when it cowered away from him he retreated sheepishly, walking a few steps backward on his hands before righting himself. His nostrils were full of seawater; he emptied them noisily, then pressed his tongue against his stinging palate. It felt as if he'd had a tube rammed down his nose.

Madhusree was twenty meters ahead of him. "Hey!" He fought down his alarm; the last thing he wanted to do was panic her. He swam after her with long, slow strokes, reaching her quickly enough, and calming himself. "Want to turn back now, Maddy?"

She didn't reply, but a grimace of uncertainty crossed her face, as if she'd lost confidence in her ability to do anything but keep swimming forward. Prabir measured the depth with one glance; there was no point even trying to stand. He couldn't just snatch her and wade back to the shore, ignoring her screams, her pummeling, and her hair-pulling.

He swam beside her, trying to shepherd her into an arc, but he was far more wary of colliding than she was. Maybe if he just grabbed her and spun her around, making a game of it, she wouldn't be upset. He trod water and reached toward her, smiling. She made a whimpering noise, as if he'd threatened her.

"Sssh. I'm sorry." Belatedly, Prabir understood; he felt

exactly the same when he was walking on a log over a stream or a patch of swampy ground, and his father or mother grew impatient and reached back to grab him. Nothing could be more off-putting. But he only ever froze in the first place when someone was watching him, hurrying him along. Alone, he could do anything—casually, absentmindedly—even reversing high above the ground. Madhusree knew she had to turn back, but the maneuver was too daunting to think about.

Prabir cried out excitedly, "Look! Out on the reef! It's a water man!"

Madhusree followed his gaze uncertainly.

"Straight ahead. Where the waves are breaking." Prabir pictured a figure rising from the surf, stealing water from each collapsing crest. "That's just his head and shoulders, but the rest will come soon. Look, his arms are breaking free!" Prabir imagined dripping, translucent limbs rising from the water, fists clenched tight. He whispered, "I've seen this one before, from the beach. I stole one of his shells. I thought I'd got away with it . . . but you know what they're like. If you take something from them, they always find you."

Madhusree looked puzzled. Prabir explained, "I can't give it back. I don't have it with me, it's in my hut."

For a moment Madhusree seemed about to protest that this was no real obstacle; Prabir could simply promise to return the shell later. But then it must have occurred to her that a creature like this wouldn't be so patient and trusting.

Her face lit up. Prabir was in trouble.

The water man lowered his arms and strained against the surface, forcing more of his body into existence. Bellowing from the pain of birth, baring glistening teeth.

Prabir turned a nervous circle. "I have to get away before his legs are free. Once you see a water man running, it's too late. No

6

one's ever lived to describe it. Will you guide me back to shore? Show me how to get there? I can't think. I can't move. I'm too frightened."

By now Prabir had psyched himself up so much that his teeth were chattering. He only hoped he hadn't gone too far; Madhusree could gouge agonizing furrows in his skin without the slightest qualm, ignoring his screams of protest, but she'd also been known to burst into inconsolable tears when anything else distressed him.

But she gazed at the water man calmly, assessing the danger. She'd been treading water since the creature appeared, and she'd already drifted around to face sideways. Now she simply leaned toward the shore and started swimming, all difficulties forgotten.

It was hard work feigning panic without overtaking her, when her arms were about a quarter as long as his own. Prabir glanced over his shoulder and shouted, "Faster, Maddy! I can see his ribs now!" The water man was leering angrily, already assuming a kind of eager parody of a sprinter's crouch. Rocking back and forth on the tips of his splayed fingers, he dragged more of his torso out of the waves. Prabir watched as the creature inhaled deeply, driving water from his lungs through his glassy skin, preparing himself for the world of air.

Madhusree was beginning to slap the water open-handed, the way she did when she was tired. Prabir suspected that he'd be able to stand soon, but it didn't seem right to intervene before he had to. "I'm going to make it, aren't I? I just have to breathe slowly, and keep my fingers together." Madhusree shot him an irritated don't-patronize-me look, and clawed the water in an exaggerated fashion before accepting his advice and powering ahead.

Prabir stopped dead and turned to examine their would-be pursuer. The last stage was always difficult; it was awkward trying to brace yourself as you dragged your legs up beneath you. Prabir closed his eyes and imagined that he was the water man. Crouching lower, forearms to the waves, he strained with his whole body until his muscles expelled a visible surge of brine. Finally, he was rewarded: he felt the warm air on the back of his knees, on his calves. His right foot broke free; the sole rested lightly on the surface, tickled by the choppy water as if each tiny crest was a blade of grass.

He opened his eyes. The water man was rising up, ready to spring forward, with just one foot trapped below the waves to hold him back.

Prabir cried out and started swimming after Madhusree. Within seconds, he knew the chase had begun. But he didn't dare look back: once you saw a water man running, you were lost.

The violence of his strokes made Madhusree turn; she lost her rhythm and began to flounder. Prabir caught up with her as her head dropped beneath the surface; he scooped her into his arms and reached for the bottom with his feet. His toes hit the sand with Madhusree cradled safely against his chest.

Running through the water was nightmare-slow, but he pushed his leaden body forward. He tramped right over a bed of brown sea-grass, shuddering with each step; it wasn't that the blades were sharp, or slimy, but it always felt as if something was hiding among them. Madhusree clung to him, uncomplaining, staring back, transfixed. Skin crawled on Prabir's scalp. He could always declare that the game was over, there was nothing following them, it was all made up. In his arms Madhusree was a passenger, immune to the rules, but if he turned and looked for himself now, the simple fact of his survival would prove beyond doubt that the water man had never been real.

But he didn't want to spoil the game for Madhusree.

His legs almost folded as he hit the beach, but he caught

himself and took a dozen more steps; just walking on dry land made him feel stronger. Then he crouched down and stood Madhusree on her feet before turning to sit facing the sea, his head lowered to help him catch his breath.

He was dizzy from the sudden end to his exertion, and his vision was marred with dark after-images. But Prabir was almost certain that he could make out a damp patch glistening on the sun-baked sand, one step beyond the water's edge, evaporating before his eyes.

Madhusree declared calmly, "Want Ma."

Prabir wasn't allowed inside the butterfly hut. Because the malaria vaccine didn't work for him, he'd had a pellet inserted beneath the skin of one arm that made him sweat mosquito repellent. The mere smell of the stuff probably wouldn't harm the butterflies, but it could affect their behavior, and any risk of serious contamination would be enough to invalidate all of his parents' observations.

He put Madhusree down a few meters from the doorway, and she waddled toward the sound of her mother's voice. Prabir listened as the voice rose in pitch. "Where have you been, my darling? Where have you been?" Madhusree began to deliver an incoherent monologue about the water man. Prabir strained his ears long enough to check that he wasn't being libeled, then went and sat on the bench outside his own hut. It was mid-morning, and the beach had grown uncomfortably hot, but most of the kampong would remain in shade until noon. Prabir could still remember the day they'd arrived, almost three years before, with half a dozen laborers from Kai Besar to help them clear away vegetation and assemble the prefabricated huts. He still wasn't sure whether the men had been joking when they'd referred to the ring of six buildings with a word that meant "village," but the term had stuck.

A familiar crashing sound came from the edge of the kampong; a couple of fruit pigeons had landed on the branch of a nutmeg tree. The blue-white birds were larger than chickens, and though they were slightly more streamlined in their own plump way it still seemed extraordinary to Prabir that they could fly at all. One of them stretched its comically extensible mouth around a nutmeg fruit the size of a small apricot; the other looked on stupidly, cooing and clacking, before sidling away to look for food of its own.

Prabir had been planning to try out his idea for altitude measurement as soon as he was free of Madhusree, but on the way back from the beach he'd thought of some complications. For a start, he wasn't confident that he could distinguish between the shore of a distant island and part of a cliff or an inland mountain, visible over the horizon because of its height. Maybe if he could persuade his father to let him borrow the binoculars he'd be able to tell the difference, but there was another, more serious problem. Refraction due to atmospheric temperature gradients—the same effect that made the sun appear swollen as it approached the horizon—would bend the light he was trying to use as one side of a Pythagorean triangle. Of course, someone had probably worked out a way to take this into account, and it wouldn't be hard to track down the appropriate equations and program them into his notepad, but even if he could find all the temperature data he needed—from some regional meteorological model or weather satellite thermal image—he wouldn't really understand what he was doing; he'd just be following instructions blindly.

Prabir suddenly recognized his name among the murmuring coming from the butterfly hut—spoken not by Madhusree, who could barely pronounce it, but by his father. He tried to make out the words that followed, but the fruit pigeons wouldn't shut up. He scanned the ground for something to throw at them, then decided that any attempt to drive them away would probably be a long, noisy process. He rose to his feet and tiptoed around to the back of the hut, to press one ear against the fiberglass.

"How's he going to cope when he has to go to a normal school back in India, in a real solid classroom six hours a day, when he's barely learned to sit still for five minutes? The sooner he gets used to it, the less of a shock it will be. If we wait until we're finished here, he could be . . . what? Eleven, twelve years old? He'll be uncontrollable!" Prabir could tell that his father had been speaking for a while. He always began arguments dispassionately, as if he were indifferent to the subject under discussion. It took several minutes for this level of exasperation to creep into his voice.

His mother laughed her who's-talking laugh. "You were eleven the first time you sat in a classroom!"

"Yes, and that was hard enough. And at least I'd been exposed to other human beings. You think he's being socialized properly through a satellite link?"

There was such a long silence that Prabir began to wonder if his mother was replying too softly for him to hear. Then she said plaintively, "Where, though? Calcutta's too far away, Rajendra. We'd never see him."

"It's a three-hour flight."

"From Jakarta!"

His father responded, quite reasonably, "How else should I measure it? If you add in the time it takes to travel from here, anywhere on Earth will sound too far away!"

Prabir felt a disorienting mixture of homesickness and fear. *Calcutta.* Fifty Ambons worth of people and traffic, squeezed into five times as much land. Even if he could grow used to the crowds again, the prospect of being "home" without his parents and Madhusree seemed worse than being abandoned almost anywhere else—as surreal and disturbing as waking up one morning to find that they'd all simply vanished.

"Well, Jakarta's out of the question." There was no reply; maybe his father was nodding agreement. They'd discussed this before: throughout Indonesia, violence kept flaring up against the ethnic Chinese "merchant class"—and though the Indian minority was tiny and invisible in comparison, his parents seemed to think he'd be at risk of being beaten up every time there was a price rise. Prabir had trouble believing in such bizarre behavior, but the sight of uniformed, regimented children singing patriotic songs on excursions around Ambon had made him grateful for anything that kept him out of Indonesian schools.

His father adopted a conciliatory tone. "What about Darwin?" Prabir remembered Darwin clearly; they'd spent two months there when Madhusree was born. It was a clean, calm, prosperous city—and since his English was much better than his Indonesian, he'd found it easier to talk to people there than in Ambon. But he still didn't want to be exiled there.

"Perhaps." There was silence, then suddenly his mother said enthusiastically, "What about *Toronto*? We could send him to live with my cousin!"

"Now you're being absurd. That woman is deranged."

"Oh, she's harmless! And I'm not suggesting that we put his education in her hands; we'll just come to some arrangement for food and board. Then at least he wouldn't be living in a dormitory full of strangers."

His father spluttered. "He's never met her!"

"Amita's still family. And since she's the only one of my relatives who'll speak to me—"

The conversation shifted abruptly to the topic of his mother's parents. Prabir had heard this all before; after a few minutes he walked away into the forest.

He'd have to find a way to raise the subject and make his feelings plain, without betraying the fact that he'd been eavesdropping. And he'd have to do it quickly; his parents had an almost limitless capacity to convince themselves that they were acting in his best interest, and once they made up their minds he'd be powerless to stop them. It was like an ad hoc religion: The Church of We're Only Doing It for Your Own Good. They got to write all the sacred commandments themselves, and then protest that they had no choice but to follow them.

"Traitors," he muttered. This was his island; they were only here on his sufferance. If he left, they'd be dead within a week: the creatures would take them. Madhusree might try to protect them, but you could never be sure what side she was on. Prabir pictured the crew of a ferry or supply ship, marching warily into the kampong after a missed rendezvous and days of radio silence, to find no one but Madhusree. Waddling around with a greasy smile on her face, surrounded by unwashed bowls bearing the remnants of meals of fried butterflies, seasoned with a mysterious sweet-smelling meat.

Prabir trudged along, mouthing silent curses, gradually becoming aware of the increasing gradient and the dark rocks poking through the soil. Without even thinking about it, he'd ended up on the trail that led to the center of the island. Unlike the path from the beach to the kampong—cut by the Kai laborers, and now Prabir's job to maintain—this was the product of nothing but chance, of rocky outcrops and the natural spacing of the trees and ferns.

It was hard work moving up the sloping ground, but he was shaded by the forest, and the sweat that dripped from his elbows or ran down his legs was almost chilly. Blue-tailed lizards darted rapidly out of his way, barely registering on his vision, but there were purple tiger beetles as big as his thumb weaving over one

13

fallen trunk, and large black ants everywhere; if he hadn't smelled as vile to the ants as the tiger beetles did to him he might have been covered in bites within minutes. He stuck to bare soil where he could find it, but when he couldn't he chose the undergrowth rather than volcanic rock—it was more forgiving on the soles of his feet. The ground was covered with small blue flowers, olive-green creepers, low ferns with drooping leaves; some of the plants were extremely tough, but they were rarely thorny. That made sense: there was nothing trying to graze on them.

The ground became increasingly steep and rocky, and the forest began to thin out around him. More and more sunlight penetrated between the trees, and the undergrowth became dry and coarse. Prabir wished he'd brought a hat to shield his face, and maybe even shoes; the dark rocks were mostly weathered smooth, but some had dangerous edges.

The trees vanished. He scrambled up the bare obsidian slope of the volcano. After a few minutes in the open, his skin had baked dry; he could feel tiny pulses of sweat, too small to form visible droplets, appear on his forearms and instantly evaporate. In the forest his shorts had been soaked through with perspiration; now the material stiffened like cardboard, and issued a curious laundered smell. He'd sprayed himself with sunscreen before leaving for the beach with Madhusree; he hoped he hadn't lost too much of it in the water. They should have added some UV-absorbing chemical to his mosquito pellet, sparing him the trouble of applying the stuff externally.

Come the revolution.

The sky was bleached white; when he raised his face to the sun it was like staring into a furnace—closing his eyes was useless, he had to shield himself with his arms. But once he was high enough above the forest to see past the tallest trees, Prabir emitted a parched whoop of elation. The sea stretched out beneath him, like the view from an airplane. The beach was still hidden, but he could see the shallows, the reef, the deeper water beyond.

He'd never climbed this high before. And though his family certainly hadn't been the first people to set foot on the island, surely no stranded fisherman would have struggled up here to admire the view, when he could have been carving himself a new boat down in the forest?

Prabir scanned the horizon. Shielding his eyes from the glare allowed enough perspiration to form to run down his brow and half-blind him. He mopped his eyes with his handkerchief, which had already been marinated in seawater and an hour's worth of sweat in the forest; the effect was like having his eyelids rubbed with salt. Exasperated, he blinked away tears and squinted, ignoring the pain, until he was convinced that there was no land in sight.

He continued up the side of the volcano.

Visiting the crater itself was beyond him; even if he'd brought water and shoes, the approach was simply too steep. On the basis of vegetation patterns in satellite images, his mother had estimated that the volcano had been dormant for at least a few thousand years, but Prabir had decided that lava was circulating just beneath the surface of the crater, waiting to break free. There were probably fire eagles up there, pecking through the thin crust to get at the molten rock. They could be swooping over him even as he climbed; because they glowed as brightly as the sun, they cast no shadows.

He stopped to check for land every five minutes, wishing he'd paid more attention to the appearance of various islands from the ferry; the horizon was such a blur that he was afraid he might be fooled by a bank of clouds, a distant thunderstorm approaching. He'd cut his right foot, but it wasn't very painful, so he avoided examining it in case the sight of the wound put him off. The soles of his feet were thick enough to make the heat of the rock bearable, but he couldn't sit to rest, or even steady himself with his palms.

When an ambiguous gray smudge finally appeared between the sky and the sea, Prabir just smiled and closed his eyes. He didn't have the energy to feel properly triumphant, let alone indulge in any kind of victory display. He swayed for a moment in the surreal heat, acknowledging his stupidity at coming here unprepared, but still defiantly glad that he'd done it. Then he found a sharp-edged rock and scraped a line at the place, as best he could judge, where the distant island first appeared.

He couldn't write the altitude; it probably wasn't all that different from the five hundred meters he'd naively calculated, but he'd have to return with his notepad to read the true figure off the GPS display. Then he could work backward to determine the effects of refraction.

The bare line wasn't enough, though. No natural markings on the rock looked similar, but it wasn't exactly eye-catching; he'd be pushing his luck to find it again. Carving his initials seemed childish, so he scratched the date: 10 DECEMBER 2012.

He headed back toward the forest in a happy daze, slipping and cutting his hands on the rocks twice, not really caring. He hadn't merely named the island, he'd begun to measure it. He had as much claim to stay as his parents, now.

The afternoon thunderstorm came from the north, behind him as he descended. Prabir looked up as the first swollen droplets splashed onto the rocks around him, and saw dazzling beads of white light against the clouds. Then the fire eagles rose up out of the storm, leaving the sky a uniform gray.

He tipped his head back and drank the rain, whispering, "Teranesia. Teranesia."

Prabir arrived back in the kampong around three. No one had missed him; when there was no school he went where he pleased, with his watch to call for help if he needed it. He was exhausted, and slightly nauseated; he went straight to his hut and collapsed into his hammock.

His father woke him, standing by the hammock in the gray light of dusk, speaking his name softly. Prabir was startled; he was supposed to help prepare the evening meal, but he could already smell it cooking. Why had they let him sleep so late?

His father put a hand on Prabir's forehead. "You're a bit hot. How are you feeling?"

"I'm all right, Baba." Prabir balled his fists to hide the cuts on his palms; they weren't serious, but he didn't want to explain them—or lie about them, if he could help it. His father looked unusually solemn; was he going to announce the decision to pack him off to boarding school, here and now?

His father said, "There's been a coup in Jakarta. Ambon's been placed under martial law." His tone was deliberately neutral, as if he were reporting something of no consequence. "I haven't been able to get through to Tual, so I'm not sure what's happening there. But we might not be able to bring in supplies for a while, so we're going to plant a small garden. And we'll need you to help look after it. Will you do that?"

"Yes." Prabir examined his father's half-lit face, wondering if he seriously expected Prabir to be satisfied with this minimal account. "But what happened in Jakarta?"

His father made a weary, disgusted noise. "The Minister for Internal Security has declared himself 'Emergency Interim Leader,' with the backing of the army. The president's under house arrest. Sittings of the MPR have been suspended; there are about a thousand people holding a vigil outside. The security forces have left them alone so far, which is something." He stroked his mustache, discomforted, then added reluctantly, "But there was a big protest march in Ambon when the news came through. The police tried to

stop it. Someone was shot, then the crowd started trashing government buildings. Forty-six people died, according to the World
Service."

Prabir was numb. "That's terrible."

"It is. And it will be the last straw for many people. Support
for ABRMS can only increase now."

Prabir struggled to read between the lines. "You think they'll
start sinking ferries?"

His father winced. "No, no! It's not that bad. Don't start
thinking like that!" He put a hand on Prabir's shoulder and rubbed
it soothingly. "But people will be nervous." He sighed. "You
know how whenever we want to go out and meet the ferry, we
have to pay the captain to make the detour? We're quite a way off
the normal route between Saumlaki and Tual; the money makes
up for the extra fuel, and the inconvenience, with a little left over
for every member of the crew."

Prabir nodded, though he'd never actually realized before
that they were paying bribes for a favor, rather than purchasing a
legitimate service.

"That could be difficult now. No one's going to want to
make unscheduled stops in the middle of nowhere. But that's all
right; we can get by on our own for as long as we have to. And it's
probably better that we make ourselves inconspicuous. No one's
going to bother us if we stay out of their way."

Prabir absorbed this in silence.

His father tipped his head toward the door. "Come on, you'd
better wash up. And don't tell your mother I upset you."

"You didn't." Prabir climbed out of the hammock. "But
where's it all headed?"

"What do you mean?"

Prabir hesitated. "Aceh. Kalimantan. Irian Jaya. Here." Over
the years, as they'd listened to the news together, his father had

explained some of the history of the region, and Prabir had begun to pursue the subject for himself on the net. Irian Jaya and the Moluccas had been annexed by Indonesia when the Dutch withdrew in the middle of the last century; both were Christian to some degree, and both had separatist movements determined to follow East Timor into independence. Aceh, at the northwest tip of Sumatra, was a different case altogether—the Muslim separatists there considered the government to be too secular by far—and Kalimantan was different again, with a long, complicated history of migrations and conquests. The government in Jakarta had been talking reassuringly about "limited autonomy" for these outlying provinces, but the Minister for Internal Security had made headlines a few weeks before with a comment about the need to "eliminate separatists." The President had told him to moderate his language, but apparently the army had decided that this was exactly the kind of language they liked.

His father squatted down beside him, and lowered his voice. "Do you want to know what I think?"

"Yes." Prabir almost asked, Why are we whispering? But he knew why. They were stuck on the island for the foreseeable future, and he'd had to be told something of the reasons why, but his father had been instructed, above all else, not to risk frightening him.

"I think the Javanese empire is coming to an end. And like the Dutch, and the Portuguese, and the British, they're finally going to have to learn to live within their own borders. But it won't come easily. There's too much at stake: oil, fisheries, timber. Even if the government were willing to walk away from the more troublesome provinces, there are people making vast amounts of money from concessions that date back to the Suharto era. And that includes a lot of generals."

"Do you think there'll be a war?" Even as he spoke the word,

Prabir felt his stomach turn icy, the way it did when he saw a python on a branch in front of him. Not out of any real fear for his own safety, but out of a horror at all the unseen deaths the creature's mere existence implied.

His father said cautiously, "I think there'll be changes. And they won't come easily."

Suddenly he scooped Prabir into his arms, then lifted him up, right over his head. "Oh, you're too heavy!" he groaned. "You're going to crush me!" He wasn't entirely joking; Prabir could feel his arms trembling from the strain. But he backed out of the hut smoothly, crouching down to fit the two of them through the doorway, then spun around slowly as he carried Prabir laughing across the kampong, under the palm leaves and the wakening stars.

Chapter 2

Prabir had stolen his father's life, but it was his father's fault, at least in part. And since no one had been deprived of the original, it wasn't really an act of theft. More a matter of cloning.

When Prabir had begged permission to start using their satellite link to the net for more than schoolwork, his father had made him promise never to reveal his true age to even the most innocuous stranger. "There are people whose first thought upon meeting a child is to wish for things that should only happen between adults," he'd explained ominously. Prabir had decoded this euphemism immediately, though he still had trouble imagining what harm anyone could do to him from a distance of several thousand kilometers. He'd been tempted to retort that if he pretended to be an adult there'd be even more people who'd want to treat him like one, but he'd had a sudden intuition that this was not a subject on which his father would tolerate smart-arsed replies. In any case, he was perfectly happy to conceal his age; he didn't want to be talked down to.

On his ninth birthday, when access was granted, Prabir joined discussion groups on mathematics, Indonesian history, and Madagascan music. He read or listened to other people's contributions carefully before making his own, and no one seemed to find his remarks particularly childish. Some people signed their posts with photographs of themselves, some didn't; his failure to do so gave nothing away. The groups were tightly focused on their chosen topics, and no one would have dreamed of straying into personal territory. The subject of his age, or what he did for a living, simply never came up.

It was only when he began exchanging messages directly with Eleanor, an academic historian living in New York City, that Prabir found himself painted into a corner. After two brief notes on the Majapahit Empire, Eleanor began telling him about her family, her graduate students, her tropical fish. She soon switched from plain text to video, and began sending Prabir miniature home movies and guided tours of Manhattan. This could all have been faked, but not easily, and it probably would have been enough to convince his father that Eleanor was an honest and entirely benign correspondent to whom Prabir could safely confess his true age. But it was already too late. Prabir had responded to Eleanor's first, written description of her family with an account of his journey from Calcutta to an unnamed island in the Banda Sea—accompanied by his wife and young son, for the purpose of studying butterflies. This exotic story had delighted her, and triggered a barrage of questions. Prabir had felt unable to refuse her answers, and he hadn't trusted himself to fabricate an entire adult biography, consistent with the things he'd already told her, out of thin air. So he'd kept on cannibalizing his father's life, until it became unthinkable to confess what he'd done either to Eleanor, or to his father.

Rajendra Suresh had been abandoned on the streets of Calcutta when he was six years old. He'd refused to tell Prabir what he remembered of his earlier life, so Prabir declared to Eleanor that his past was veiled by amnesia. "I could be the son of a prostitute, or the lost scion of one of the city's wealthiest families."

"Wouldn't wealthy parents have gone looking for you?"

Eleanor had wondered. Prabir had hinted at revelatory dreams of scheming evil uncles and fake kidnappings gone wrong.

Rajendra had survived as a beggar for almost five years when he first encountered the Indian Rationalists Association. (Outside the family—Prabir had had this drummed into him from an early age—the organization was never to be referred to by its initials, unless they were swiftly followed by some suitable clarifying remark.) They couldn't grant him the protection of an orphanage—their resources were stretched too thin—but they'd offered him two free meals a day, and a seat in one of their classrooms. This had been enough to keep him from starvation, and to save him from the clutches of the Mad Albanian, whose servants prowled the city hunting down children and lepers. Prabir had had nightmares about the Mad Albanian—far too disturbing to share with Eleanor—in which a stooped, wrinkled creature pursued him down alleys and into open sewers, trying to wash his feet with a cloth drenched in lamb's blood.

The IRA's avowed purpose was to rid the country of its mind-addling legacy of superstition, along with the barriers of caste and gender that the same gibberish helped prop up. Even before they'd begun their social programs—feeding and educating street children, teaching women business skills and self-defense—the Calcutta Rationalists had taken on the gurus and the god-men, the mystical healers and miracle workers who plagued the city, and exposed them as frauds. At the age of twelve, Rajendra had witnessed one of the movement's founders, Prabir Ghosh, challenge a local holy man, who made his living curing snake bites, to save the life of a dog who'd been thrust into a cage with a cobra. In front of an audience of a thousand enthusiastic believers, the holy man had waved his hands over the poor convulsing animal for fifteen minutes, muttering ever more desperate prayers and incantations, before finally confessing that he had no magical powers at all, and that anyone bitten by a snake should seek help from the nearest hospital without delay.

Rajendra was impressed by the man's honesty, however belated; some charlatans kept bluffing and blustering long after they'd lost all credibility. But the power of the demonstration impressed him even more. It was common knowledge that many snakes were not poisonous, and that a shallow enough bite or a strong enough constitution could enable some people to survive an encounter with a truly venomous species. The holy man's reputation must have flourished on the basis that he'd "cured" people who would have survived anyway—each success a joyous miracle worth trumpeting loudly, to be retold with embellishments a hundred times, as opposed to each sad and unsurprising death. But this simple trial had cleared away all the confounding issues: the snake was poisonous, the bites were deep and numerous . . . and the victim had died in front of a thousand witnesses.

In the minute's silence for the dog that followed, Rajendra had chosen his vocation. Life and death were mysteries to him, but no mystery was impenetrable. The earliest attempts to understand these things, he reasoned, must have foundered against obstacles that seemed insurmountable, leaving behind failed systems of knowledge to ossify or degenerate. That was the source of religion. But someone, somewhere had always carried on the search in good faith; someone had always found the strength to keep on asking: Are the things I believe true? That was the legacy he'd claim. Hindus, Muslims, Buddhists, Sikhs, Jains, Parsees, and Christians, from the most sincere self-deluding mystics to the most cynical frauds, could never do more than parody the search for truth. He would put the truth above every faith, and hunt down the secrets of life and death.

He would become a biologist.

Four years later, Rajendra was working as a bookkeeper in a

warehouse, studying in the evenings and helping out at the IRA school on Sundays, when Radha Desai took over the women's self-defense class. Each week he'd see her arriving, dressed in a plain white karate uniform, chauffeured by a man in his early thirties who was clearly not a servant. It took Rajendra a month to discover that she was neither married nor engaged; the chauffeur was her elder brother, and the only reason she wasn't driving herself was fear of the car being vandalized.

Prabir had trouble keeping a straight face when he described his parents' courtship, but he knew it was the kind of thing Eleanor would want to hear about, even if he was short of authentic details and had to improvise. In Prabir's version, Rajendra would synchronize the chants of his class of beggars reciting their multiplication tables with the shouts of Radha from the courtyard as she counted out push-ups and sit-ups, allowing him to hang on her every word without neglecting his students. And then just before lunchtime she'd walk right past his classroom window, and he'd stare at the floor, or feign a migraine and cover his eyes, lest their gazes meet accidentally and his face betray everything to the worldly children.

Prabir's mother described her parents as "upper-middle-class pseudo-socialist hypocrites." For their daughter to teach karate to Scheduled Caste women and brush shoulders with infamous atheists could be considered progressive and daring. To say that she'd married a bookkeeper three years younger than herself who'd fought his way up to live in the slums wouldn't have had quite the same value as a throwaway line at parties. His father was milder, merely saying that "given their background, what could you expect?"

Radha was studying genetics at the University of Calcutta. They'd meet secretly in parks and cafés early in the morning, before Rajendra started work—long before Radha's first lecture, but she always had the excuse of karate training. Rajendra was still struggling with high school biology, but Radha tutored him, and they set their sights on a distant goal: they'd work together as researchers. Somewhere, somehow. Prabir was confident that it had been love at first sight—though neither of them had ever said as much—but it was biology that kept them together, in more than the usual way.

Prabir snorted with laughter as he described clandestine meetings on park benches, hands fumbling with the pages of textbooks, recitations of the phases in the life cycle of a cell. But for all that it amused and embarrassed him, and nagged at his conscience now and then, he never really felt like a thief and a traitor as he gave away secrets that weren't his to give. Though all of this was supposedly for Eleanor's benefit, imagining his parents' lives became, for Prabir, something akin to staring into Madhusree's eyes and trying to make sense of what he saw. In this case, though, he had no memories to guide him, just books and films, instinct and guesswork, and his parents' own guarded confessions.

Rajendra won a scholarship to attend the university. With so many more opportunities to be together, they became less discreet. Their affair was discovered, and Radha left home, severing all ties with her family. She was still not qualified for an academic job, but she was able to support herself as a lab assistant. Four men ambushed Rajendra on the campus one night and put him in the hospital; there was never any proof of who sent them. When he'd recovered, Radha tried to teach him to defend himself, but Rajendra turned out to be her worst student ever, strong but intractably clumsy, possibly as a result of early malnutrition.

Lest Eleanor think less of his father for this—the whole question of exactly whose honor was at stake was somewhat blurred in Prabir's mind by now—he sent her a picture of

Rajendra in an IRA parade, dragging a truck through the center of Calcutta with a rope attached to his body by two metal hooks through the skin of his back. Not quite single-handed; a friend marched beside him, sharing the load. The visible tension in the ropes and the pyramids of skin raised by the hooks made it look as if both men were on the verge of being flayed alive, but they were smiling. (Smiling over gritted teeth, but anyone pushing a truck through the heat of Calcutta would have clenched their jaws as much from sheer exertion.)

A similar feat was performed as part of certain religious festivals, in which devotees would whip themselves into a frenzy of body piercing, hot-coal walking, and other supposedly miraculous acts of potential self-harm—protected by purification rituals, the blessing of a holy man, and the intensity of their faith. But Rajendra and his fellow human bullock had received no blessing from anyone, and loudly professed their complete lack of faith in everything but the toughness and elasticity of ordinary human skin. Positioned correctly, the hooks drew little blood, and a thick fold of skin could take the load easily, even if the tugging sensation was disturbing to the uninitiated. There was no need for "trance states" or "self-hypnosis"—let alone supernatural intervention—to block out the pain or stop the bleeding, and the greatest risk of actual harm could be eliminated by carefully sterilizing the hooks. It still required considerable courage to participate in such a gruesome-looking act, but knowing the relevant anatomical facts was as good an antidote to fear as any amount of religious hysteria.

Prabir spared Eleanor the picture of his mother with cheeks and tongue skewered, though like the hooks it was safe and painless enough if you knew how to avoid the larger nerves and blood vessels. The sight of his mother performing this exacting feat made Prabir intensely proud, but it also induced more complicated feelings. You couldn't tell from the picture, and she hadn't known it at the time, but on the day of the parade she was already carrying him. It added a certain something to his cozy images of amniotic bliss to see steel spikes embedded in the same sheltering flesh.

Rajendra had learned of the butterfly as he was completing his doctorate in entomology. A Swedish collector, in the country on a buying expedition, had come to the university seeking help in identifying a mounted specimen he'd bought in the markets; he'd been handed down the academic ranks until he'd reached Rajendra. The butterfly—a female, twenty centimeters across, with black and iridescent-green wings—clearly belonged to some species of swallowtail: the two hind wings were tipped with long, narrow "tails" or "streamers." But there were puzzling quirks in certain anatomical features, less obvious to the casual observer but of great taxonomic significance: the pattern of veins in the wings, and the position of the genital openings for insemination and oviposition. After a morning spent searching the handbooks, Rajendra had been unable to make a positive identification. He told the collector that the specimen was probably a mildly deformed individual, rather than a member of an unknown species. He could think of no better explanation, and he had no time to pursue the matter further.

A few weeks later—having successfully defended his doctoral thesis—Rajendra sought out the dealer who'd sold the specimen to the Swedish collector. After chatting for a while, the dealer produced another, identical butterfly. No fewer than six had arrived the month before, from a regular supplier in Indonesia. "Where, exactly, in Indonesia?" Ambon, provincial capital of the Moluccas. Rajendra negotiated the price down to something affordable and took the second butterfly to the lab.

Dissection revealed more anomalies. Whole organs were displaced from their usual positions, and features conserved across the entire order Lepidoptera were missing, or subtly altered. If all of these changes were due to a barrage of random mutations, it was hard to imagine how the creature could have survived the larval stage, let alone ended up as such a beautifully formed, perfectly functioning adult. You could expose generations of insects to teratogens until half of them grew heads at both ends of their bodies, but nothing short of a few million years of separate evolution could have produced so many perfectly harmless—or for all Rajendra knew, beneficial—alterations. But how could this one species of swallowtail have been isolated longer than any other butterfly in the world?

Radha carried out genetic tests. Attempts to determine the butterfly's evolutionary genealogy with standard markers yielded nonsensical results—but old, degraded DNA couldn't be trusted. Rajendra begged the dealer to try to obtain a living specimen, but nothing doing, that was too much trouble. However, he did reluctantly reveal the name of his supplier in Ambon. Rajendra wrote to the man, three times, to no avail.

By 2006, the couple had scraped together enough money for Rajendra to travel to Ambon in person, and he'd taught himself enough Bahasa Indonesia to speak to the supplier without an interpreter. No, the supplier couldn't get him live specimens, or even more dead ones. The butterflies had been collected by shipwrecked fishermen, killing time waiting to be rescued. No one visited the island in question intentionally—there was no reason to—and the supplier couldn't even point it out on a map.

"Fishermen from where?"

"Kai Besar."

Rajendra phoned Radha. "Sell all my textbooks and wire me the money."

With the help of the bemused fishermen, Rajendra collected dozens of pupae from the island; he had no idea what the chrysalis stage would look like, so he grabbed a few examples of every variation he could find. Back in Calcutta, fifteen of the pupae completed metamorphosis, and three yielded the mysterious swallowtail.

Fresh DNA only confirmed the old puzzles, and added new ones. Structural differences in the genes for neotenin and ecdysone, two crucial developmental hormones, suggested that the butterfly's ancestors had parted company from other insects three hundred million years ago—roughly forty million years before the emergence of Lepidoptera. This conclusion was obvious nonsense, and other genes told a far more believable story, but the discrepancy itself was remarkable.

Radha and Rajendra coauthored a paper describing their discoveries, but every journal to which they submitted it declined publication. Their observations were absurd, and they could offer no explanation for them. Most of their peers reviewing the work for the journals must have decided that they were simply incompetent.

One referee who'd read the paper for *Molecular Entomology* thought differently, and contacted Radha directly. She worked for Silk Rainbow, a Japanese biotechnology firm whose specialty was using insect larvae to manufacture proteins that couldn't be mass-produced successfully in bacteria or plant cells. Her employers were intrigued by the butterfly's genetic quirks; no immediate commercial applications were apparent, but they were prepared to fund some blue-sky research. If Radha was willing to send her DNA samples, and her own tests confirmed the unpublished results, the company would pay for an expedition to study the butterflies in the wild.

Prabir had pieced together most of this story long after the events had taken place—even when he'd been old enough to understand the fuss over the butterfly, he hadn't been paying much attention—but he could remember the day the message arrived from Tokyo, very clearly. His mother had grabbed his hands and danced around their tiny apartment, chanting, "We're going to the island of butterflies."

And Prabir had pictured the green-and-black insects by the millions, carpeting the ground in place of grass, nesting in the trees in place of leaves.

A month after the coup, Prabir received a message from Eleanor. He closed the door to his hut and lay on his hammock with his notepad beside him, turning down the volume until he was certain that no one outside could hear. The message was video, as usual, but this time Eleanor hadn't roamed the city with the camera, or even prowled her own apartment cornering her irritated teenage children. She simply sat in her office and spoke. Prabir felt guilty that he'd never been able to repay her in kind for the tours of New York, but if he'd owned up to having a suitable camera at his disposal it would have been impossible to justify the pure text messages that concealed his true age.

Eleanor said, "Prabir, I'm worried about you. I understand that you don't want to interrupt your work—and I know how difficult and expensive it would be to charter a boat now—but I still hope you'll reconsider. Will you hear me out?

"I've been looking at the latest State Department report on the crisis." A URL came through on the data track, and the software automatically attempted to open it, but the ground station in Sumatra through which Prabir was connected to the wider world was blocking the site. "Kopasus troops are being flown in to Ambon; I'm sure you know the kind of things they've been doing in Aceh and Irian Jaya. And you're in a typical hiding place for an ABRMS base; I know you're there with official permission, but if you're relying on bureaucrats in Jakarta to dig up the relevant file and instruct the army to stay out of your way . . . I think that might be a bit too optimistic."

Eleanor hunched toward the camera unhappily. "This isn't going to blow over in a month or two; even if the president is restored to office, there's almost nothing the government could do now to put things right. For the past sixty years, people in the provinces have tolerated rule from Jakarta so long as there was some token respect for the customary power structures, and some token spending on things like health and education in return for all the timber, fishing, and mineral rights being handed over to the cartels. But after fifteen years of austerity programs—with every spare rupiah going to subsidize the cost of living in the major cities, to stave off riots—the imbalance has become impossible to ignore. Forget religious and ethnic differences; the provinces have been bled dry, and they're not going to put up with it any longer."

There was more in the same vein. Prabir listened to it all with a mixture of unease and annoyance. His parents had decided that the safest thing to do was stay put, attract no attention, and ride out the storm. Teranesia had no strategic importance, so neither side had reason to come here. Who was Eleanor to think she knew better, from twenty thousand kilometers away?

Still, it was clear that she was genuinely worried about him, and Prabir didn't like to see her upset. He'd send back a confident, upbeat reply that would put her mind at ease . . . without casting doubt on her conclusions, or questioning her expertise.

Prabir pressed one foot against the wall of the hut and rocked the hammock gently while he composed his reply. He began by mentioning the garden, and how well it was doing, though in truth it was full of starchy native tubers that would probably taste like cardboard. "Rajendra is weeding it diligently every day. He's such a good boy!" He dictated the words to the notepad and it converted them into text; he'd almost patched the software to add random typing errors, but then he'd decided that even the oldest, cheapest keyboard-driven notepad would have corrected them as they were made.

He added a few vaguely positive words about "my work," but there was nothing new to report. His parents had gathered a wealth of data as they observed generation after generation of the butterfly in the setting that had, presumably, shaped its strange adaptations, but as far as Prabir could tell they were still no closer to an explanation. Nothing about Teranesia was wildly different from other islands in the region, and even eighty kilometers of water—and much less during ice ages—was no real barrier to migration on a time scale of tens of millions of years.

He left any mention of politics to the end, and ran through the words in his head a dozen times before committing a first draft to the notepad. He had to sound like his father, but firmer and clearer, so Eleanor wouldn't keep questioning his decision to stay. Instead of dismissing her fears that the worst might happen, he'd welcome the possibility with open arms.

"By the way, I checked out that State Department report you mentioned, and I agree completely with your analysis of the situation. The brutal, corrupt Javanese empire is finally coming to an end! Like the Portuguese, and the Dutch, and the British, they're going to have to learn to live within their own borders. And if they can't read the lessons of history, ABRMS is going to have to teach them the hard way.

"But please don't worry about me and my family. The army will never even think of coming here. We have all the equipment and supplies we need, so we can stay holed up here for as long as we have to. And it's not as if Radha and I have nothing to do! We'll continue with our work, until it's safe to leave."

Safe to leave? That wouldn't inspire much confidence. He

slid the cursor back across the screen with his finger. "Until victory is accomplished!"

Prabir hesitated. It still sounded a bit like whistling in the dark. He needed to sign off on a positive note, or Eleanor would think it was all bluster.

He closed his eyes and swung the hammock, sighing with frustration.

Then inspiration struck.

"As ever, your friend Prabir. Long live the Republik Maluku Selatan!"

Chapter 3

B e careful!" Prabir's mother shaded her eyes and looked up at him, shifting Madhusree to one side to free her arm. Prabir stepped off the ladder onto the gently sloping roof. There were no gutters, so there was nothing to stop him falling if he started to slide, but the surface of the photovoltaic composite felt reassuringly rough beneath his feet. The modified fiberglass gained efficiency from its lack of polish; the polymer strands could gather more light if they stuck out in random tufts.

Prabir crouched down slowly, legs spaced, balancing carefully. He'd managed to convince his parents that they were both too heavy to walk on the roofs of the huts, and though he'd been arguing entirely for the sake of doing the job himself, it seemed he'd been right: he could feel the panels flexing beneath his feet. They still felt springy, but it probably wouldn't have taken much more force to buckle them.

He shook the spray can and began to paint an *I*. His parents had argued it through the night before: no elaborate messages proclaiming neutrality, no Indian flag, no sycophantic declarations of loyalty to either side, no praise-be to Allah or Jesus. Just one word on every wall and every roof of every hut: ILMUWAN. Scientist.

The hope remained that no sign was needed. No one had troubled them so far, and since it seemed unlikely that their presence had gone unnoticed, perhaps their purpose was already known. Jets had flown over the island a few times, tiny soundless metallic specks, so small that Prabir could almost believe that they were just flaws in his vision, like the swimming points of distortion he saw when he stared too long into a cloudless sky. Whether they were scanning the island for rebel bases, or merely passing over on their way elsewhere, it was hard to feel threatened when all you could see was a glint of sunlight.

The whole Emergency was becoming like that: distant, hallucinatory, impossible to resolve in any detail. Their access to the net had been cut off since the beginning of February; presumably Jakarta had pulled the plug on the entire province. They could still get BBC shortwave, but the reception was very patchy, and there was only so much you could cram into an hour-long bulletin that covered all of East Asia. It was clear that the regional independence movements were taking advantage of each other's actions: the separatists in Aceh were now fighting government troops for control of the district capital, and in Irian Jaya the OPM had bombed an army base in Jayapura—an unexpected move from a group whose weapons were usually described as "neolithic." But while dramatic events like that made it into the bulletins, the day-to-day situation in Tual or Ambon never rated a mention. A web site in the Netherlands had been offering individual reports for every inhabited island group in the Moluccas, and its operators had successfully evaded the Indonesian censors with some fancy rerouting tricks, right up to the moment of the uniform blackout. Prabir's father had warned him that the site was probably run by expatriate ABRMS members, but Prabir didn't care. He wasn't interested in the voice of neutrality. He wanted a flood of propaganda washing over the islands, proclaiming bloodless victory to the rebels. He wanted everyone in Indonesia to talk themselves into believing that they could walk unharmed out of the ashes of the burning empire.

Prabir completed the final *N* and sidled back toward the ladder. The paint would reduce their power supply by about one-fifth, but with the satellite link switched off they'd still have enough to keep everything else running. As he approached the ground, Madhusree started wailing because she wasn't allowed to climb up and see what he'd written. His mother began fussing over her as if she were in genuine distress, cooing and stroking her brow. Prabir said mischievously, "She can do the next one. I don't mind. Would you like that, Maddy?" He gave her an aren't-you-adorable look, and she stared back at him in amazement, her bawling dying down to a half-hearted wheezing sound.

His mother said wearily, "Don't be stupid. You know she can't." Madhusree started screaming. Prabir moved the ladder over to the next hut.

"I wish you'd grow up! You're such a baby sometimes!" Prabir was halfway up the ladder before he realized that these words were directed at him. He continued on, his face burning. He wanted to shout back: *It was only a joke. And I look after her better than you do!* But there were some buttons he'd learned not to push. He concentrated on his sign writing, and kept his mouth shut.

When he came down, Madhusree was still whimpering. Prabir said, "She can help me do one of the walls."

His mother nodded, and stooped to put Madhusree down. Madhusree gazed resentfully at Prabir and clung on, sensing a chance to milk the situation further. Prabir gave her a warning look, and after a moment she changed her mind and waddled over to him. He handed her the spray can, then crouched behind her, guiding her arm while she squeezed the button.

"You know we almost sent you off to boarding school this year. Would you have liked that?" His mother spoke without a trace of sarcasm, as if the answer weren't obvious.

Prabir didn't reply. It was no thanks to her that he'd been spared; only the war had saved him from exile.

She said, "At least you would have been out of all this."

Prabir kept his eyes on the job, doing his best to compensate for Madhusree's enthusiastic random cross-strokes, but he thought back over the conversation he'd heard between his parents in the butterfly hut. It was true that his mother had suggested sending him to her cousin in Toronto . . . but that had only served to put his father off the whole idea, a response that might not have come as a great surprise to her. So maybe he'd judged her too harshly. Maybe she'd actually been fighting to keep him here.

He said, "If I was away I'd be worried about everyone. This way I know you're all safe."

"That's true."

Prabir glanced over his shoulder; his mother was smiling, pleased with his answer, but she still looked uncharacteristically fragile. It made him very uneasy to think that she might need reassurance from him. Ever since she'd gone soppy over Madhusree he'd longed for some kind of power over her, some means of extracting revenge. But this was too much. If an ill-chosen word could truly hurt her, it was like being handed the power to shut off the sun.

The sign on the wall resembled one of Prabir's attempts to write with his foot, but the word was recognizable. He said, "Well done, Maddy. You wrote *Ilmuwan*."

"Mwan," Madhusree declared confidently.

"Ilmuwan."

"Ilwan."

"No, *Il-mu-wan*."

Madhusree screwed her face up, ready to cry.

Prabir said, "Don't worry about it. We'll be back in Calcutta soon, and no one speaks Indonesian there. It's a language you'll never use again."

Prabir woke in the middle of the night, his stomach churning. He staggered half-awake to the lavatory hut. He'd suffered bouts of diarrhea ever since they'd started eating homegrown yams, but it had never woken him before.

He sat in the dark, with the door open slightly. There was a faint electrical hum from the treatment tank beside him. It took him no time to empty his bowels, but then he still ached, almost as badly. He was breathing strangely, much faster than usual, but if he tried to slow down that made the pain worse.

He washed his hands, then walked out into the middle of the kampong. The view through the gaps in the trees was like deep space. In Calcutta the stars had seemed tame, almost artificial— drab enough to pass for a halfhearted attempt to supplement the street lighting. Here there was no mistaking them for anything human.

Back in his hammock the pain refused to fade. He didn't need to vomit, or shit more, but his stomach was knotted with tension, as if he was about to be found out for some crime. But his conscience was no more troubled than usual. He hadn't teased Madhusree badly, or upset his mother that much. And he'd made up for it to both of them, hadn't he?

When they'd first arrived on the island, and the unfamiliar sounds had woken him nightly, Prabir had cried out until his father came and rocked him back to sleep. This had gone on for weeks, though for the last few nights he'd been doing it out of habit, not fear. His father had never shouted at him, never complained. In the end, just the knowledge that his father would come if he needed him was enough; Prabir didn't have to keep testing him in order to feel safe.

But he was too old to cry out for Baba now. He'd have to find another way to calm himself.

Prabir slid off his hammock and walked over to the screen door. The butterfly hut was directly opposite, gray and indistinct in the shadows. He knew the door to the hut would be bolted, to make sure no animals got in, but it wouldn't be locked. Nothing ever was.

Cool sweat was gathering behind his knees. He moistened his fingers and sniffed them; he was so used to the smell of the mosquito repellent that he could barely detect it any more. But he doubted that anyone in the family found it so pungent that a few drops could incriminate him.

He opened the screen door just enough to slip through, then headed across the kampong, bare feet silent on the well-trodden ground. He was determined to act before he changed his mind. When he reached the butterfly hut, he didn't hesitate: he slid the bolt open in one smooth motion. But when he began gently pushing the door, the whole fiberglass panel squeaked alarmingly, picking up the vibrations as its bottom edge scraped across the floor. He knew at once how to remedy this—the door to the kitchen made the same kind of noise—but he remained frozen for several heartbeats, listening for a sound from his parents' hut. Then he steeled himself and flung the door open; the panel flexed enough to gain the necessary clearance, and there was nothing but the sigh of moving air.

Prabir had seen most of the inside of the hut through the windows, by daylight, but he'd never had reason to commit the layout to memory. He stood in the doorway, waiting to see how well his eyes would adapt. Anywhere else it would have barely mattered; he could have marched in blindfolded. "This is my island," he whispered. "You had no right to keep me out." Even as he said the words, he knew they were dishonest—he'd never actually resented the fact that the butterfly hut was out-of-bounds—but having stumbled on the lame excuse, he clung to it.

A patch of floor a meter or so ahead of him was gray with starlight, preceded by what he guessed to be his own shadow, unrecognizably faint and diffuse. The darkness beyond remained impenetrable. Switching on the light would be madness; there were no blinds or shutters for the windows, the whole kampong would be lit up. He might as well wave a torch in his father's face.

He stepped into the hut. Groping around with outstretched arms would have been a recipe for sending glassware flying; he advanced slowly with one hand in front of him, just above waist height, close to his body. He inched forward for what seemed like minutes without touching anything, then his fingers struck Formica-coated particle board. It was the stuff of all their furniture: his own desk, the table they ate from. Unless he'd veered wildly off course, this was the main bench that ran along the length of the hut, not quite bisecting it. He glanced over his shoulder; he appeared to have walked straight in. The gray after-image of the doorway took forever to fade, and when it did he could still see nothing ahead of him. He turned to the left and walked beside the bench, his right hand brushing the side of the benchtop, the left on guard for obstacles.

After sidestepping a stool and a chair on casters, Prabir came to a patch of starlight falling on the bench from one of the windows. He moved his right hand tentatively into the faint illumination, complicating the already baffling shadows and hints of surfaces. He touched cool metal, slightly rough and curved. A microscope. He could smell the grease on the focusing rack-and-pinion; it was a distinctive odor, summoning memories. *His father propping him up on a stool so he could peer into a microscope, back in Calcutta. Showing him the scales on the butterfly's wings, glinting like tiny emerald prisms.* Prabir's stomach tightened until he could taste acid, but that only strengthened his resolve. The worse he felt about doing this, the more necessary it seemed.

He pictured the daylight view through the window. He'd seen his father hunched over the microscope; he knew where he was now, and where he needed to go. Opening a cage full of adults in the dark would be asking for trouble; he could hardly expect to find their bodies by touch without waking them, and even if none escaped, their wings were easily damaged. The larvae were covered with sharp bristles and spurted a malodorous brown irritant. He could probably have overcome his reluctance to touch them—they were only caterpillars, after all; it wouldn't be like thrusting his hand into a cage full of scorpions—but he'd seen the kind of stains the irritant left on his father's skin. He'd be hard-pressed to explain an equally bad case as the product of a chance encounter.

A couple of meters farther along the bench, he found what he hoped was the right cage. He flicked the taut mesh a few times, and listened for a response. No nervous fluttering, no angry hiss. He put his face to the mesh and inhaled; behind the metallic scent there was sap and leaves. Prabir had seen the pupae hanging by narrow threads from the branches in the cage, lumpy orange-black-and-green objects, each supported by a coarse silk net—what his father called a "girdle"—like small, misshapen, fungus-rotted melons in individual string bags. The larvae spun no proper cocoon to hide their metamorphosis; they did it naked, and it was not a pretty sight. But however ugly their jumble of dissolving parts, they wouldn't be half as unpleasant to handle as they were before the process began.

Prabir opened the cage and reached in.

He pulled his hand back. *Idiot.* He couldn't trust a vague memory of how the cage had once looked to guide him. He had to start near the bottom and work his way up, lest he sever one of the supporting threads. And he needed sweat on his fingers now, so the first touch would count.

His arms and sides were dripping from the night's humidity; he soaked his right hand and placed it, palm up, on the bottom of the cage. Then he raised his arm slowly. The empty space above the floor of the cage seemed to go on forever; he could feel his palm drying while the rest of his skin shed nervous rivulets. He tried to remember what his father had told him about the breeding cycle. Maybe there were no pupae in the cage at all.

When his hand was shoulder-high, his wrist finally touched something.

It was cool and springy. One of the branches.

He withdrew his arm. It was trembling.

One more time, he decided. If he failed again, he'd walk away.

As he stood beside the cage, trying to remember exactly where he'd placed his hand the first time, Prabir became aware of a faint, unfamiliar drone coming from somewhere outside the hut. He was puzzled; he knew the sound of every machine in the kampong, whether they were working smoothly, laboring against an overload, or seizing up completely. If there were any mysteries left, they'd be in here with him: some automated piece of lab equipment or refrigeration pump, too quiet to hear from the outside. But the source of this sound was not in the hut, he was sure of that.

It was a jet. Flying lower than usual. Or maybe not; maybe the night air changed the acoustics. The sound was so faint it would never have woken him. He couldn't be sure that this was anything new.

He stood in the dark, listening to the aircraft approaching. *If it was flying lower, what did that mean?* If he ran and woke his parents, no one would demand to know what he'd been doing. He'd been woken by stomach pains, that was all he'd need to say.

The drone grew louder, then suddenly dropped in pitch. Prabir remained paralyzed, picturing bombs tumbling through the air, falling toward their target as the plane accelerated away. But as the retreating engines faded, nothing followed. Only frog calls from the jungle.

Prabir almost laughed with relief, but the sound stuck in his throat. Maybe the signs had protected them, the paint visible against the warmth of the roof panels, black-on-green in the false colors of an infrared display. But if the plane's destination had been elsewhere all along—if Teranesia had meant nothing to the pilot but a fleeting piece of scenery beneath the flight path—then the bombs could still fall tonight. On some other island.

Prabir stared into the darkness, a hollow ache in his chest. He put his hand into the cage again, and continued the search. This time he was rewarded: his fingertips brushed against the side of a chrysalis. The impact set it swinging, but the silk thread holding it was resilient. He waited for the oscillations to die down, then cupped it gently in the palm of his hand. The surface was cool and smooth, like shellac.

He wasn't sure now how much sweat he'd had on his palm, and he didn't want to try to move his left hand into the cage as well—that would mean twisting his body, and worrying about new obstacles. He stood perfectly still for a while, fixing the position of the chrysalis in his mind. Then he withdrew his hand, coated it thoroughly, and wiped a second, surer dose of poison across the surface of the sleeping insect.

He closed the cage and walked out of the hut the way he'd come. Belatedly, he crouched to check for footprints, but there was enough grass along the route he'd taken to keep him from making any impression in the soil, and to keep his feet from being dusty enough to have left a visible trail indoors.

As he lay down in his hammock, he felt physically drained, more exhausted than when he'd half-climbed the volcano. But everything he'd done in the butterfly hut already felt less real than a dream. Not having seen the crime would make it easier to keep the guilt from his face when he heard the news. By the time the poisoned butterfly failed to emerge—or unfurled its wings and died in the sunlight—no memory would remain of the faint mental image of his hand inside the cage.

Prabir was walking back from the beach, Madhusree in his arms, when he heard a loud, dull thud from the direction of the kampong. It could almost have been a tree toppling, but there'd been no screech of tearing wood, no rustle of branches.

Madhusree gave him a puzzled look, but didn't press him for an explanation; she was perfectly capable of inventing one herself. They'd all get to hear it at dinner: a new creature on the island, probably, blundering around in search of children to eat.

Prabir heard his mother cry out "Rajendra!", her voice rising in horror. Madhusree looked startled, then her mouth curled. Prabir put her down on the path. "Stay here." He began running toward the kampong. Madhusree screamed wordlessly after him; he turned and saw her flapping her arms in distress. He stopped and gazed back at her, torn. What if there was danger here, too? *If soldiers had parachuted from the plane, they could be anywhere.*

He ran back to her and lifted her up. She clawed at his cheeks and pummeled his neck, tears and mucus streaming down her face. Prabir ignored the assault and started jogging down the path again, indifferent to her weight and her struggling. It was like running in a dream; the jungle flowed past him, but it took no will, no effort to move. The dream itself propelled him forward.

His mother was standing alone in the middle of the kampong, distraught, looking around as if searching for something. When she spotted Prabir she started banging her fist on her forehead. She screamed at him angrily, "Take her away! She mustn't see!"

Prabir stopped at the edge of the kampong, confused, fighting back tears. *Where was his father?* "What happened? Ma?"

His mother stared at him as if he were an idiot. "Where's the ladder?" she wailed. "What did you do with the ladder?"

Prabir couldn't remember. He'd meant to put it in the storage hut when they'd finished painting the roofs, but that would have been the first place she'd checked.

He stepped forward uncertainly. "I'll help you look."

His mother waved him away miserably, then started walking in circles around the middle of the kampong.

Madhusree was scarlet-faced, screaming and trying to slither out of his grip. Prabir ran over to his parents' hut and placed her in her cot. She was tall enough now to climb over the sides if she wanted to, but smart enough to realize that the fall would do her serious harm. Prabir knelt down and pressed his face against the bars. "I'll be back soon, I promise. With Ma. OK?" He didn't wait for an answer.

He found the ladder in the undergrowth behind the butterfly hut, the last place he'd used it. He picked it up one-handed and started running toward his mother; it wasn't all that heavy, but it swayed sideways as he moved, throwing him off balance.

He called out nervously, "Where should I take it? Where's Baba?"

She stared at him blankly for several seconds, then put her hand over her mouth and closed her eyes. Prabir stood watching her, his skin growing icy.

When she opened her eyes she seemed calmer.

She said softly, "Baba's been hurt. I'm going to need your help. But you have to do exactly what I tell you."

Prabir said, "I will."

"Wait there." She vanished into the storage hut, then emerged with two empty wooden packing crates. "Listen to me carefully. I want you to follow five meters behind me. Walk where I walk, nowhere else. Bring the ladder, but don't let it touch the ground."

As she spoke, Prabir heard doubt rising in her voice, as if she was beginning to think this was too much to ask of him. He said firmly, "Follow five meters behind you. Walk where you've walked. Don't let the ladder touch the ground."

She smiled reluctantly. "OK. I know you're not stupid, I know you'll be careful. Can you be brave for me, too?" She searched his face, and Prabir felt his chest tightening.

"Yes."

His father was lying in a shallow crater in the middle of the garden behind the storage hut. His legs were mangled, almost shredded. Dark blood was spurting from his thighs, welling up through a layer of sand that must have rained down on top of him from the blast. His eyes were closed, his face set against the pain. Prabir was too shocked for tears, and when he felt a plaintive cry of "Baba!" rising in his throat, he silenced it.

His mother spoke almost in a whisper. "I'm back, love. It won't be much longer." His father showed no sign of having heard her.

She turned to Prabir. "There could be more mines buried in the garden. So we'll put the ladder between the crates, like a bridge. Then I'll walk across to Baba and bring him back. Do you understand?"

Prabir said, "I can do it. I'm lighter." The ladder was aluminum, and he was afraid that it might not take the weight of two adults.

His mother shook her head impatiently. "You couldn't lift him, darling. You know that. Just help me get the ladder in position."

She placed one of the crates squarely on the ground at the edge of the garden, at the point nearest his father. Then she walked a couple of meters away, and motioned to Prabir to approach the crate. When he was standing beside it, he swung the ladder toward her, and she took hold of the end. She was still carrying the second crate in her left hand, gripping it by one exposed side.

As his mother walked around the edge of the garden, Prabir fed her more of the ladder, until he was holding it by the opposite end. She smiled at him encouragingly, but he felt his heart pounding with fear for her. Staying out of the garden was no guarantee of safety. The rectangle of cleared soil must have looked like an ideal target from the air—and maybe it was easier for a self-laying mine to penetrate the ground and cover its tracks where there was no vegetation—but there could still be others, buried anywhere at all.

As his mother approached the far corner, they both had to stretch their arms to keep their hold on the ladder, and it was soon clear that even this wouldn't be enough. She seemed to be about to cut across the garden, but Prabir shouted out to her, "*No!* I can move closer to you!" He gestured toward the corner nearest to him, where she'd already proved the ground safe. "I'll stand over there. Then once you've turned the corner I can walk back toward the crate, keeping step with you."

His mother shook her head angrily, but she was cursing herself for not thinking clearly. "You're right. We'll do it that way."

Once they were holding the ladder across the full width of the garden, carrying it straight toward his father, Prabir began to feel hopeful. Just a few more steps and his mother would have no untried ground left to walk. He kept his eyes averted from his father's legs, but a cool voice in his head was already daring to counsel optimism. People had survived these kinds of injuries, in remote villages in Cambodia and Afghanistan. His mother had studied human anatomy and performed surgery on experimental animals; that had to be of some use.

Prabir waited for her to put the second crate on the ground, then they lowered the ladder into place together. He didn't doubt that the crates would take the load; there were a dozen of them scattered around the kampong, and he'd seen his father standing on them to reach things. If the ladder didn't buckle, the one remaining problem was the far end sliding off the crate.

His mother followed his gaze.

She said, "You watch that, and tell me if it moves. If I shift it one way by accident, I can always shift it back."

She took off her shoes and climbed onto the crate.

The ladder's steps were sloped so as to be horizontal when the ladder was a few degrees off vertical; the sides they presented now were curved metal, with none of the non-slip rubber that covered the tops. But as Prabir looked on, his mother found a way to balance with her feet resting on both the supporting rails and the sides of the steps. Still above the crate, she screwed her eyes shut and began swaying slightly, her arms partly raised at her sides—rehearsing the moves that would restore her equilibrium without compromising her footing, so she wouldn't have to guess them when she was halfway across. Prabir's throat tightened, his fear for her giving way to love and admiration. *If there was anyone in the world who could do this, it was her.*

She opened her eyes and started walking along the ladder.

Prabir kept his hands on his end of the ladder, pushing it down firmly against the top of the crate, and kept his gaze on the other, unattended crate. He could feel a slight vibration with each step his mother took, but the ladder wasn't trying to jerk sideways out of his grip. He risked a quick glance at his mother's face; she was staring sightlessly over his head. He looked down at the opposite crate again. A wooden plank might have bowed enough to push the crates apart, its curvature redirecting the load, but the ladder was far too rigid for that. It would take the weight of both of them, easily; he was sure of that now.

His mother paused. Prabir watched her feet as she took one more step forward on her left, turning her body partly sideways so she could face his father. She dropped slowly to a crouch, then reached down toward him. The ladder was about half a meter from the ground; she could just touch his face with her fingertips.

"Rajendra?"

He moved his head slightly in acknowledgment.

"I'm too high to lift you from here. You're going to have to sit up."

There was no response. Prabir pictured his father rising from the sand into her arms, like a water man rising from the waves. But nothing happened.

"Rajendra?"

Suddenly his father emitted a sobbing noise, and reached up with one hand and touched her forearm. She clasped his hand. "It's all right, love. It's all right."

She turned to Prabir. "I'm going to try sitting down, so I can get Baba on to the ladder. But then I might not be able to stand up with him, to carry him. If I leave him on the ladder and walk back to my end, do you think the two of us could carry the ladder to the side of the garden with Baba on it—like a stretcher?"

Prabir replied instantly, "Yes. We can do it."

His mother looked away, angry for a moment. She said, "I want you to think about it. Don't just tell me what you'd like to be true."

Chastened, Prabir obeyed her. *Half his father's weight. More than twice as much as Madhusree's.* He believed he was strong enough. But if he was fooling himself, and he dropped the ladder . . .

He said, "I'm not sure how far I could carry him without resting. But I could slide the crate along the ground with me— kick it along with one foot. Then if I had to stop, I could rest the ladder on it."

His mother considered this. "All right. That's what we'll do." She shot him a half-smile, shorthand for all the reassuring words that would have taken too long to speak.

She gripped the ladder with her hands on either side, raised herself slightly with her arms, then brought her legs forward and lowered herself until she was sitting. She was still facing at an angle to the ladder; she curled her right leg up behind her and hooked her foot over one of the steps. Prabir pushed down nervously on the opposite rail. He had no way of sensing any change in the balance of forces as his mother shifted her weight, but he had a sickening feeling that the ladder might suddenly flip over sideways if he wasn't ready to prevent it.

She reached down and took hold of his father by the chest, one hand beneath each armpit, her own arms fully extended. Prabir had imagined her wrapping his father in a bear hug and hefting him up in one smooth motion—he'd seen her handle ninety-kilogram gas cylinders that way, in her lab in Calcutta— but it was clear now that she could stretch no closer. She took a few deep breaths, then attempted to lift him.

The geometry could not have been more awkward; that she could hold him at all was miracle enough, but everything she'd had to do with her body in order to reach him worked to undermine her strength. As Prabir watched, the top of the foot that she'd hooked over the ladder turned pale, then darkened with violet bruises. A resonant sound started up in her throat, an almost musical droning, as if she'd caught herself on the verge of an involuntary cry of pain and decided to make this sound instead, full of conscious anger and determination. Prabir had only heard her do this once before: in the hospital in Darwin, during labor.

His father lifted his head slightly, then managed to raise his shoulders a few centimeters off the ground by curving his spine. His mother took advantage of this immediately, bending her arms, moving her shoulders back, bracing herself more efficiently. With her arms stretched as far as they'd go, her whole upper body had been dead weight, but now the muscles in her back and arms could come into play. Prabir watched in joy and amazement as she pulled his father up, her arms closing around his back, until he was sitting.

She rested for a moment, catching her breath, repositioning her damaged foot. Prabir realized that his hands were shaking; he fought to steady them, to prepare himself for the task of stretcher-bearer.

Rajendra's eyes were still closed, but he was smiling, his arms around Rahda's waist. She tightened her embrace, clasped her hands together behind him, and lifted him off the ground.

A wall of air knocked Prabir backward onto the grass, then a soft rain of sand descended on him. He opened his mouth and tried to speak through the grit, but his ears were ringing and he couldn't tell if any sound was emerging.

As he brushed his face clean with his arm, something beneath the sand scratched his forearm, then his face began to throb with pain. When he tried to open his eyes, it felt as if the point of a knife was being held against the lids.

He cried out, "Baba! Baba! *Baba!*"

He could feel the air resonating in his throat; he knew he was shouting at the top of his lungs. His father would hear him; that was all that mattered. His father would hear him, and come.

Chapter 4

We're going on a trip, Maddy! South, south, south! To the Tanimbar Islands!" Prabir undressed her as he spoke, dropping her soiled clothes on the mattress of the cot. He didn't think his mother would mind if he left them there unwashed; the whole point of the exercise was deciding what was important and what wasn't. That was why he hadn't wasted time burying the "bodies" his parents had left in the garden; if something ever really did happen to them, they'd want him to think of Madhusree, rather than fussing over their meaningless remains.

He hoped his appearance wasn't too alarming. He'd washed away all the dirt, but he'd given up trying to dig the metal from his skin, and simply drenched his face and chest with Betadine in the hope of warding off infection. Naturally, his parents had made sure that none of the shrapnel would penetrate too deeply; they would have calculated the size and placement of the charge so that no fragment would carry enough energy to harm him.

Madhusree had apparently cried herself dry in his absence. When she fingered a wound on Prabir's face and he smacked her hand sharply, all she could manage was a whimpering sound, and even that soon faded. She remained sulky and irritable, but the idea of a trip seemed to intrigue her.

He carried her to the lavatory hut, wiped her backside, then cleaned her a bit more with moistened toilet paper.

"Where's Ma?" she demanded.

"I told you. South. On the Tanimbar Islands. She's waiting for us there with Baba."

Madhusree regarded him skeptically. "She didn't."

"Didn't what? Didn't leave the island? Where is she then, smart-arse?"

Madhusree opened her mouth to reply, but she couldn't hear her mother's voice, so she had no ready answer.

Prabir said soothingly, "I know it was rough of them to sneak off without saying good-bye to you, but they had to do it that way. They wanted to see if I could look after you. If I do a good job, they'll let me stay. If I don't, I'll have to go to boarding school. Sounds fair, doesn't it?"

Madhusree shook her head unhappily, but Prabir suspected that this had more to do with the absence of Ma than the threat of him being sent away. He said, "Don't worry, it won't be for long. I worked out what they wanted, straight away. They want us to leave Teranesia."

He took her back to his parents' hut, put clean underpants on her, then started packing the bag they used to carry her things when they went on the ferry. It was hard to decide what was essential. Warm clothes, obviously, in case they were still at sea when night fell, but what about diapers, lotions, and powder? She'd been using the toilet for months now, climbing up on the steps his father had made for her, but how would she cope on the boat? He decided to bring her old potty along; diapers were too bulky, but he couldn't expect her to piss over the side.

In the kitchen, he filled all six of her old baby bottles with fruit juice. She normally drank from a cup now, but when she was tired or moody his mother sometimes offered her a bottle, and it would make things easier on the boat. He grabbed three packs of the biscuits she ate, and a tin of powdered milk, then hesitated over her canned food. If they didn't find their parents on the first night, they'd be camping out on land, so it wasn't absurd to think about heating things in saucepans. He'd take the tiny methylated-spirits cooker that they kept in case of power failure.

Madhusree followed him from hut to hut as he gathered everything they'd need into a pile at the edge of the kampong. It made him nervous to see her running about freely, but it would have slowed him down too much to carry her everywhere, and after visiting the kitchen and peering through the doorway of the butterfly hut, she could see for herself that Ma and Baba were no longer in the kampong. He resisted the urge to warn her sternly to keep away from the garden; if he didn't mention it, she wouldn't even think of going there.

When he dragged the motorboat out of the storage hut, Madhusree finally seemed to accept that they were leaving.

"Ambon!" she shouted.

"No, not Ambon. The ferry's not running. We're going south, all by ourselves."

The boat and its outboard motor were both made of ultra-light carbon-fiber composites. Normally his father carried the motor in his arms, to and from the beach, while his mother carried the hull over her head. Prabir had planned to push the hull all the way to the beach, fully loaded, but his first exploratory shove was enough to convince him that he'd never succeed. He'd have to make at least four trips: the hull, the motor, fuel and water, then food, clothing, and everything else.

"Shit!" He'd almost forgotten. He went back into the storage hut and pulled down the two smaller life jackets from their hooks on the wall. He stared uncomprehendingly at the two larger ones remaining, then he turned and walked out.

He couldn't put Madhusree back in her cot; even if she didn't start screaming, he wasn't willing to leave her alone again. So he carried the hull to the beach with Madhusree following him on foot. The hull was incredibly light, but since his arms couldn't quite stretch between the sides of the upturned boat at its center of gravity, he either had to hold it nearer to the bow, where the sides were closer together—in which case he had to fight the unbalanced weight—or walk with his arms straight up and his palms supporting the floor of the boat, which was almost as awkward and tiring. He ended up alternating between the two methods, but he still had to stop and rest after ever shorter stretches. This did have one advantage: Madhusree had no trouble keeping up with him.

He rested on the beach for a few minutes, then carried Madhusree back to the kampong and started out with the motor. A third of the way to the beach she sat down on the path and refused to walk any farther. Prabir knelt down and coaxed her into putting her arms around his neck and clinging to his back with her legs. He usually hooked his arms under her legs when he carried her this way, reinforcing her grip and taking some of her weight, but the motor made that impossible. As her legs grew tired, she ended up virtually hanging on to him by her arms alone, and though Prabir leaned forward to try to shift some of her weight on to his back, by the time they reached the beach she was crying from exhaustion.

For a moment he was tempted to leave her on the beach—*what harm could come to her, sleeping beneath a palm tree?*—but then he wrapped her in his arms and trudged back to the kampong. He managed to hang the three bags of clothes and food from his neck and shoulders, leaving his arms free.

Down to the beach, back to the kampong. Two cans of fuel and two cans of water remained—each weighing about ten kilograms. He'd been fooling himself: even without Madhusree, he'd never have been able to move them all in one trip. Cradling her in his right arm, holding her against his side the way his mother did, he carried the cans to the beach one by one.

By the time he dropped the last can of fuel on to the sand beside the boat, it was almost three o'clock. Prabir dug his notepad out of one of the bags: it was fully charged, which meant eight hours' normal operation, but the battery drained three times faster when the screen had to be electronically illuminated. Still, even if they were at sea in darkness he wouldn't need the map constantly visible.

Madhusree had grown resentful; she'd never been dragged back and forth like this for the sake of a boat trip before. She sat in the shade at the edge of the beach, calling for Ma every minute or two. Prabir replied soothingly, but equally mechanically, "We're going to Ma."

The notepad's GPS software included a respectable world map, but Teranesia wasn't on it; as far as the software was concerned they were already in the middle of the Banda Sea. The Tanimbar Islands were shown, but the smaller islands in the group were just blobs of two or three pixels, and the coastlines of the larger ones appeared crudely rendered, as if they'd been extracted automatically from a satellite image or a cheap printed map. With access to the net Prabir could have substituted the official navigation chart for the region, complete with water depths and information on currents; he'd viewed it a dozen times, but never thought to keep a copy in his notepad. But there was no use dwelling on that. At least Jakarta hadn't been able to block the GPS signals; if he'd been left with dead reckoning, the sun and the stars, he would have been afraid to leave the island at all.

He fitted the motor to the hull, filled the fuel tank, then dragged the empty boat into the shallows. An image came to him suddenly, from a video his parents had watched back in Calcutta; he'd been asleep in his mother's arms for most of it, but he'd woken near the end. A man on a deserted beach had tried to drag a wooden boat into the ocean, to make his escape from some war or revolution. But the boat had been too large, too heavy, and no matter how he strived it had remained firmly beached. Prabir shuddered at the memory, but at least he knew they wouldn't share that fate. Whatever else happened, they wouldn't be stranded.

He loaded everything into the boat. It sank dismayingly low in the water, but his parents' combined weight must have been more than the weight of these provisions, and the boat had carried the whole family safely out to the ferry dozens of times. He fetched Madhusree; she didn't struggle or complain as he fitted her into her life jacket, merely glaring at him suspiciously.

Prabir put her in the boat, then climbed in himself and stood looking back across the beach. He wouldn't be gone long; if he completed the test his parents would have no reason to send him away, and everything would be back to normal within a couple of days. The poisoned chrysalis would be forgiven; it was only one butterfly out of all the thousands on the island. Anything could be forgiven if he proved he was capable of getting Madhusree to safety.

He started the motor. The boat rose up in the water and sped away from the beach, like an amphibious creature suddenly revived from a dormant state. Having the tiller firmly in his hand gave Prabir no immediate sense of control; he'd never been allowed to steer the boat. Nervously, he shifted the tiller back and forth a few degrees. The boat responded smoothly enough, turning more readily than he'd anticipated. This was encouraging, though it made his balance seem all the more precarious; if he stumbled and made the boat swerve sharply, the acceleration might knock him right off his feet.

He had to remain standing to watch for the gap in the reef. Prabir was used to recognizing the gap as they passed through it, when safe passage was a fait accompli. The breaking waves approached with alarming speed; he hunted for a stretch of darker water, leading to a region where the waves raised less foam. He spotted one candidate, but he had no clear memories of the approach to confirm his choice, and the signs were far from convincing.

Madhusree looked up at him, disoriented, rubbing her eyes. "Baba should!" she exclaimed accusingly. When Prabir ignored her she started crying. Tears flooded down her face, but Prabir was unmoved; she could make the slightest fit of pique sound like gut-wrenching anguish. He'd done it himself, countless times. He could remember that much very clearly.

"Shut up, Maddy," he suggested mildly. "You're not fooling anyone." She redoubled her efforts, and gave herself hiccups. Now Prabir felt sorry for her; hiccups were awful.

They were approaching the reef. The channel he'd picked looked more promising than ever, but now that he had a target to aim for, steering was proving to be harder than he'd realized. The boat was headed too far to the left; he struggled to picture their motion from above, and the turning arc that would neatly convert their present course into the one they needed.

He glanced down at his notepad on the floor of the boat. He hadn't thought he'd have any use for it until they hit the open sea; the software knew nothing of the reef, and at the present magnification the record of their entire journey so far was just a speck. *But it was the map that was crude, not the navigation system.* The commercial GPS that had superseded the U.S. military version gave unencrypted signals that resolved the receiver's position to the nearest centimeter.

Prabir shouted, "Notepad: zoom in. More . . . *more* . . . stop!" The speck became a crooked line against a blank background; all landmarks had vanished from the screen, but the magnified trail of the boat itself gave him his bearings. He glanced back toward the beach, then compared how far they'd come with the distance remaining to the reef. The image at his feet made perfect sense now; he could place the channel on it in his mind's eye.

He leaned gently on the tiller, and observed the effect: in reality, and on the map. The curve was still too shallow; he nudged the tiller, watching the growing arc and visualizing its extension.

The boat shot through the reef without a bump, without a scratch. Prabir was overcome with pride and happiness. He could do this, it wasn't beyond him. He'd be reunited with his parents soon—and whether it was midnight or dawn when he finally tracked them down, it would be long before they'd expected him. They'd teasingly beg his forgiveness for ever doubting him, then they'd take him in their arms and spin him around, lifting him up toward the sky.

His elation lasted until sunset.

By daylight, everything worked as planned. The sea felt far rougher than it did from the ferry—and in bad weather it might have been suicidal to attempt the crossing in such a small vessel—but it was still *musim teduh*, the calm season, and for all its relentless lurching the boat didn't take much water. Setting the right course was a matter of trial and error—quite apart from the current, the waves themselves seemed to deflect the boat as it cut across them—but by the time Teranesia's volcanic peak had shrunk to insignificance the GPS software showed that they were making steady progress south-southeast, at about ten kilometers an hour.

Once she'd recovered from the shock of finding herself at sea—with no Ma, no Baba, no ferry full of strangers, and no real conception of where they were headed—Madhusree grew positively entranced by the experience. The expression of delight on her face reminded Prabir of the way he felt in the middle of a wonderfully surreal dream. He was nauseated himself, but her fearlessness shamed him into stoicism. Madhusree sucked her bottles of fruit juice, ate a whole packet of biscuits, and used her potty without complaint. Prabir had no appetite, but he drank plenty of water, and urinated overboard to Madhusree's scandalized laughter.

As darkness fell, the wind rose and the waves grew higher. Madhusree vomited as Prabir was dressing her against the chill, and from that moment her mood worsened steadily. His shallow wounds were aching and itching; he wanted the metal out, whether it was harming him or not.

When Madhusree fell fitfully asleep, Prabir felt a strong urge to hold her. He picked her up and wrapped her in a blanket, but there seemed to be no way to keep his hand on the tiller that wouldn't make them both uncomfortable, so he laid her down again gently. He watched her for a while, half wishing she'd wake and keep him company. But she needed to sleep—and a few hours alone was a small price to pay to save himself from years of exile.

The blackness around the boat was impenetrable, untouched by the dazzling hemisphere of stars, but Prabir felt no sense of physical danger lurking in the gloom. The chance of an encounter with a pirate ship or any vessel involved in the war seemed slender. He'd glimpsed a couple of small sharks by daylight, but as far as he could tell they'd been passing by, uninterested in pursuit. And though he knew that the boat might yet meet a wave large enough to overturn it, there was no point worrying about that.

It was the dark water itself, stretching to the horizon—and for all he knew as far beneath him—that chilled him with its emptiness. There was nothing to recognize, nothing to remember.

The monotony of the view and the chugging of the motor could never have made him drowsy; his whole body had forsworn the possibility of sleep. But even wakefulness here felt blank and senseless, robbed of everything that made it worthwhile.

He glanced down at Madhusree, and hoped she was dreaming. Strange, complicated dreams.

The moon rose, swollen and yellow, not quite half full. With nothing else in sight it was hard not to stare at it, though its glare made his eyes water. The sea around the boat became visible for forty or fifty meters, but it looked as unreal as the jungle looked at the edge of the light from the kampong.

Prabir held his notepad up to the moonlight. The map showed them less than ten kilometers from their destination. Instead of heading straight for the northernmost island, he decided to aim slightly to the west of it. If the map turned out to be perfect he'd still spot the land, and then he could turn toward it. But he couldn't trust the map to be accurate down to the last kilometer, so it seemed safer to risk missing their target by veering too far west; they'd still hit the main island of the group, Yamdena, in another fifty kilometers. Going too far east would send them down through the Arafura Sea, toward the northern coast of Australia, six hundred kilometers away. The error would eventually become obvious, but he didn't have the fuel for much backtracking.

When the cliffs came into view, Prabir wondered if he was hallucinating, conjuring up the sight out of sheer need. But the land was real; the journey was almost over. He checked the notepad: the software showed the boat northwest of the island . . . but the cliffs were to his right. If he'd aimed true, they would have missed the islands completely.

As they drew nearer, Prabir saw that the cliffs didn't quite meet the water; there was a narrow, rocky beach below. He had no idea whether this island was inhabited, but he felt sure that his parents would be waiting here: it was the nearest land, the simplest possible choice. He thought of circumnavigating the island, looking for the boat they'd used to make the crossing, but he didn't trust himself to spot it in the dark. If he'd had any reason to believe that there was a harbor or a jetty he would have searched for that, but he wasn't prepared to chase after the mere possibility.

He steered straight for the beach.

There was a grinding sound at his feet and the boat came to a shuddering halt. Madhusree rolled off the bench where she'd been sleeping, into the gap between the bench and the bow. Prabir grabbed the food bag beside him, dropped his notepad in, zipped it closed and draped the handle around his neck. Then he leaped forward and reached for Madhusree; she was only just waking, whimpering and confused. He lifted her up, wrapped his arms around her, and jumped into the water.

His feet touched rock. The water was waist high.

Prabir started crying, shaking with relief and unused adrenaline. Madhusree gazed at him uncertainly, as if trying to decide between a show of sympathy and a competitive display of tears.

She said tentatively, "I bumped my head."

Prabir wiped his eyes with the heel of one palm. "Did you, darling? I'm sorry."

He waded to the shore and put her down, then went back for the other two bags, then again for the unopened water can. The boat was dented, but the floor appeared dry; the composite hull was tougher than he'd realized.

He rested on the pebble-strewn beach, using the clothes bag as a pillow, cradling Madhusree on top of him. They were both still wearing their life jackets; when he closed his eyes, the universe shrank to the smell and squeak of plastic.

• • •

Prabir was woken by someone shouting a single word, far away. He listened for a while, but there was nothing more. Maybe he'd dreamed it.

It was still dark. He maneuvered Madhusree on to one side, and checked his watch. It was just after four.

He'd dreamed that his father was standing at the top of the cliffs, calling his name. But if the image had only been a dream, the sound might still have been real.

Prabir rose to his feet, leaving Madhusree lying where he'd been. He'd have to take her with him if he explored the top of the cliffs. He couldn't bring much else, though. He'd make do with a canteen of water.

He urinated into the sea, shivering. The stones were cold beneath his feet. He'd forgotten to bring shoes.

He walked along the beach for fifteen minutes before he found a break in the cliff wall, with a steep rocky path to the top. He scrambled up, nearly losing his footing half a dozen times. Madhusree slept on in his arms, oblivious.

There was thick coarse grass at the top of the cliff, and what he guessed was dense jungle in the distance. There was no fire, no light, no sign of life. The moonlight seemed to reveal that there was no one but the two of them from the cliff edge to the jungle, but then Prabir heard the voice again.

It was a man's voice, but it wasn't his father. The word he was shouting was "Allah!"

Prabir walked toward the sound, aware of the danger but tired of thinking of nothing else. His parents should have been there to meet him on the beach. He'd done all he could to get Madhusree to safety; anything that happened now was their fault.

He found the man lying on his back in the grass. He was an Indonesian soldier, almost shaven-headed, dressed in neat green camouflage and combat boots. He looked about nineteen. Some kind of long-barreled weapon lay by his side.

Prabir said, in his halting Indonesian, "We're friends, we won't hurt you."

The man turned on his side, fear in his eyes, clutching at his weapon. His face shone with sweat. There was a huge, dark stain in his shirt over his abdomen.

Prabir said, "I'll get help. Tell me where to go."

The man stared at him mistrustfully. Finally he said, "I don't know where they are. I don't know where to send you."

Prabir squatted down and offered him the canteen. The man hesitated, then took it and drank from it. When he offered it back, Prabir said, "Keep it." He still had ten liters on the beach.

It was hard to know how to talk to the soldier without angering him, but Prabir suggested tentatively, "The local people might help you."

The man shook his head, grimacing, closing his eyes against the pain.

Madhusree woke, yawning and befuddled. She took in her new surroundings, then gazed at Prabir with intense disappointment. "I want Ma!"

The man opened his eyes and smiled at her. He propped himself up and held out his arms. Madhusree shook her head, unafraid but unwilling to indulge this stranger. He gave an understanding shrug, then screwed up his face suddenly and cried out again, "Allah!" Tears escaped his eyelids and flowed down his cheeks.

Prabir felt his legs grow weak. He sat down in the grass, clutching Madhusree to his chest. There were so many things he'd forgotten to bring from the island: bandages, painkillers, antibiotics.

Madhusree dozed off again. The man fell silent; he seemed

to have lost consciousness, though he was still breathing loudly. Prabir wondered if he really believed in Allah—an Allah who could send his comrades back to help him, or at least welcome him into paradise—or if he'd merely been shouting the word from habit, like a curse. When Prabir had asked his father why so many people believed in gods, his father had said, "When things are hard, there's a part of everyone that wants to believe there's someone watching over them. Someone ready to help, or even just to judge their actions and acknowledge that they've done their best. But that's not the way the world is."

Prabir put Madhusree down on the grass; she stirred unhappily, but didn't wake. He walked over to the soldier and sat beside him, cradling the dying man's head in his arms.

Just before dawn, with birds screaming in the jungle, two heavily bearded men in ragged clothes approached.

Prabir said, "Don't kill us. He won't hurt anyone. He just needs a doctor. He can still be saved."

One of the men lifted Madhusree into his arms, then grabbed Prabir by the shoulder and jerked him to his feet. The other man squatted by the soldier and drew a knife. As Prabir was being led away, he heard a choking sound, like a swimmer coughing up seawater. He didn't look back, and after a few seconds it stopped.

Chapter 5

The detention camp was ten kilometers out of Exmouth, a small town on the northwest coast of Australia. Prabir found this puzzling, because almost everyone in the camp had come ashore at least a thousand kilometers farther north. He knew that Darwin was home to a large community of Indonesian exiles, sympathetic people with invaluable local knowledge who would have happily visited the camp and offered advice, if it had only been closer. And though the government provided legal aid to help the detainees apply for refugee status, there were no lawyers in Exmouth, so they all had to travel great distances from Perth or Darwin. The camp had only one phone for twelve-hundred inmates, so the lawyers had little choice but to make the trip in person, and this ate away at the time they might otherwise have spent on actual casework—not least because the cost of travel came out of each applicant's legal aid allocation.

It was several weeks before it occurred to him that the location had been chosen for precisely these reasons.

The ABRMS guerrillas had dumped Prabir and Madhusree on Yamdena, where a Chinese woman from eastern Java had taken pity on them and paid for them to join her family on a boat south. But the family had relatives in Sydney to sponsor them, and they'd left the camp after a month.

Six months later, Prabir overheard a social worker telling one of the guards, "I'm sure we can adopt out the girl; she's young enough, and she's pretty cute. But her brother's a complete basket case. You're going to be stuck with him for years."

The next time the lawyers made their trek into the wilderness, Prabir spoke his first words to anyone but Madhusree since the Chinese family had left.

He said, "I've changed my mind. I don't want asylum here. We have to go to my mother's cousin Amita, in Toronto."

The lawyer said, "Cousin Amita? Do you know her full name?"

Prabir shook his head. "But she teaches at a university there. She'll be in their directory. You could find her e-mail address in no time."

The lawyer looked skeptical, but she slid her notepad across the desk to Prabir. "Why don't you do the honors?"

He stared down at the machine. "I'll look up her address, but would you talk to her, please?" Prabir had never met Amita, or even spoken to her. "I might say something foolish and ruin everything."

Amita and her partner Keith met them at the airport, signing for them and taking them from the social worker. Madhusree allowed them each a turn at holding her and pulling baby faces; Prabir had lectured her for hours on the need to make a good impression.

In the car, Keith drove, and Amita rode in the back with them. Madhusree—who'd stayed awake for all five flights, entranced by the views—fell asleep in Prabir's arms. Keith pointed out Toronto's landmarks, and seemed to expect Prabir to be amazed by every large building.

Amita said, "I have something for you, Prabir." She handed him a small, molded-plastic object that looked like a hearing aid.

Prabir said, "Thank you." He was too nervous to ask what it was. He slipped it into his pocket.

Amita smiled indulgently. "Put it in your ear, darling. That's what it's for."

Reluctantly, Prabir fished it out and complied. A woman's voice said, "Don't be sad." *What was it, a radio?* He waited for something more. After a few seconds, the voice repeated, "Don't be sad."

Amita was watching him expectantly. Prabir thought it best to tell her straightaway, lest he be blamed for damaging the gift. "I think it's broken. It just keeps repeating itself."

Amita laughed. "That's what it's meant to do. It's a sample mantra: it reads your mood, and gives you a message to cheer you up, whenever you need it."

"Don't be sad," said the earpiece.

"I chose the sample myself," Amita explained proudly. "It's taken from an old Sonic Youth song. But of course you can reprogram it with anything you like."

Prabir tried hard to look grateful. "Thank you, Amita. It's wonderful." He had to wait until they were home and he was safely in the toilet with the door locked before he could free himself from the inane chant. He unscrewed the device easily, and his first thought was to drop the battery into the toilet bowl, but then he feared it might resist flushing, or Amita might ask for the device back to show him how to load a new sample, and realize what he'd done from its diminished weight.

Inspiration struck: he reversed the button-shaped cell, swapping positive for negative, and reassembled the earpiece. It was mute. It also rendered him partially deaf, but that was a small price to pay. He could find out later how to wipe the sample while still running the circuitry that let him hear normally.

Prabir stared down at his shoes. He was shaking with anger, but he had to be polite to Amita and Keith, or they'd separate him from Madhusree.

The house was an endless succession of cavernous rooms painted white; it made him feel disembodied. Amita had put Madhusree down to sleep, in a room all her own. Now she showed Prabir his room; it was even larger than Madhusree's, and despite all the furniture and gadgets it contained, there was a vast amount of unused floor space. Prabir thanked Amita for everything—struggling to conceal his dismay at the sense of debt he felt from being showered with gifts like this—before suggesting that they move Madhusree in with him. "She's not used to being alone."

Amita and Keith exchanged glances. Amita said, "All right. Maybe for a week or two."

After dinner, Keith bid them goodnight and drove away. Prabir was confused. "Doesn't he live here?"

Amita shook her head. "We're separated. But we're still good friends, and he's agreed to spend some time here now that you and Madhusree have arrived."

"But why?" Prabir wanted to kick himself as soon as the words escaped his lips. Amita had made great sacrifices for his sake; he had to put things more diplomatically.

Amita explained, "I decided that you and your sister should be exposed to both male and female narratives."

"You mean . . . he'll help you read to us?" Prabir didn't want to sound ungrateful, but surely Amita would be relieved to hear that there was no need to have her ex-lover hanging around just to do the male voices in bedtime stories. "I can read for myself. And we could take turns reading to Madhusree."

Madhusree interjected, "I can read, too!" This wasn't true, but Prabir had taught her the Latin alphabet in the camp, and her spoken English was already as good as her Bengali.

Amita sighed with amusement and tousled Prabir's hair. "I *meant* our personal narratives, funny boy. Though all such texts are fluidly gendered, in order to decode and contextualize your own experiences you'll benefit from familiarity with at least the fundamental binary templates."

Prabir glanced discreetly at the wine bottle in the middle of the table.

In bed, he lay awake for hours, cocooned in crisp sheets and a heavy blanket. It was cold, he needed the bedclothes, but he felt like he was in a straitjacket. He wasn't troubled by the unfamilar shadows in the room, or the faint traffic sounds that faded into silence, though he'd grown used to listening to the chain-smoking men in the camp hawking up mucus all night. It wasn't just pointless feeling homesick, it was meaningless: there was no right way the room could have looked, no comfort the sounds of the night could have delivered. From his hammock on the island, or his bed in Calcutta, his parents would still have been dead.

He watched Madhusree sleeping. They would never reach the shore, they would never reach safety. There was no such thing. It had all been in his head.

The next time Keith was in the house, Prabir took the opportunity to interrogate him.

"How did you meet Amita?" he asked innocently. Amita was out on some errand, so they were alone in the living room with Madhusree, who was playing delightedly with the puppy Keith had brought for her.

"It was at a performance space in the city," Keith began tentatively. "Twelve years ago." He frowned, struggling to dredge up details. "The Anorexic Androgynes were reciting the Unabomber Manifesto, with backing music by Egregious Beards." He added helpfully, "They were a Country Dada band, but they broke up years ago."

Prabir wasn't interested in any of this; he wanted to hear about the couple's passion for knowledge. "So how did you end up working at the university together?"

"Well, I'd already done a Ph.D. in X-Files Theory at UCLA, and Amita was just starting her Master's in Diana Studies with the University of Leeds, via the net. U Toronto was in the process of opening its own Department of Transgressive Discourse—at last!—so it was only natural that we both applied for positions."

When Prabir pressed Keith for explanations of all the phrases he didn't understand in this account, his heart sank. "And this is what Amita has done for the last twelve years?"

Keith laughed. "No, no, of course not! That was just her Master's; she's moved on. For her doctorate she tackled an entirely different subject: developing an interactive graphic novel of Conrad's *Nostromo*, as an exercise in post-colonial transliteracy. Nostromo becomes a comic-book superhero in Lycra, who loses his powers whenever he's exposed to radiation from silver ingots. This ironizes and recontextualizes Conrad's own highly ambiguous relationship with the economic benefits of imperialism, and cleverly undermines the whole myth of the artist as quasi-divine standard-bearer for transcendent morality."

Prabir was beginning to wonder if Keith was playing an elaborate joke on him. "And what is she studying now?"

Keith smiled proudly. "For the past four years, she's been working on a radical new paradigm in computing. She's still had no luck getting funding to build a prototype, but that can only be a matter of time."

"Amita has designed a computer?" Now Prabir knew he was being taken for a ride. "When did she find time to study engineering?"

"Oh, she'll hire an engineer when she gets funding." Keith waved a hand dismissively. "Her contribution is purely intellectual. *Mathematical*."

"Mathematical?"

Keith regarded him dubiously. "You might be a bit young to understand this. Do you know how computers work, Prabir?"

"More or less."

"Zeroes and ones. You understand the binary system?" Keith grabbed a notepad that was lying on the coffee table in front of them, and drew the two digits.

Prabir tried not to sound offended. "Yes, I understand."

"Have you ever wondered why computers are so hostile to women?"

"Hostile?" Prabir had some trouble deciding what Keith was most likely to mean by this claim. Paranoid delusions of artificial intelligence weren't necessarily out of the question. "You mean . . . why do some men harass women on the net?"

Keith said, "Well, yes, but it goes far deeper than that. Amita's work not only reveals the fundamental reason for the problem, it offers a stunningly simple solution." He jabbed at the notepad with his finger. "Zero and one. Absence and presence. *And just look how they're drawn!* 'Zero' is female: the womb, the vagina. 'One' is male: unmistakably phallic. The woman is absent, marginalized, excluded. The man is present, dominant, imperious. This blatantly sexist coding underpins all modern digital technology! And then we ask ourselves why women find it an unwelcoming space!

"So Amita proposed a new paradigm, for both hardware and software. The old, male-dominated hardware is replaced by the transgressive computer, or *transputer*. The old, male-dominated software is translated into a brand new language, called *Ada*—after Ada Lovelace, the unsung mother of computing."

Prabir ventured, "I think someone's already named a language after her."

But Keith refused to be distracted. "What is this new paradigm? It's simple! Every one becomes a zero, every zero becomes a one: a universal digital gender reassignment! And the beauty of it is, on the surface everything *looks like* business as usual. If all hardware and all software undergoes the same inversion, programs continue to produce the same results—there is no change whatsoever to the naked eye. But deep inside every microchip, the old phallocentric coding is being subverted, billions of times per second! The old power structures are turned on their head every time we switch on our computers!"

Prabir had had enough; Keith must think he was some kind of uneducated hick who'd swallow anything. If he'd been feeding him these increasingly tall tales to see how much he could get away with, it was time to call his bluff.

"Computers don't have little numerals inside them," Prabir said flatly. "Zero is usually coded in memories by the absence of electrical charge in a capacitor, and one by the presence of charge, but sometimes even that's reversed. And even when it's not reversed . . . absence is coded as absence, presence is coded as presence. There are no diagrams of vaginas and penises, or anything else to do with people's sex."

Keith said uncertainly, "Well, maybe not literally. But you can hardly deny that *the symbols themselves* permeate technological culture. No one *lives* in the so-called 'physical' world of electrons and capacitors, Prabir! The true space we inhabit is cultural!"

Prabir stood and picked up the notepad, exasperated. "These are *Hindu-Arabic numerals*! People have used them for centuries; they have nothing to do with computers! If you really imagine that they're drawings of private parts, it's not technology that should offend you—it's mathematics!"

Keith shouted, "Yes, yes! You're absolutely right! Don't move; I'll be back in five seconds!" He ran from the room.

Madhusree gave Prabir a questioning look. Prabir said, "Don't worry, we're just playing a game." *And I'm winning.*

Keith returned, carrying a book, flicking through it, looking for something. "Aha!" He held the cover up for Prabir. "From the *Proceedings of the Fifteenth Annual Conference of Cyberfeminist Discourse.* This was the paper Amita gave last year, which made the *New York Times* describe her as 'Canada's most exciting living intellectual.'"

He read, "'The transputer will only be the first stage in a revolution that will transform the entire gendered megatext of technology and science. The next hegemony to fall, long overdue for its own hyperqueer inversion, will be mathematics itself. Once again we will need to rebuild the discipline from the ground up, rejecting the flawed and biased axioms of the old, male dispensers of truth, transforming their rigid, hierarchical approach into one that is organic, nurturing, and playful. Proof is dead. Logic is obsolete. The next generation must be taught from childhood to ridicule Russell's *Principia,* to tweak the beard of Carl Friedrich Gauss—to *pull down* Pythagoras's trousers!'"

Prabir stretched his hand out and took the book. The passage was exactly as Keith had read it. And Amita's name was at the top of the article.

He sat down, light-headed, still disbelieving. In the camp, when he'd recalled the things his father had said about Amita, he'd feared that she might be religious, but it was even worse than that. She was opposed to everything his parents had stood for: the equality of men and women, the separation of scholarship from self-interest, the very idea of an honest search for truth.

And he'd delivered Madhusree into her hands.

• • •

Prabir had been dreading the start of school, but by the end of the first week all his worst fears had proved groundless. The teachers spoke like sane human beings; there was no Keith-and-Amita-babble in sixth grade. And he'd been allowed to sit in on Madhusree's first morning in child care, which seemed equally harmless. Madhusree had played with other children in the camp, so it had come as no great shock to her to meet the same kind of strange beings again, and though she'd cried when Prabir left her on the second day, when he came home she'd been full of enthusiastic reports of her activities.

Prabir had expected to be beaten up at school, but the other students kept their distance. One boy had started taunting him about his face, but then another boy had whispered something to the first that had made him fall silent. Prabir fervently hoped that they only imagined they knew the story behind the scars; he'd rather have been laughed at than have these strangers discussing anything that had happened on the island.

There were three other students in his class who looked like they might have had Indian parents, but they all spoke with Canadian accents, and when Prabir was around them he thought he sensed an even greater unease than he produced in everyone else. Amita had come to Canada when she was three, and her parents had stopped speaking Bengali immediately; she remembered almost nothing of the language. He was determined to keep Madhusree bilingual, but in her presence he sometimes found himself halting in the middle of sentences, suddenly doubting that he was speaking correctly. He could have tried to contact some of his old classmates from the Calcutta IRA's net school, but he couldn't face the prospect of explaining the reasons for his changed circumstances.

In the months that followed, he grew used to the routine: waking at seven, washing and dressing, catching the bus, sitting through lessons. It was like sleepwalking on a treadmill.

On the weekends, there were outings. Keith took him to a festival screening of a film called *The Four Hundred Blows*. Prabir went along for the novelty of finally experiencing celluloid technology, with its giant image and communal audience. Though he remembered Calcutta being full of movie houses, he'd never been inside one; his parents had preferred to rent a disk, and he'd been far too young to go on his own.

"So what did you think?" Keith asked as they crossed the foyer on their way out. He'd been talking about the event for weeks beforehand; apparently this was his all-time favorite film.

Prabir said, "I think the spoiled brat was treated far better than he deserved."

Keith was scandalized. "You do know it's autobiographical? You're talking about Truffaut!"

Prabir considered this new information. "Then he was probably being too gentle on himself. In reality, he was probably even more stupid and selfish."

Amita had very different tastes, and took him to *BladeRunner*™ *OnIce*™ with *MusicInTheStyleOf*™ *GilbertAndSullivan*™. He'd heard that the show was distantly derived from a halfway decent science fiction novel, but no evidence of that survived among the fog, laser beams, and black rubber costumes. During the interval, a disembodied voice calling itself "Radio KJTR" cackled inanities about sex with amputees. The McDonald's in the foyer was offering a free game/soundtrack/novelization ROM with every MacTheBlade™, which turned out to be a frothy pink drink like liquefied Styrofoam. The worst thing was Amita humming "I Am the Very Model of a Modern Mutant Replicant" for the next six weeks.

By the end of their third month in Toronto there was a perceptible change in the household, as if it had been decided that their settling-in period was over. Amita began hosting dinner parties, and introducing her foster children to her friends. The guests made goo-goo noises over Madhusree, and handed Prabir calling cards with Dior web sites embedded in the chips.

Keith and Amita's acquaintances were drawn from almost every profession, but remarkably they all had one thing in common. Arun was a lecturer, writer, editor, social commentator, and poet. Bernice was a sculptor, performance artist, political activist, and poet. Denys was a multimedia consultant, advertising copywriter, film producer . . . and poet. Prabir flipped through all the cards one night, to be sure he hadn't left someone out, but there were no exceptions. *Dentist, and poet. Actor, and poet. Architect, and poet. Accountant, and poet.*

Thankfully, none of these visitors ever raised the subject of the war with him, but that left them with little choice but to ask about school. To Prabir's dismay, confessing that his best subjects were science and mathematics almost invariably triggered a baffling stream of non sequiturs comparing him with the famous Indian mathematician Ramanujan. Could they really not tell that he was too old for this kind of grow-up-to-be-an-astronaut flattery? And why did they always invoke Ramanujan? Why not Bose or Chandrasekhar, why not Salam or Ashtekar, why not even (perish the thought) someone Chinese or European or American? Prabir eventually discovered the reason: an Oliver Stone biopic that had been released in 2010. Amita rented it for him. The story was punctuated with sitar-drenched hallucinatory visits from Hindu deities, dispensing cheat notes to the struggling young mathematician. In the end, Ramanujan steps from his deathbed into a desert strewn with snakes, all biting their tails to form the symbol for infinity.

There were worse things in the world than being patronized by the And Poets. Prabir knew that he was a thousand times better off than most of the war's orphans—and if this fact had ever slipped his mind, the TV was full of harrowing footage from Aceh and Irian Jaya to rub his face in it. The fighting was over, the leaders of the coup had been overthrown, and five provinces had gained independence, but ten million people were starving across the archipelago. He'd been deprived of nothing—save the one thing that no one could restore. Amita not only fed, clothed, and sheltered them, she bestowed endless physical affection on Madhusree, and she would have done the same for him if he hadn't recoiled from her touch.

Prabir found himself growing almost ashamed of his lack of respect for her, and he began to wonder if his fears for Madhusree were unfounded. Amita hadn't tried to brainwash him with her bizarre theories; maybe Madhusree would be left to make up her own mind.

Maybe Amita really was harmless.

In the summer of 2014, Amita asked Prabir if he'd come to a rally, organized in response to a recent spate of racially motivated bashings, at which she'd been invited to speak. Prabir said yes, happily surprised to learn that Amita wasn't as detached from reality as he'd imagined, locked away in the university battling colonialism with *Nostromo* comics and undermining the patriarchy by pointlessly flipping computer bits. At last, here she was doing something of which he could be unequivocally proud.

The rally took place on a Sunday; they marched through the streets beneath a cloudless sky. Prabir liked summer in Toronto; the sun only climbed two-thirds of the way to the zenith, but it made the trip last. Keith seemed to think that thirty-two degrees was sweltering; when they reached the park and sat down on the grass, he opened the picnic hamper they'd brought and consumed several cans of beer.

In front of two thousand people, Amita took her place at the lectern. Prabir pointed her out to Madhusree. "Look! There's Amita! She's famous!"

Amita began, "We're gathered here today to deplore and denounce racism, and that's all well and good, but I believe the time is long overdue for a more sophisticated analysis of this phenomenon to reach the public sphere. My research has shown that antipathy toward people of other cultures is in fact nothing but a *redirection* of a far more basic form of oppression. A careful study of the language used in Germany in the 1930s to describe the Jews reveals something quite striking, and yet to me, deeply unsurprising: every term of racial abuse that was employed was also a form of *feminization*. To be weak, to be shiftless, to be untrustworthy—to be *the Other* at all, under patriarchy—what else can this possibly mean, but to be *female*?"

If the Nazis had triumphed, Amita explained, they would eventually have run out of distracting false targets, and started feeding their true enemy—German women—into the gas chambers. "Forget all those Riefenstahl Rhine maidens; the real core of Nazi propaganda films was always a celebration of *male* strength, *male* beauty. In the Thousand-Year Reich, women would have been retained only for breeding, and only for as long as it took to supplant them with a technological alternative. Once their last essential role was gone, they too would have vanished into the ovens.

"I was invited here to address you today because of the color of my skin, and the country of my birth, and it's true that these things make me a target. But we all know that there's more violence directed against Canadian *women* than there is against every ethnic minority combined. So I stand here before you and say: *as a woman* I too was in Belsen, *as a woman* I too was in Dachau, *as a woman* I too was in Auschwitz!"

Prabir waited anxiously for a riot to start, or at least for someone to shout her down. Surely there were children or grand-children of Holocaust survivors in the crowd? And even if there weren't, there had to be someone with the courage to cry "thief!"

But the crowd applauded. People stood up and cheered.

Amita rejoined them on the grass, lifting Madhusree into her arms. Prabir watched her with a curious sense of detachment, wondering if he finally understood why she'd agreed to shelter them. She'd made it clear what her idea of compassion was: to denounce violence, and to show real generosity toward its victims, but then to cash it all in for a cry of "Me, too!" like an infant competing for sympathy. That was what the death of six million strangers meant to her: not a matter of grief, or horror, but of envy.

She smiled down at him, jiggling Madhusree. "What did you think, Prabir?"

"Will you show me your tattoo?"

"I'm sorry?"

"Your number from the camp."

Amita's smile vanished. "That's a very childish form of humor. Taking everything literally."

"Maybe you should take a few more things literally yourself."

Keith said sharply, "You can apologize now."

Amita turned to him. "Would you stay out of this, please?"

Keith balled his fists and glared down at Prabir. "We're not going to make allowances for you forever. There are plenty of institutions that'd take you; it wouldn't be hard to arrange." Before Amita could respond he turned and walked away, cupping his hands over his ears, blocking out everything but his sample mantra.

Amita said, "I'd never do that, Prabir. Just ignore him."

Prabir looked past her face, into the dreamy blue sky. The fear racing through his veins was welcome. The whole problem was, he'd let himself feel safe. He'd let himself pretend that he'd arrived somewhere. He'd never forget where he stood, now.

Nowhere at all.

He said softly, "I'm sorry, Amita. I'm sorry."

"Do you want to know where Ma and Baba went?"

Prabir stood beside Madhusree's bed in the dark. He'd waited there silently for almost an hour, until by chance she'd stirred and the sight of him had brought her fully awake.

"Yes."

He reached down and stroked her hair. In the camp he'd evaded the question, telling her useless half-truths—"They can't be here now," "They'd want me to look after you"—until she'd finally given up asking. The social workers had told him, "Say nothing. She's young enough to forget."

He said, "They've gone into your mind. They've gone into your memories."

Madhusree gave him her most skeptical look, but she seemed to be considering the claim.

Then she said decisively, "They have not."

Prabir wiped his eyes with the heel of his hand. He said, "All right, smart-arse. They've gone into mine."

Madhusree looked annoyed. She pushed his hand away. "I want them, too."

Prabir was growing cold. He lifted her out from under the covers and carried her to his bed. "Don't tell Amita." Madhusree scowled at him disdainfully, as if he was an idiot even to raise the possibility.

He said, "Do you know what Ma's name was, before you were born?"

"No."

"She was called Radha. And Baba was called Rajendra.

They lived in a huge, crowded, noisy city called Calcutta." Prabir repeated himself in Bengali.

He turned his bedside lamp on low, then took his notepad from his desk and summoned up a picture of his mother. It was the shot taken at the IRA parade, the only image he had of her, rescued from the net workspace where he'd placed it before deciding not to mail it to Eleanor.

Madhusree's eyes lit up in amazement.

Prabir said, "Radha knew everything about the human body. She was the smartest, strongest person in Calcutta. Her Ma and Baba had a big, beautiful house, but she didn't care about that." He scrolled the notepad's window to reveal the picture of his father; Madhusree had apparently grown nonchalant about metal through skin, but she leaned forward eagerly to examine Rajendra's face, more recognizable than her mother's. "So she fell in love with Rajendra, who had nothing, but he was smart and strong like Radha. And he loved her, too."

Prabir thought: *I'm ruining it.* He didn't want to fill her head with sugar-coated stories that might as well be fairy tales. He could still feel his father's hands around him, holding him up to the sky. He could still hear his mother's voice, telling him they were heading for the island of butterflies. *How could he ever make them as real again for Madhusree?*

Madhusree was having second thoughts about the picture of Radha. "Why isn't she crying?"

Prabir put his fingers to his cheek. "There's a spot where there's hardly any nerve endings." He'd checked one of the virtual bodies on the net. "There are lots of tiny threads in your skin for feeling pain, but if you don't cut them it doesn't hurt."

Madhusree looked doubtful.

There were kebab skewers in the kitchen. He could sterilize one in a gas flame, or use disinfectant from the medicine cabinet.

The thought of pushing the metal right through his own flesh made his stomach clench; he wouldn't have minded someone else performing the trick on him—that could hardly have been worse than the injections he'd had to dissolve the scar tissue on his face—but the prospect of having to apply the force himself was daunting.

But his mother had done it; that wasn't a fairy tale, the proof was right in front of him. It was just a matter of being confident that you understood what you were doing.

He said, "I'll show you." He put the notepad down on the pillow and climbed off the bed. "Just the cheeks, though, not the tongue. And when you're older, you have to help me pull the truck."

Madhusree didn't make commitments lightly; she examined the picture of her father again. Prabir leaned over her. "Look at their faces. If it hurt, they wouldn't be smiling, would they?"

Madhusree considered the merits of this argument, then nodded solemnly.

"OK."

Chapter 6

P rabir worked late to finish a project, to keep it from nagging at his thoughts all weekend. It was nothing out of the ordinary, but there were some minor problems that demanded his concentration; he lost himself in the details and the time flew by. But when he was done, instead of dashing for the elevators with a clear conscience, gleefully consigning the bank to oblivion, he sat for fifteen minutes in a kind of stupor, staring out across the rows of deserted cubicles.

He turned back to his work station and reran the tests on the credit card plug-in, one more time. It was a standard piece of anthropomorphic software: an "investment adviser" with voice and appearance tailored to the customer's psychological and cultural profile, who appeared on the card and offered suggestions for shuffling money between various financial instruments. It was a sales gimmick, more than anything else. People who played the markets seriously had to arm themselves with far more sophisticated tools, and know how to use them; anyone who didn't want to waste time becoming an expert was better off relying on one of the bank's standard low-risk algorithms. And most people did just that. But the bank had identified a demographic of potential customers who'd be attracted by this kind of novelty: the illusion of technology laboring ceaselessly on their behalf, but only to put the facts at their fingertips, always leaving the final decision to them.

It was worth doing anything well. Even this. But as Prabir watched the array of sixteen sample advisers reacting flawlessly to a barrage of test data, he just felt tired and ridiculous, as if he'd stayed back to straighten all the pictures in the corridors. He wasn't even impressing his superiors, making his position more secure; the only way to do that would be to spend his evenings studying advanced financial voodoo at quant school, a prospect he found dispiriting beyond words. But he'd probably be idle now for half the day on Monday, before the sales consultants and market researchers made up their minds on the next gimmick.

As he stepped out of his cubicle, the screen and the desk light flickered off; a sprite in the ceiling guided him through the darkness to the elevators. Wasting a few hours on a Friday night was no great tragedy, but he felt the same sense of anticlimax every time he went looking for some kind of satisfaction from the job. He had to be stupid, or morbidly compulsive, to keep on acting as if there were any to be found.

It was only half past nine, but as he walked out onto Bay Street he suddenly felt light-headed with hunger, as if he'd been fasting all day. He bought a glutinous foil-packed meal from a vending machine and ate it waiting for the bus. It was a crisp winter night; the sky looked clear, but it was a blank starless gray behind the street lights.

When he arrived home, Madhusree's door was closed, so he didn't disturb her. As he sank into the couch the TV came on, with no sound and the picture half-sized. Watching an image three meters wide was fine if you wanted to get drawn in, but all that activity in your peripheral vision was counterproductive if you were really just hoping to doze off as soon as possible. Prabir kept thinking about work—even with the adviser finished, there were half a dozen things he could be tinkering with—but the bank had a strict policy of no remote access for software development.

Someone rang the doorbell down on the street; a window appeared in the corner of the screen, showing Felix shuffling his feet against the cold. Prabir felt a rush of guilt; he'd been meaning to call him all week. Felix spread his arms and looked straight into the camera, comically imploring. Prabir said, "Come on up."

Felix entered the apartment smiling, looking around. "So what are you up to?"

Prabir indicated the TV. "Stupefaction therapy."

"Do you want to go somewhere?"

"I don't know. I just got home; I'm pretty tired."

Felix nodded sympathetically. "Me too." He didn't look tired. "I came straight here; I had a batch of coins in a reducing bath I couldn't leave."

"Have you eaten?" Prabir took a few steps toward the kitchen. "We've got plenty of food, if you don't mind something reheated."

"No, it's OK. I grabbed something at work." Felix took off his jacket and they sat on the couch.

Prabir said, "What kind of coins?"

"English. Eighteenth century. Nothing very interesting." Felix was a preservationist at the Royal Ontario Museum; his job was a mixture of everything from art history to zoology. He often complained that most of what he did was mundane lab work, but he seemed to have a very different notion of "mundane" than anyone who'd worked in retail banking.

He leaned forward and kissed Prabir, then moved closer and put an arm around him. Prabir did his best to respond enthusiastically, kissing back, trying to loosen the muscles in his shoulders. He wanted nothing more than to be at ease, to be as unselfconscious as

Felix was, but his heart still skipped a beat out of sheer panic at the first touch.

Even when Madhusree had first moved in with him, nine years before, Amita hadn't fought him for custody; she'd resigned herself to Madhusree's decision. But Prabir had never felt confident that there wouldn't be a legal challenge from somewhere, and an eighteen-year-old guardian who slept with men under the same roof as his ten-year-old sister would hardly have been placing himself in the most secure position imaginable. He'd heard of established, respectable gay couples winning custody battles, but his own situation could not have been more different, and the prospect of his first clumsy attempts to find a partner not only costing him Madhusree but ending up as evidence in court was all the discouragement he needed.

The risk had begun to seem far less dramatic when Madhusree was a few years older, but Prabir still hadn't been willing to gamble. By the time she'd turned eighteen and the danger of losing her had evaporated, Prabir had grown so accustomed to celibacy that he'd had no real idea how to end it. He'd had no social life for eight years; aside from not wanting to leave Madhusree with sitters in the early days, everything his old schoolfriends or colleagues had been into had seemed to demand either that he faked being straight, or that he tempted fate. But once there was nothing holding him back, he felt like a stranger in the country all over again. He knew he could have found Toronto's gay bars and nightclubs listed in any tourist guide, but he had no reason to believe that he'd belong in that world, any more than anywhere else.

Felix began unbuttoning Prabir's shirt. Prabir came to his senses and pulled away. He whispered, "What are you doing? She's just in the next room."

"Yes?" Felix laughed. "Somehow I don't think your sister has a problem with us." It was Madhusree who'd introduced them. "And I wasn't planning to tear all your clothes off until we were in your bedroom."

"I'm serious. She's trying to study."

"I can be as quiet as you like."

"*Quiet* just makes it obvious."

Felix shook his head, more amused than annoyed.

Prabir protested, "Don't try telling me it's not distracting, knowing that someone's having sex ten meters away. She has a cladistics test on Monday."

"That's why Darwin invented Sunday afternoons. Listen, I did my entire degree sharing a house with six other students. It was quadraphonic fucking twenty-four hours a day. Madhusree has it easy." Felix stretched his legs and sat back on the couch.

"Yeah, well I'm sorry you were stranded in a bohemian nightmare, but it's not my role to put character-building hurdles in front of her. She's entitled to some peace in her own apartment when she needs it."

Felix said nothing. He glanced at the TV.

Prabir said, "If you'd called me at work we could have met at your place."

Felix kept his mouth shut, refusing to prolong the argument. He reached over and ran the back of his hand along Prabir's forearm, a gesture that seemed both conciliatory and erotic, but Prabir wasn't willing to let the matter drop. He said, "Just admit that I'm not being unreasonable."

Madhusree emerged from her room. "Hi, Felix." She bent down and kissed him on the cheek, then addressed Prabir. "I'm going out. Don't wait up."

"Where are you headed?"

"Nowhere special. I'm just meeting some friends."

"That sounds good." Prabir tried to read her clothes, but he didn't know the codes anymore. She could have been on her way to a diplomatic reception in a five-star hotel or a demolition party, for all he could tell.

He said, "Have fun."

She smiled at him, *you too*, then raised a hand good-bye to Felix.

When she was gone, Felix feigned interest in the TV. The Zeitgeist Channel—a redirection filter that automatically displayed whatever the greatest number of people in the same town or city were watching—was showing a bland office comedy. Prabir said, "Did I ever tell you that one of my foster parents wrote a ten thousand word academic paper called 'Second-Level Mutual Inter-Sitcom Self-Reference as a Signifier for the Sacred'?"

Felix cracked up. "Who published it? *Social Text*?"

"How did you know that?"

In the bedroom, Felix said, "Any chance of a visual-cortex massage?" Prabir knelt over him and gently peeled the electrode sheet from his back. The skin beneath was slightly pale, but it wasn't waxen like the skin beneath a cast or a bandage; the polymer let through plenty of oxygen. Felix claimed to wash the twenty-thousand-dollar device in the Laundromat along with his shirts, but Prabir had never actually witnessed this.

When Felix had been born with malformed retinas, in 2006, artificial replacements were just coming into use. But there'd been no prospect then of wiring the photosensor arrays directly to his brain. Instead, circuitry in the sheet received the signals from his eyes, and the electrodes stimulated nerves in his back. From infancy, he'd learned to interpret the sensations as images.

Prabir started kneading, cautiously. Felix said, "You can be a lot rougher. It's not hypersensitive. It's just skin."

"But . . . do you feel my hands, or do you see something?"

"Both."

"Yeah? What do you see?"

"Abstract patterns. Rows of dots, starbursts. But it's all pretty faint and unconvincing. The whole point is to get a strong sensation that's more compelling as touch than as imagery, so I don't lose the original function of the nerves."

Prabir had found software on the net that let him transform a camera's image into something comparable to the information flowing through the sheet. The impressionistic, monochrome version of his own face that it had shown him had barely been recognizable as a face at all, but Felix could spot people from fifty meters. Experience made all the difference. An operation to connect the artificial retinas directly to his brain had been available for about five years, but he would have found it as hard to adjust to the new way of seeing as Prabir would have found adjusting to the sheet.

Prabir's hands began to stray. After a while, Felix rolled onto his back and pulled Prabir down on top of him. As they kissed, Prabir felt a warmth like liquid fire spreading through his veins, and a growing tightness in his chest, as if he'd been robbed of his breath by the sight of something astonishing. This was what he wanted, more than sex itself. He had no word for it: it was far too physical to be mere tenderness, far too tender to be mere desire.

He said, "You know what I like most about being with you?"

"No."

"Stealing this together." Prabir hesitated, afraid of sounding foolish. But if he couldn't speak now, when could he? "Sex is like a diamond forged in a slaughterhouse. Three billion years of unconscious reproduction. Half a billion more stumbling toward animals that weren't just compelled to mate, but were happy to do it—and finally knew that they were happy. Millions of years spent honing that feeling, making it the most perfect thing in the world. And all just because it worked. All just because it churned out more of the same." He reached down and slid his palm over

Felix's penis. "Anyone can take the diamond; it's there for the asking. But it's not a lure for us. It's not a bribe. We've stolen the prize, we've torn it free. It's ours to do what we like with."

Felix was silent for a while, just smiling up at him. Then he said, "Do you know what an oxbow lake is?"

"No."

"When a river meanders sharply, sometimes the water in the bend ends up cut off from the flow. The river throws off an oxbow lake. That's how I've always thought of it: we're in an oxbow lake, we're not part of the flow. But the river keeps making those lakes. There's something still in it, generation after generation, that makes it happen."

Prabir conceded, "Maybe that's a more honest way of putting it. We had no choice; we're just stranded here by chance." He shrugged. "But I'm glad I'm cut off, I'm glad I'm stranded."

Felix reflected on this, then suggested cryptically, "Maybe you're not, though. Maybe it just looks that way."

Prabir laughed. "You think I'm moonlighting as a sperm donor?"

"No. But you have to ask yourself: Why are there genes in the river that keep making the lakes? What does any lineage have to gain by retaining that trait, in the long run? Swapping the sex of the object of attraction might be the least risky way to make someone infertile; it's less dangerous than messing with anatomy or endocrine function—and a hundred thousand years ago it might not even have entailed getting the crap beaten out of you."

Prabir had his doubts, but he was willing to accept the premise for the sake of the argument. "What's the advantage of being infertile, though?"

Felix said, "Under the right conditions, infertile adults might be able to contribute more to the survival of the lineage by devoting their resources to close relatives, rather than children of their own. It takes so long to raise a human child that it might be worth having the occasional infertile offspring as a kind of insurance policy—to look after the others if something happens to the parents."

Prabir disentangled himself and sat on the side of the bed. His heart was pounding, and there was a red streak across his vision, but he'd pulled away without even thinking. He still lost his temper too easily, but through eight long years with Keith and Amita he'd trained himself to withdraw, not lash out.

"Prabir? *Shit.* I didn't mean—" Felix swung his legs around and sat beside him.

Prabir waited until he could speak calmly. "I really set myself up for that one."

"Come on, you know I didn't mean it like that."

"Didn't you?"

"No!" Felix managed to sound both contrite and indignant. "Even if the theory's true . . . all it's describing is the survival of the trait through a statistical advantage. It says nothing about the actions of individuals." There was an awkward silence, then he conceded, "But it was pretty crass of me to bring it up like that. I'm sorry."

"Forget it." Prabir stared down at the worn linoleum at his feet, his anger draining away. "You know, in high school I used to try to start relationships with girls I thought Madhusree would look up to?" He laughed, though the memory of it still made him cringe. "Which probably would have been enough to doom the entire endeavor, even if I'd been straight. And when I finally stopped kidding myself that there was any chance of that . . . I just felt like I'd fucked up again. I couldn't even give her a sister-in-law with attitude, to make up for my stupidity in bringing her to Amita."

Felix said, "You should have trusted her more. You should have known she didn't need it."

Prabir snorted derisively. "That's easy to say now! But why should you trust a child to overcome being brought up by fools? Was I supposed to assume that she was genetically endowed with so much innate good sense that nothing anyone could do would harm her?"

"Hmm." Felix seemed genuinely lost for a reply, though maybe he was just being diplomatic.

"But you're right," Prabir admitted. "Madhusree didn't need *role models*. By the time we left Amita, I understood that. And I finally stopped worrying about all the ideology Amita would have tried to foist on me if she'd ever found out that I was gay. I started thinking about what it meant for me, instead of what it meant for everyone else." He stopped abruptly, his courage waning; he'd already made enough of a fool of himself.

But Felix squeezed his shoulder and said, "I'm listening. Go on."

Prabir kept his eyes on the floor. "I thought: Maybe I should be glad. Evolution is senseless: the great dumb machine, grinding out microscopic improvements one end, spitting out a few billion corpses from the other. If I'd dragged just one good thing clear of it—if I'd found a way to be happy that cheated the machine— then that was a kind of victory. Like dragging Madhusree clear of the war." He looked up and asked hopefully, "Does that make any sense to you?"

"It makes a lot of sense."

"But you don't believe it's true, do you? You don't believe I've cheated the machine."

Felix hesitated, then made an exasperated noise, as if he'd been trapped into a choice between arguing with him or humoring him.

He said, "I don't believe it matters."

Prabir was suddenly sick of talking. He'd bared his soul, and it had brought them no closer. He took Felix by the shoulders and drew him down onto the bed.

"Ah, that's what I like: less theory, more practice." Felix kissed him deeply, then ran a hand down the center of his body. "You've got a lot of catching up to do."

Prabir said, "I'll race you to the edge of the lake."

"I have a favor to ask you."

Madhusree was washing the breakfast dishes; Prabir was drying. Felix had left, but they'd arranged to meet in the evening. Winter sunlight filled the kitchen, revealing every speck of dust and every imperfection on the room's worn surfaces. Prabir felt utterly contented. He had no problems in his life, just invented complications. They were safe, they were happy. What more did he want?

He said, "Go ahead."

"I need some money."

"Sure. How much?"

Madhusree grimaced, bracing herself. "Five thousand dollars."

"Five *thousand*?" Prabir laughed. "What are you planning to do? Start a business?"

Madhusree shook her head apologetically. "I know, it's a lot to ask." She added, deadpan, "That's why I was so glad when Felix showed up last night. I've been waiting all week to catch you in a good mood."

Prabir flicked her on the arm with the tea towel. "Don't be impertinent. And it makes no difference. I'm always in a good mood."

"Ha."

"So what's the money for?"

"I should be able to pay you back within a couple of years. Once I've graduated—"

Prabir groaned. "You don't have to *pay me back*. Just tell me what you want it for." He scrutinized her face; she stared back at him with exaggerated nonchalance, but she couldn't quite pull it off. She was actually nervous.

He was worried now. "If you're in some kind of trouble, just tell me. I'm not going to be angry."

Madhusree said, "I've been invited to go on a field trip. A joint expedition being mounted by several universities. It's twenty-one people, mostly postdocs, but they're taking two undergraduates. Only the funding doesn't really cover us, so we have to pay our own way."

"But . . . that's fantastic!" Prabir's anxiety gave way to relief, then pride. "Just two places for undergraduates, and they offered you one?" He put down the plate he was drying and embraced her tightly, lifting her off the floor. "Of course you can have the money, you idiot! What did you think I'd say?"

When he drew away from her, Madhusree was blushing. Prabir berated himself silently; he hadn't meant to go overboard and embarrass her.

"So where's the expedition going?" he asked. "Not the Amazon, I hope. Apparently they're so sick of naturalists there that they shoot them on sight."

"Not the Amazon. The South Moluccas."

Prabir said, "That's not funny." Neither was getting murdered in Brazil, actually, but he felt as if she'd responded to a playful jab by kicking him in the head.

"It's not meant to be." She met his gaze; she was more nervous than ever, but she wasn't lying, or teasing him. "That's where we're going."

"Why?" Prabir folded his arms awkwardly; he suddenly felt ungainly, his body strangely skewed. "Why there?"

"Don't get upset."

"I'm not upset. I just want to know."

Madhusree led him to her room and picked up her notepad. "This screen's too small. I'll show you on the TV." They sat on the couch and she summoned up a succession of images from news reports and scientific papers.

The first discovery to attract the attention of the world's biologists had been a fruit pigeon with strange coloration, a hitherto unseen mottled camouflage of green and brown. MRI scans and DNA analysis had yielded more radical differences; Prabir listened in a dreamlike state as Madhusree described structural anomalies in the bird's internal organs, and a catalog of useful mutations in key blood proteins. The Javanese zoologist who'd brought the specimen to light six months ago had only traced it as far as a bird dealer in Ambon, but after word had spread that anything unusual would fetch good money, two other genuine cases had emerged from a torrent of fakes and minor novelties. There was a dead tree frog with young that had apparently been maturing in a water-filled pouch. And there was a bat with the bones in its wings rearranged in an efficient, albeit unspectacular, fashion—thanks to a fully functioning gene for a protein controlling embryological development that did not exist in any other species on the planet. Both had been found on the island of Ceram, more than three hundred kilometers north of Teranesia.

Madhusree had to fight to contain her enthusiasm. "These are amazing discoveries—just like the butterflies, but who knows how many species are involved now? And there *is no* explanation. There's no way of making sense of this. Whatever the cause turns out to be, it's going to shake up biology like nothing since Wallace." Madhusree would have none of this Darwin nonsense; Alfred Wallace might have been too much of a doormat to take the credit he was due, but that wasn't going to stop her putting the record straight.

Prabir was numb. "You didn't tell anyone? About the butter-flies?" The reports made no mention of any earlier find; apparently neither his parents' academic colleagues in Calcutta, nor their sponsor at Silk Rainbow, had felt inclined to volunteer anecdotal evidence about their unpublished work.

Madhusree said, "I probably should have, but I was afraid they'd suspect I was making it up just to get in on the act." She smiled proudly. "But I'm on the team by merit alone. I even said 'no' on the questionnaire when they asked about 'jungle experience.'" She mused, "Maybe the best thing would be for me to keep my mouth shut, and let the expedition stumble on the evidence. I mean, the huts should still be standing, and most of the equipment should be recognizable. There might even be some records intact."

Prabir regarded her stonily. She took his hand and said, "Don't you think they'd be glad if one of us went back? Now that it's safe?" Prabir felt a chill at the base of his spine: whether by choice or out of habit, she'd slipped into the hushed voice she'd used when they'd talked about their parents in his room at Amita's.

He said, "It's not safe. Why do you think it's safe?"

Madhusree examined his face. "Because the war's been over for almost eighteen years."

Prabir pulled his hand free, irritated. "Yeah, and there are lunatics in government in West Papua—"

"I'm not going to West Papua—"

"Who want to claim half the islands—"

"That's *nowhere near* where we're going!"

Prabir's head was beginning to pound. If this wasn't a dream, it was some kind of test. He'd brought her to safety, and now she was standing on the edge of the cliffs, babbling childish nonsense about diving back into the water.

He said, "There are still mines on those islands. Do you think someone's gone through and de-mined them all?"

Madhusree rummaged through files, then waved her notepad at the TV. "You strap this device to your belt. If there's any chemical explosive within twenty meters, it tells you."

The gadget was about as big as a matchbox. Prabir said, "I don't believe you. Buried explosives? *How?* You know the Indonesians had NQR-aware mines? If you send out a radio pulse, they'll triangulate your position and give you a gut full of shrapnel."

"It doesn't use Nuclear Quadrupole Resonance; it's entirely passive. There's a radiation signature from the explosive: secondary particles emitted from the constituent atoms due to background and cosmic radiation."

"And . . . *that thing's* sensitive enough to identify chemical composition from secondary radiation?"

Madhusree nodded earnestly.

Prabir stared at the screen, feeling like a doddering centenarian who'd blinked and missed a decade. "I've been in banking too long."

"Isn't that a tautology?"

Prabir laughed, and felt something tearing inside. He could give in; it would be easy. He could shout, "Go! Go!" and dance around the room with her, playing proud supportive big brother. Then she'd fly off to salvage her parents' reputation and complete their work, like a fairy-tale princess returning from exile to right all wrongs and avenge all injustices.

He said, "I can't afford it."

"I'm sorry?"

He turned to her. "Five thousand dollars? I don't know what I was thinking. I don't even have that much in my account. And without collateral . . ." He raised his hands apologetically.

Madhusree bit her lip and eyed him with frank disbelief, but Prabir was almost certain that she wouldn't call his bluff. She might have argued all weekend about the risks the expedition would face, but she wouldn't make a scene over money.

She said, "OK. I knew it was a lot. I'll have to see about raising it some other way."

"Some other way? How long do you have?"

"Two months."

Prabir frowned sympathetically. "So what were you thinking of doing?"

Madhusree shrugged and said casually, "I've got some ideas. Don't worry about it." She stood and left the room abruptly.

Prabir put his face in his hands. He hated lying to her, but he was certain now that he'd made the right decision. Even if there really was some revolutionary discovery waiting to be made on the island—and not just a very unpleasant mutagen that left a vast number of stillborn victims rotting in the jungle for every spectacular survivor—she could read about it like everyone else.

That would make her angry. But it wouldn't kill her.

"Are you sure it's all right for me to be here?" Felix's workroom looked like a biology lab in which an eclectic art thief had stashed a few million dollars worth of stolen goods. Prabir didn't recognize any of the paintings awaiting assessment, hanging in a rack like posters in a shop, but the richness of the pigments and the skill of the execution was enough to make him nervous just being near them. "I don't want to get you into trouble."

"Don't be stupid." Felix was glued to a microscope, manually removing the last flakes of corrosion from an arrowhead after electrochemical treatment. "We have visitors back here all the time. You can't steal anything; the building's too smart.

Try swallowing one of those coins and see how far you get."

"No, it's the frog collection that's starting to look tempting."

Felix groaned. "I know, the booking's for nine. I won't be much longer."

Prabir watched him working, envious and admiring. Anything involving fine visual detail was tricky for Felix, but with stationary objects he could build up a mental picture with higher resolution than the electrode sheet provided at any given moment, accumulating extra data as his eyes swept back and forth across the scene. Apparently the process had become partly instinctive, but it still required a certain amount of sheer doggedness, a constant mental effort to maintain the model in his head.

Prabir said, "I wish I'd met you nine years ago."

Felix replied without looking up. "I was fifteen. You would have gone to prison."

"This is a hypothetical: we both get to be eighteen."

"That would have been even worse. You wouldn't have wanted to know me then."

Prabir laughed. "Why?"

"Oh . . . I did a lot of stupid things."

"Like what?"

Felix didn't respond immediately; Prabir wasn't sure whether the question discomforted him, or whether he was merely concentrating on his work. "I used to go out with the sheet off, just to prove I didn't need it. To convince myself that I could have lived a hundred years ago, and still got by."

"What's so stupid about that?"

"It wasn't true. I'd grown up with it, I didn't have the skills to cope without it. I knew that, but I kept pushing my luck." He laughed. "I met this guy in a club one night. He hung around talking to me for about three hours. There was a lot of touching: hands on shoulders, guiding me through the crowd. Nothing overtly sexual, but it was more than just polite. He was pretty evasive, but after a while I was almost certain that he was coming on to me—"

"Three hours of this, and he wasn't?"

"I found out later that he had some complicated theory about picking up women. You know: outdoors you can walk a dog as a kind of character reference, but they don't let you do that in nightclubs. It's just a pity he didn't tell me I was meant to be playing tragically disabled spaniel." Prabir was outraged, but Felix started laughing again. "I lured him out into an alley to see what he'd do with no one else around. I ended up spending a month in hospital."

"Shit." As Prabir's anger subsided, a fierce core of protectiveness remained. But anything he said would have sounded melodramatic now that Felix had reached the point where he could laugh the whole thing off.

"Madhusree told me about the expedition." Felix kept his eyes on the arrowhead. "She can't understand why you're so set against it."

Prabir was about to deny this and stick to his claim of insufficient funds, but then it occurred to him that Felix would probably offer to help. He said, "It's a dangerous place. There are still pirates all around those islands."

Felix didn't contradict him, directly. "The expedition's being led by experienced local scientists; I'm sure they'll take sensible precautions. And I can't think of many places a biologist would want to go that aren't potentially dangerous, one way or another."

Prabir shifted awkwardly on the lab stool. It was easy to laugh off the sense of betrayal he felt, at the thought of Madhusree and Felix ganging up against him. But when he brushed aside his paranoia and told himself that Madhusree was entitled to seek other

allies—it couldn't always be the two of them against the world—
that realization still left him feeling almost unbearably lonely.

Felix looked up and said bluntly, "She was a lot younger
than you when your parents died. If she's not worried about
going back, why can't you just accept that?" He seemed genuinely puzzled. "You're the one who always wanted her to be
proud of them. Now she wants to carry on their work! And even
if there'd been no new discoveries . . . don't you think she might
have wanted to return eventually? Just to see where everything
happened? However much you've told her, it's not the same."

Prabir said, "Can we get out of here? They're going to give
our table to someone else."

"Yeah, I've finished." Felix packed up quickly, then grabbed
his jacket. "I'm sorry; I'm not going to harangue you all night.
But I promised her I'd talk to you."

"And now you have."

Felix led the way out of the workroom, into a maze of corridors. "If you don't want to talk to me, talk to her. Properly. You
owe her that."

"*I* owe *her*? I've only given her eighteen years of my life!"

Felix snorted with amusement. "That's one thing I love
about you: you could have given her a lung and a kidney, and you
still wouldn't be able to milk it for sympathy with any convic-
tion."

Prabir was caught off balance. "Don't be so fucking patron-
izing." The compliment pleased him, but this wasn't the time to
admit that.

Felix said, "This is a good thing for both of you, any way
you look at it. And if you think it's dangerous for Madhusree to
go traipsing through the jungle for a couple of weeks, you can't
have much idea of what most nineteen-year-olds get up to."

"Oh, so now you're an expert on that, too?"

"No, but I can still remember what it was like."

Prabir had no reply. He'd always imagined that was how he understood Madhusree: by being young enough to remember. But nothing about his own life at nineteen resembled hers. It wasn't just the fact that he'd had a child to look after; he'd also had any adolescent attraction to risk knocked out of him, well in advance. His entire adulthood had been devoid of excitement. *Why should Madhusree have to pay the same price?* The whole point had been to make things better for her, to try to give her something like a normal life.

No, the whole point was to keep her safe.

Prabir stopped dead. There was a dusty display case full of tropical butterflies hanging on the wall, with fading labels that looked like they'd been produced on a manual typewriter. It had probably been hanging there since some era when this corridor lay on a route between public exhibits, long before the latest round of rebuilding.

He said, "Getting her away from there was the one good thing I've done in my life. And now everyone expects me to pack her bags and buy her a ticket. It's surreal. Why don't you just ask me to blow my brains out while you're at it? I'm not going to do it."

Felix backtracked, and saw what he was looking at. "What you did was get her away from the war. She wouldn't be going back to that."

Prabir had lost interest in trying to justify himself. He said flatly, "You weren't there. You don't know anything about it."

Felix wasn't that easily intimidated. "No, but I'll listen to whatever you want to tell me. It'd be a fucking lonely world if that never worked."

Prabir aimed lower. "Doesn't it ever cross your mind that there are things I don't want you to understand?"

• • •

Prabir worked late, to keep his mind blank for as long as possible. He tinkered for five hours with a perfectly good class definition template for tellers, trying to improve its eye contact and shave a few milliseconds off its response times. In the end he gave up, discarding everything he'd done, trawling through the automatic backups and erasing them all manually—the closest he could get to the physical experience of crumpling up a sheaf of paper.

As he walked out of the building he felt a kind of defiant pride, in place of the usual sense of regret at his stupidity. It wasn't as if he had better things to do. He didn't want to be with Felix or Madhusree. He didn't want to be alone with his thoughts. Numbing himself with a few hours of vacuous make-work every night until he was safely asleep on his feet was infinitely preferable to taking up alcohol.

Sitting in the bus, he ached all over. He was shivering, too, though he'd felt the usual blast of warm air as he'd stepped on board. With a shock he realized that he probably had some kind of mild viral infection. Despite the change of climate he hadn't suffered so much as a cold since arriving in Toronto; the immigration authorities had inoculated him against everything in sight. But he hadn't kept up to date with booster shots, and it looked as if some new strain had finally broken through his defenses.

When he entered the apartment, Madhusree's door was open, but her room was in darkness. Even from a distance, as Prabir's eyes adjusted he could see that her desk had been tidied, everything cleared away or straightened into neat piles.

There was a note taped to the fridge. She'd never told him exactly when the expedition was leaving, but he'd been half expecting something like this for days.

He read the note several times, compulsively, as if he might have missed something. Madhusree explained that she'd raised part of the money working in a café, and borrowed the rest from friends. She apologized for doing everything behind his back, but pointed out that this had made it easier for both of them. She promised to reveal nothing about their parents' work until she returned and they'd had a chance to discuss the matter properly; in the meantime, the expedition would have to rely on its own discoveries. She'd be back within three months. She'd be careful.

Prabir sat in the kitchen with tears streaming down his cheeks. He'd never felt happier for her, or more proud of her. She'd overcome everything now. Even him. She'd refused to let him smother her with his paranoia and insecurity.

He suddenly recalled the night they'd resolved to leave Amita. At the start of the week, Madhusree had announced that her class had begun studying the civil rights movement. Then, at dinner on Friday, she'd informed Keith and Amita that she finally understood what their work at the university was all about.

Keith had flashed Prabir a victorious smirk, and Amita had cooed, "Aren't you clever? Why don't you tell us what you've learned."

Madhusree had expounded with her usual nine-year-old's volubility. "In the 1960s and '70s, there were people in all the democratic countries who didn't have any real power, and they started going to the people who did have all the power and saying, 'All these principles of equality you've been talking about since the French Revolution are very nice, but you don't seem to be taking them very seriously. You're all hypocrites, actually. So we're going to make you take those principles seriously.' And they held demonstrations and bus rides, and occupied buildings, and it was very embarrassing for the people in power, because the other people had such a good argument, and anyone who listened seriously had to agree with them.

"Feminism was working, and the civil rights movement was working, and all the other social justice movements were getting more and more support. *So*, in the 1980s, the CIA—" she turned to Keith and explained cheerfully, "this is where X-Files Theory comes into it—hired some really clever linguists to invent a secret weapon: an incredibly complicated way of talking about politics that didn't actually make any sense, but which spread through all the universities in the world, because it sounded so impressive. And at first, the people who talked like this just hitched their wagon to the social justice movements, and everyone else let them come along for the ride, because they seemed harmless. But then they climbed on board the peace train and threw out the driver.

"So instead of going to the people in power and saying, 'How about upholding the universal principles you claim to believe in?' the people in the social justice movements ended up saying things like, 'My truth narrative is in competition with your truth narrative!' And the people in power replied, 'Woe is me! You've thrown me in the briar patch!' And everyone else said, 'Who are these idiots? Why should we trust them, when they can't even speak properly?' And the CIA was happy. And the people in power were happy. And the secret weapon lived on in the universities for years and years, because everyone who'd played a part in the conspiracy was too embarrassed to admit what they'd done."

After a long silence, Amita had suggested in a strained voice, "You might not have understood that lesson properly, Maddy. These are difficult ideas, and you're still quite young."

Madhusree had replied confidently, "Oh no, Amita. I understood. It was very clear."

Late that night, she'd snuck into Prabir's room. When they'd finally stopped laughing—with their faces pressed into pillows and hands to muffle the sound—Madhusree had turned to him and pleaded solemnly, "Get me out of here. Or I'll go mad."

Prabir had replied, "That's what I do best."

He'd found a job the following weekend. But after six months working three nights a week filling vending machines—telling Amita he was studying with friends—he'd finally accepted what he'd known all along: part-time work would never be enough. A week before he graduated from high school, he'd smooth-talked his way into an interview at the bank, and demonstrated on his own notepad that he had all the skills required for a software development position they'd advertised. When the personnel manager conceded his technical abilities but started raising other hurdles, Prabir pointed out that his lack of tertiary qualifications would save them a third of the salary.

He'd gone straight from the interview to a real-estate agent, and whispered the news to Madhusree that night by the light of the TV.

"We're heading south."

Felix arrived just after eleven. As he entered the apartment he explained warily, "I just wondered how you were taking the news."

"You knew she was leaving tonight?"

"Yeah. She thought she had to tell me, because I loaned her some money."

Felix waited for a response. Prabir recoiled with mock indignation. "Traitor!" He shook his head, smiling abashedly. "No, I'm OK. I'm just sorry I screwed you both around so much."

They sat in the kitchen. Felix said, "She's going to be independent soon. She'll have money of her own. A place of her own."

Prabir was wounded. "You think that's what this was all about? You think I get some kick out of holding the purse strings, telling her what she can and can't do?"

Felix groaned, misunderstood. "*No*. I just wanted to know

what your plans were. Because once she's supporting herself, you're going to be free to do anything you want. Quit the bank. Travel, study."

"Oh yeah? I'm not that rich."

Felix shrugged. "I'll help you."

Prabir was embarrassed. "I'm not that poor, either." He mused, "If I can hang on at the bank until she graduates, that'll be ten years. I'll have access to part of my pension fund." He shivered, suddenly aware of the fact that he was babbling on about money while Madhusree was flying straight for the one place on Earth he'd sworn to keep her away from. "It's strange. I didn't think I'd be so calm. But she's really not in any danger, is she?"

"None at all."

"Ceram, Ambon, Kai Besar . . . they're just islands like any other now."

"Safer than Mururoa."

Prabir said, "Did I ever tell you about the time she debated a Texan creationist minister on the net, and he publically admitted that she'd changed his mind?"

Felix smiled and shook his head stoically. "No. Go on, tell me."

"He was a brave man, actually. He got excommunicated, or whatever it is they do to lapsed creationists."

"I believe the technical term is 'lynching.'"

They sat talking until four A.M. When they staggered into bed, Felix was asleep within seconds. Prabir stared blearily at the open door of his room; even with the apartment to themselves he felt exposed, but he was too cold to get up and close it.

He dreamed that his father was standing in the doorway, looking in. Prabir couldn't see his face in the darkness, and struggled to decide whether his stare was reproachful. Everything he knew about Rajendra suggested that he wouldn't have been angry, but Prabir was still ashamed that he'd let his father stumble upon him like this, without warning.

But as the silhouette in the doorway took on more detail, Prabir realized that his father was oblivious to Felix. There were more important things on his mind. Rajendra was holding an infant in his arms, rag-doll limp. He was rocking her back and forth, weeping inconsolably with grief.

Prabir lay in the bath so long that he ran out of room to add hot water. He climbed out, shivering, and pulled the plug.

As the bath refilled, he picked up the paper knife, closed his eyes, rehearsed the strokes. He'd deliberately avoided testing the blade on his skin; the only part of the knife he'd touched was the plastic handle. Anyone who could stick a kebab skewer through his cheeks ought to be able to lull the relevant part of his brain into believing that there was no real threat from a couple of scrapes with this toy.

He stepped into the bath again, scalding his legs, swearing irritably. He didn't want to feel any discomfort at all now; he wanted to die as pleasantly as possible. But every kind of potentially lethal legal pharmaceutical he could imagine getting his hands on came with a dose-limiting enzyme, and he couldn't bring himself to buy street drugs that would turn him into a stranger as he went. Drain cleaner was even less attractive, and he didn't trust himself to have the courage to jump from a bridge.

He lay down in the bath, submerged up to his chin. He went over the message to Felix and Madhusree one more time; it was sitting in his notepad in the kitchen, waiting to be sent, but Prabir knew it by heart. He was happy with the wording, he decided. Neither of them were idiots: they'd understand his reasons, and they wouldn't blame themselves.

He'd done what he'd set out to do: he'd carried her to safety.

He was proud of that. But it wouldn't do either of them much good if he kept on going through the motions for another fifty years, just because it was the only thing that felt worthwhile to him.

He'd very nearly kept her from joining the expedition, which would have ruined her whole career. Two days after she'd left, he'd almost followed her, which would have humiliated her in front of all her colleagues. And though he knew that she'd be safe, there was nothing he could do, nothing he could tell himself, to banish the feeling that he was standing idly by while she walked across a minefield.

There was only one way to cut the knot.

Prabir dragged the blade across his left wrist. He barely felt it pierce the skin; he opened his eyes to check the extent of the wound.

A red plume, already wider than his hand, was spreading through the water. The dark core looked almost solid, like some tightly packed blood-rich membrane uncoiling from the space beneath his skin. For several long seconds he lay motionless and watched the plume growing, observing the effect of his heartbeat on the flow, following the tongues of fluid at the edges as they diffused into the water.

Then he declaimed loudly, to remove all doubt, "I don't want to do this. I'm not going to do this."

He scrambled to his feet and reached for a towel. The wound was even more shocking when it hit the air, spraying blood down over his chest and legs. He wrapped it in the towel, almost slipping on the floor of the bath, his paralysis turning to panic.

He stumbled out of the bathroom. *It was only a cut, a paper-thin slit.* There had to be something he could do to stop the bleeding. *Tie a tourniquet.* But where, exactly? And how tight? If he got it wrong, he could still bleed to death. Or lose his arm.

He knelt in front of the TV. "Search: emergency first aid."

The entire screen was filled instantly with tiny icons; there must have been thirty thousand of them. It looked like a garden of mutated red crosses, stylized flowers in some toy-world evolution program. Prabir swayed on his knees, appalled but mesmerized, trying to think what to do next. *Help me, Baba.*

"No sacred, no mystic, no spiritual." The garden thinned visibly. "No alternative. No holistic." The towel was turning red. "No *yin*, no *yang*, no *chi*, no *karma*. No nurturing, no nourishing, no numinous . . ."

The TV remarked smugly, "Your filtering strategy is redundant," and displayed a Venn diagram to prove its point. The first three words he'd excluded had eliminated about a quarter of the icons, but after that he'd just been re-lassoing various subsets of the New Age charlatans he'd already tossed out. Whatever pathology had spawned the remainder of the noise employed an entirely different vocabulary.

Prabir was at a loss as to how to proceed. He pointed to an icon at random; a pleasant, neuter face appeared and began to speak. "If the body is a text, as Derrida and Foucault taught us—"

Prabir closed the site then fell forward laughing, burying his face between his forearms, pressing down on the wound with his forehead. "Thank you, Amita! Thank you, Keith!" How could he have forgotten everything they'd taught him?

"No *transgressive*."

He looked up. Thousands of icons had vanished, but tens of thousands remained. Half a dozen new fads had swept the anti-science world since Amita's day. *Liberation Prosody. Abbess Logic. Faustian Analysis. Dryad Theory.* Prabir hadn't bothered to track their ascent or learn their jargon; he was free of all that shit, it couldn't touch him anymore.

He stared at the screen, light-headed. There had to be genuine help, genuine knowledge, buried in there somewhere. But he'd die before he found it.

As he'd meant to. So why fight it? There was a comforting drowsiness spreading through his body, a beautifully numbing absence flowing in through the wound. He'd made the whole business messier than it might have been, but in a way it seemed far less bleak, far less austere, to die like this—absurdly and incompetently—than if he'd done it in the bath without a hitch. It wasn't too late to curl up on the floor and close his eyes.

No, but it was almost too late to do anything else.

He staggered to his feet and bellowed, "Call an ambulance!"

"You might not find her," Felix warned him. "Are you prepared for that?"

Prabir glanced up nervously at the departure list; he'd be boarding the flight to Sydney in five minutes. Madhusree had covered her tracks well, and no one at the university had been willing to provide him with the expedition's itinerary. All he could do was fly to Ambon, then start asking around.

He said, "I'm doing this to satisfy my own curiosity. It was my parents' work; I want to know where it would have led them. If I happen to run into my sister while I'm there, that will be a pleasant coincidence, nothing more."

Felix replied dryly, "That's right: stick to the cover story, even under torture."

Prabir turned to him. "You know what I hate most about you, Menéndez?"

"No."

"Everything that doesn't kill you makes you stronger. Everything that doesn't kill *me* just fucks me up a bit more."

115

Felix grimaced sympathetically. "Irritating, isn't it? I'll see if I can cultivate a few more neuroses while you're away, just to even things out a bit." He took hold of Prabir's hand between the seats, and stroked the all-but-vanished scar. "But if I'd met you when I was fucked-up myself, it probably would have killed us both."

"Yeah." Prabir's chest tightened. He said, "I won't always be like this. I won't always be dragging you down."

Felix looked him in the eye and said plainly, "You don't drag me down."

Prabir's flight was called. He said, "I'll bring you back a souvenir. Do you want anything particular?"

Felix thought about it, then shook his head. "You decide. Anything from a brand new phylum will be fine by me."

Chapter 7

The flight from Toronto touched down in Los Angeles and Honolulu before terminating in Sydney. Prabir changed planes for Darwin without leaving the airport. Choosing this route over Tokyo and Manila had been purely a matter of schedules and ticket prices, but as the red earth below gave way to verdant pasture and great mirrors of water, it was impossible not to dwell upon how close he was coming to retracing his steps away from the island. The boat full of refugees from Yamdena had landed in Darwin, and he and Madhusree had been flown back there from Exmouth before finally leaving the country via Sydney. The more he thought about it, the more he wished he'd gone out of his way to avoid these signposts; the last thing he wanted to do was descend systematically through the layers of his past, as if he was indulging in some kind of deliberate act of regression. He should have swooped down from Toronto by an unfamiliar route, and arrived in Ambon feeling as much like a stranger as possible.

He stepped out of the terminal at Darwin into a blast of tropical heat and humidity. It was barely half an hour later, local time, than it had been in Toronto when he left; even with three stops along the way, he'd almost kept pace with the turning of the

Earth. The sky was full of threatening clouds, which seemed to spread the glare of the afternoon sun rather than diminish it. February was the middle of the wet season here, as it was in most of the former Indonesia, but Madhusree's expedition wasn't mistimed; in the Moluccas the pattern of the monsoon winds was reversed, and there it would be *musim teduh*, the calm season, the season for travel.

The flight to Ambon left the next morning. Prabir slung his backpack over his shoulders and started walking, ignoring the bus that was waiting to take passengers into the city center. Once he checked into the hotel he'd probably fall asleep immediately, but if he could hold off until early evening he'd be able to start the next day refreshed and in synch. With six hours to kill and no interest in window shopping, the simplest method he could think of to stave off boredom would be to wander through the city on foot. His notepad had already acquired a local street map, so he was in no danger of getting lost.

He headed north out of the airport precinct, past playing fields and a cemetery, into a stretch of calm green tropical suburbia. At first he felt self-conscious when he passed other pedestrians—the size of his backpack marked him clearly as a tourist—but no one gave him a second glance. It felt good to stretch his legs; the pack wasn't heavy, and even the surreal heat was more of a novelty than a hardship.

There was nothing on these serene, palm-lined streets to remind him of the detention camp two thousand kilometers away, but as he passed what looked like the grounds of a boarding school, he recalled his parents discussing the possibility of sending him to Darwin to study. If they'd had their way, he might have sat out the war here. *So why hadn't he?* Had he dissuaded them somehow? Thrown some kind of tantrum? He couldn't remember.

The afternoon downpour began, but the trees along the verge

gave plenty of cover and his pack was waterproof. He kept walking north, away from the hotel. The earthy smell of the air as it rained made him ache with a kind of frustrated nostalgia: He couldn't decide whether the scent of the storm reminded him of Calcutta, the island, or just Darwin itself.

The answer came a few minutes later, when the road ended at a hospital. He stood in the rain, staring at the entrance. He would never have recognized the building by sight alone, but he knew that he'd been here before.

His mother had been in labor for eight or nine hours, starting late at night. He'd been put to bed somewhere far enough away from the delivery room that he couldn't hear a sound, and he'd fallen asleep assuming—with a mixture of resentment and gratitude—that he'd miss out on everything. But in the morning his father had woken him and asked, "Do you want to see your sister being born?"

While the violence of the birth itself had unnerved him, even his mother's suffering hadn't been able to distract him entirely from the strangest part of what he was witnessing. Two cells that might as easily have been shed from his parents' bodies like flakes of skin had instead succeeded in growing into an entirely new human being. That they'd done this deep inside his mother was clearly of no small consequence to her, but what struck Prabir even more forcefully than the realization that he'd emerged in the same dramatic fashion himself was the understanding that he too had been built from nothing but air and food and ancestry, just as this child had been built, month by month back on the island, right before his eyes.

He'd long ago accepted his parents' account of his own growth. He was not at all like a child-shaped balloon, merely swelling up with food; rather, he grew the way a city grew, with buildings and streets endlessly torn apart and reconstructed. A vast collection of templates inside him was used to assemble, from the smallest fragments of each digested meal, the molecules needed to repair and rebuild and extend every part of his body. Great fleets of microscopic couriers rode crystalline scaffolding, swam rivers thicker than treacle, and negotiated guarded portals to carry the new material to the places it was needed.

All of this was astonishing and unsettling enough, but he'd always shied away from pursuing it to its logical conclusion. Only once Madhusree had emerged, staring uncomprehendingly into a room full of faces and lights that he knew she'd never remember, had Prabir finally seen beyond the vanishing point of his own memories. The thing he knew firsthand about her was equally true of himself: he had once not existed at all. He'd been air and water, crops and fertilizer, a mist of anonymous atoms spread across India, across the whole planet. Even the genes that had been used to build him had been kept apart until the last moment, like the torn halves of a pirate's map of an island yet to be created.

While his mother cradled the child in her arms, his father had knelt by the bed, kissing them both, laughing and sobbing, delirious with happiness. Prabir had been relieved that his mother was no longer in agony, and quite smitten with his newborn sister, but that hadn't stopped him from wondering what Madhusree had actually done to deserve all this adoration. Nothing he hadn't done himself. And that would always be true: however precocious she turned out to be, he'd had too much of a head start to be overtaken. His position was unassailable.

Unless he was working from the wrong assumptions. He'd always imagined that he'd somehow earned his parents' love, but what if his sister's reception was proof that you began life not with a blank slate, devoid of either merit or blame, but with the kind of unblemished record that could only be marred? In that case, the best he could hope for would be to slip no further while he waited for her to fall as far.

He'd felt ashamed of these thoughts immediately, and though that wasn't enough to quash his jealousy, he'd resolved, there and then, never to take it out on Madhusree. If his parents continued to favor her—once the understandable fog of emotions brought on by the birth itself had cleared—then that would be their fault entirely. It was obvious that she'd played no part in it.

Nineteen-and-a-half years later, Prabir wasn't sure that any of these thoughts really had run through his head in the delivery room. He didn't trust memories of sudden revelations or resolutions; it seemed more likely that he'd reached the same conclusions over a period of months, then grafted them onto his memories of the birth. Still, it made him cringe to think that he could have been so calculating and smug, however absurd it was to judge himself in retrospect by adult standards. And in one sense he couldn't even claim to have advanced much beyond that child's perspective: he still couldn't untangle the reasons for his parents' love.

On one level it seemed utterly unmysterious: caring for your children was as indispensable as every other drive for reproduction or survival. It might be a struggle to raise a family, the way it was a struggle to gather food or find a mate, but the end result was as unequivocally satisfying as eating or fucking, as self-evidently right as breathing.

The only trouble was, this was bullshit. Even writing off as aberrations the vast number of parents who never came close to that ideal, no one's love was unconditional. Children could gain or lose favor through their actions, just like any stranger. Had the possibility of rejection itself been fine-tuned by natural selection, to improve the child's prospects of survival by instilling a suitably pragmatic moral code? Or was it all a thousand times subtler than that? Human parents weren't bundles of twitching reflexes; they agonized over every decision. And yet, you could reflect and reason all you liked, mapping out an elaborate web of consequences that might not have occurred to you if you'd acted in haste, but in the end you still had to decide what was right, and the touchstone for that was as primal as it was for any gut feeling.

Felix would have told him that none of this mattered—however fascinating it was, scientifically. In the end *we are what we are*, and it makes no difference how we got there. But that wasn't such an easy mantra to recite when you'd traveled halfway around the planet, with no clear idea why. Prabir had resigned himself to his inability to reason away the dread he felt at the thought of Madhusree setting foot on the island; whether or not it was out of all proportion to any real risk she faced, he couldn't expect to shake off the past so lightly. But he wasn't even sure what fear, or what drive, the fulcrum of Teranesia had rendered so powerful. *Was he still trying to impress his dead parents with his dedication?* He'd always relied on his memory of them for guidance—and their imagined approval had always been the one sure sign that he'd done something right—but he didn't believe that he'd reduced Madhusree to a pawn in some game with the ghosts in his head. Still less could he accept that everything between them revolved around the obscure Mendelian fact that she was the only living person who could carry half his genes into the future. Madhusree wasn't only his sister; she was his oldest friend and staunchest ally. Why wouldn't he take a few weeks' vacation from a job he hated to look out for her in a dangerous corner of the world?

Prabir turned away from the hospital and started back toward the city. However much he might have loved, admired, and respected her if they'd met for the first time under Amita's roof—if she'd been adopted from some other family entirely, but still chosen to flee that madhouse with him at the first opportunity—he was almost certain that he would never have been willing to follow her all the way to Teranesia.

• • •

Prabir had flown into Ambon once before, but he had no clear memory of the descent. This time, at least, it was startlingly apparent—as it had never been from sea level, approaching in the ferry—that the mist-shrouded island was actually a pair of distinct volcanic bodies, connected in geologically recent times by a narrow isthmus of silt. Ambon Harbor was the largest part of what had once been the strait between these two separate islands; if it had penetrated any deeper it would have come out the other side.

Pattimura Airport lay on the northwest shore of the harbor; Ambon City was ten kilometers due east. Prabir watched one speedboat crossing the water, overloaded with people and luggage, and decided to take the long way around.

Waiting on the highway for the bus, he felt self-conscious in a very different way than he had in Darwin; he was almost afraid that someone might recognize him and ask him to account for his long absence. That wasn't very likely; the people they'd met here had been friendly enough, but with his broken Indonesian and the family's infrequent visits, he'd never really had the chance to get to know anyone.

The trip around the harbor took almost an hour. The water looked much cleaner than he remembered; there'd usually been a plume of oil and floating garbage stretching out to surround the ferry before it had even entered the harbor.

He alighted in the city and set out for the hotel. The streets were cobblestone, recently refurbished, lined with tall palm trees at regular intervals; the whining scooters he remembered being everywhere had apparently been banished from the city center. There were no billboards, and no intrusively modern signs on the shops; an almost uniform row of white stone façades shone in the sun. The whole thing was probably a calculated attempt to re-create the style of the Dutch colonial period for the tourists, most traces of the real thing having been comprehensively bombed into dust during World War II.

He'd never learned his way around Ambon as a child, relying on his parents to shepherd him. He recognized none of the buildings he passed, and he had no real sense of where he was in relation to the shops and markets where they'd bought provisions. But the angle of the light, the scent of the air, were enough to evoke a discomforting sense of reconnection. He didn't need to see the past re-created brick by brick to feel the tug of it inside him.

A small group of people in brightly colored, formal-looking clothes stood at the edge of the main square, arms outstretched at their sides, eyes half closed, perspiring heavily, singing. Behind them, a sagging cardboard sign bore a few dozen words in Indonesian. Prabir was too tired to dredge his memory for an uncertain translation, and when he saw a citation at the bottom—book, chapter, and verse—he decided not to bother fishing out his notepad for help.

Hordes of evangelical Christians from the U.S. had descended on the region in the wake of the civil war, but they'd had far more success in West Papua, where even the current president had been converted to born-again psychosis. Prabir wasn't sure why the Moluccans had proved so resistant this time around; they'd been a pushover for Spanish Catholicism, then chucked it all in for Dutch Protestantism—though that must have been at least partly a matter of trying to get along with whoever held the guns to their heads from year to year. Maybe the American missionaries hadn't tried hard enough to conceal their phobia of Islam, which would not have gone down too well here. Relations between Christians and Muslims on Ambon had suffered almost irreparable damage in the early years of the post-Suharto chaos, with provocateur-led riots claiming hundreds of lives. A decade later, entire villages had been wiped out under cover of war. With independence, the government of the Republik Maluku Selatan had set about reviving a five-hundred-year-old tradition of alliances between Christian and Muslim villages; these *pela* alliances had once been famously successful at defusing interreligious tensions, and still ran so deep on some outlying islands that Christians built mosques for their neighbors, Muslims built churches. The return of *pela*, with the opportunity it provided to write off the years of violence as an aberration, was probably the main reason the ABRMS hadn't torn itself apart in an endless cycle of revenge killing.

Prabir was about to move on when he noticed the exhibit at the singers' feet, largely obscured by the pedestrians passing in front of it. Some kind of animal had been inexpertly dissected, and the parts laid out on a stained canvas sheet. Reluctantly, he moved closer. The viscera and the separated bones meant nothing to him; the intended audience had probably had more experience with butchering animals, and would at least know what was meant to impress them. The skull looked like a small marsupial's, a tree kangaroo or a cuscus. Some pieces of the hide were thickly furred; others were covered in shiny brown scales. But if the creature really had been some kind of astonishing chimera, why lessen the impact by cutting it up?

One of the evangelists opened her eyes and beamed at him. His clothes and backpack must have given him away as a foreigner; the woman addressed him in halting English. "End times, brother! End times upon us!"

Prabir replied apologetically, in Bengali, that he had absolutely no idea what she was talking about.

The desk clerk at the Amboina Hotel was far too polite to laugh when Prabir asked where he might hire a boat as cheaply as possible. The response—couched in the most diplomatic language—

was that he could forget about the "cheap" part and join the queue. Everyone who'd arrived in town for the last two months had been looking for a boat; it was a seller's market.

This was a dispiriting start, but Prabir fought down the urge to retreat into pessimism. "There was a group of about twenty people who would have passed through Ambon three weeks ago. Scientists, on an expedition being mounted by some foreign universities. Have you heard anything about that?" There were half a dozen other places they could have stayed, but he had nothing to lose by asking.

"No. But we have many guests here from foreign universities."

"You mean, in general? Or in the hotel right now?"

The man glanced at his watch. "Mostly in the bar, right now."

Prabir couldn't believe his luck. They must have completed the first stage of their work and returned to base to recuperate. They could hardly have been stranded here all this time; they would have organized transport well in advance.

He sat in his room for forty minutes, trying to decide exactly what he'd say to Madhusree. How he'd explain his presence, what he'd propose they do. If he'd picked up his notepad and called her from Toronto, she would have talked him into staying there, but this was scarcely any better. He'd imagined tracking her down somewhere so remote that she couldn't simply order him home, but here there was nothing to stop her. The next flight out of Ambon was never more than a day away.

He wouldn't push his luck: he wouldn't ask to be allowed to tag along with the expedition. He'd suggest that he stay on in the hotel, so he could see her each time she came back into town. That wouldn't embarrass her too much, surely?

The longer he thought about it, the more nervous he became. But it was no use trying to rehearse the whole encounter, writing scripts for both of them in his head. He'd go downstairs and face her, see how she reacted, and play it by ear.

The bar opened into a shaded courtyard; all the customers were out there catching the afternoon breeze. Prabir bought a syrupy fruit concoction whose contents defied translation; the bartender assured him that it was nonalcoholic, but that seemed to be based on the dubious assumption that the whole thing wouldn't spontaneously ferment before his eyes, like an over-ripe mango. Prabir took one sip and changed his mind; the sugar concentration was high enough to kill any microorganisms by sheer osmosis. He steeled himself and walked out into the court-yard.

He scanned the tables, but he couldn't see Madhusree any-where. There were only about thirty people in the courtyard; it didn't take him long to convince himself that she was not among them.

Someone stretched a hand out to him. "Martin Lowe, Mel-bourne University." Prabir turned. Lowe was a middle-aged man, visibly sunburnt—not surprising if he'd been at sea for the past three weeks. There were two other men seated at the same table, intent on some kind of printout. He shook Lowe's hand distract-edly and introduced himself.

Lowe asked amiably, "Are you looking for someone?"

Prabir hesitated; he couldn't announce his intentions baldly to one of Madhusree's colleagues, before he'd even spoken to her. "Is the whole expedition staying here? In this hotel?"

"Expedition? Ah. I think you'd better have a seat."

Prabir complied. Lowe said, "You mean the biologists, don't you? I'm afraid you've missed them; they left weeks ago. They took a boat and headed south."

"But I thought they were back." Prabir blinked at him, con-fused. He'd had nine hours' sleep in Darwin, and woken at dawn feeling perfectly normal, but now jet-lag was catching up with him again. "I thought you said you were—"

"You thought I was one of them? God, no!" The older man seated opposite glanced up from his work. Lowe said, "Hunt, this is Prabir Suresh: he's chasing the biologists, for some unfathomable reason. Hunter J. Cole, Georgetown University. And this is Mike Carpenter, one of his postdocs."

Prabir leaned across the table and shook hands with them. The desk clerk hadn't been mistaken; the bar was full of foreign academics. But if the biologists hadn't returned, who were these people?

"You're here to observe the Efflorescence?" Cole wore a fixed, slightly self-effacing smile, as if he knew from long experience that it was only a matter of time before he said something devastatingly clever, and he was already basking graciously in Prabir's anticipated response.

"I suppose so. Though I hadn't heard it called that before."

"My own terminology," Cole confessed, raising one hand dismissively as he spoke. "My *Taxonomy of Eucatastrophe* has not been widely read. And still less widely understood."

Prabir was feeling increasingly disorientated. The title sounded as if it should have made sense to him—something to do with population ecology, maybe?—but the actual meaning eluded him completely.

"Whatever terminology we choose to deploy," Lowe responded earnestly, "what we're witnessing here is a classic manifestation of the Trickster archetype, taking gleeful pleasure in confounding the narrow expectations of evolutionary reductionism. After biding its time for almost two centuries, indigenous mythology has finally given rise to the ideal means of undermining the appropriations of Wallace. This meshes perfectly with my overarching model of nature as 'The Unruly Woman': disruptively fecund; mischievously, subversively bountiful."

Cole smiled contentedly. "That's an interesting framework, Martin, but I find many aspects of it deeply problematic. The only safe assumption we can make at this point is that we're moving into a Suspensive Zone, where normal logics and causalities are held in abeyance. To reify the disruptive impulse is to presuppose that every teleological trajectory implies an agent, and ultimately to misunderstand the entire dynamic of Wrongness."

Prabir was experiencing severe déjà vu: Keith and Amita had had arguments like this, all Big Dumb Neologisms and thesaurus-driven bluster. It was like listening to two badly written computer programs trying to convince each other that they were sentient. He glanced hopefully at Cole's student, Carpenter; surely his generation had regained some mild interest in reality, if only for the sake of rebelling against half a century of content-free gibberish.

Carpenter tipped his head admiringly toward his mentor. "What he said."

The rest of the courtyard had fallen silent. Prabir looked around to see what had caught their attention. A huge black bird, fifty or sixty centimeters tall, had landed on one of the unused tables, and was sitting with its back to him, preening its feathers. Though it was dark as a raven, it was unmistakably a species of cockatoo, with a slender, almost threadlike crest. He'd seen them on the island now and then, but never in the metropolitan heart of Ambon. Maybe this was a sign that the city really had brought its pollution levels under control.

The bird turned its head to peck at its shoulder, revealing a row of sharp brown teeth embedded in the lip of its beak.

Prabir felt a small, hot trickle of urine flow across one leg. Mercifully, he'd emptied his bladder half an hour ago; there was almost nothing to soil his clothes. He glanced at Lowe, who was staring at the creature with a glazed expression. No one in the courtyard was moving or speaking. The bird emitted

129

a brief raucous cry, then began grooming under one wing.

"You're a fine boy, aren't you? You're my beautiful boy!" A woman had risen from one of the tables; she approached the bird slowly, crooning to it softly, circling around it to get a better view. Prabir watched her, horrified at first, then impressed by her presence of mind. The thing was still a cockatoo, after all, not some taloned bird of prey. As a child he'd been entirely unafraid of its equally imposing cousins, and the teeth scarcely added to the kind of damage its beak could have inflicted anyway.

The woman announced, to no one in particular, "I can see no sign of reversal of normal fusion in the vertebrae of the pygostyle. No vestigial claws on the wing tips. Naive to look for these things, I suppose, but whose instincts wouldn't tell them to *cherchez la* theropod?" Prabir found it hard to judge whether her speech was slurred—she spoke with a strong Welsh accent for which his ear was not well calibrated—but her movements seemed a bit uncoordinated.

She made a grab for the bird's legs. It squawked and ascended half a meter, then came down on the table again, lunging at her. Prabir rose to his feet, but he was too far away to help. The bird sank its teeth into the woman's forearm, shook its head vigorously to and fro half a dozen times, then opened its jaws and flew away.

"Fuck. *Fuck!*" She stared after it angrily, then glanced down at her wound. "Buccal fauna. Food residues. *Saliva!*" She tipped her head back and laughed with delight, then dashed from the courtyard.

Prabir caught up with her outside the hotel. "Excuse me. I'm sorry. Can I talk to you for a second?"

The woman scowled at him. "What's your problem? I'm in a hurry."

"I understand. I won't slow you down; I can explain while we walk."

She didn't look too happy with this, but she nodded reluctantly. "It's too crowded for me to run, and I don't want to raise a sweat." Prabir thought it unwise to point out that this was a lost cause, unless she planned to conjure up an air-conditioned limousine in the next thirty seconds.

He said, "I'm hoping to get in touch with someone on the expedition. Do you think you'd be able to let me have a copy of the itinerary?" She must have arrived late in Ambon, or succumbed to a temporary illness when the others were leaving. Since she hadn't given up and gone home, she was presumably in the process of arranging to rejoin her colleagues. If he offered to split the cost, she might even let him hitch a ride.

She took a few seconds to make sense of his question. "You mean the university biologists? I've only been here six days; they left weeks ago."

"You're not with them?"

"Hardly. I'm freelance."

"You've had no contact with them at all?"

"No." She turned to face Prabir, without slowing her pace. "Can't you just call whoever it is? There's no reason for them to be having reception problems."

"It's my sister. And no, I can't call her." He added defensively, "It's complicated."

The woman shrugged; this was none of her business. "I'm sorry. But I really don't know where they've gone."

Prabir was bitterly disappointed, but he struggled to regain some perspective. Before he'd checked into the hotel he hadn't expected to learn anything useful for days.

He said, "Well, good luck with the saliva. I can't think what possessed you to walk into a bar without a sequencer on you."

She laughed. "There's no excuse, is there? I carry a camera about the same size, and I didn't even think to use it. The sequencer would have been a thousand times more valuable . . . but no, I had to leave it on the boat."

Prabir didn't bother to conceal his amazement. "You have a *boat*? And you're still here after six days?"

"Don't get me started." She regarded him darkly. "I gave myself three days to buy provisions and hire a guide. But everyone I speak to wants to drag all their friends and family into the deal: no guide without hiring a whole crew."

"You have a crew already?"

She rolled her eyes. "It's a brand new MHD craft, not a prau with sails and masts and rigging. There'd be nothing for a crew to do, except fish and sunbathe at my expense. I brought it here from Sulawesi; I can handle it perfectly on my own. I put myself through a doctorate in Aberdeen working part-time on a North Sea fishing trawler. This whole place looks like a millpond to me."

Prabir wondered if it had occurred to her that not everyone in Ambon necessarily doubted her seacraft, or was intent on ripping her off. Most men here would consider it inappropriate to be alone on a boat with a foreign woman, and not many women would be willing to take on the job at all. The simplest thing to do would be to reconcile herself to the need to hire as many hangers-on as decorum required.

There was one cheaper alternative, though.

He said, "If you could cope with the North Sea, I'd trust you here any day. And I grew up in these islands."

"You did?"

He nodded calmly, planning to lie by omission only. "I was born in Calcutta, but my family moved here when I was six. I live in Canada now, but I still think of this as—" He trailed off, unable to say it, though a few more honest alternatives came to mind.

They were almost at the harbor. She stopped walking, and offered him her hand.

"I'm Martha Grant."

"Prabir Suresh."

She held up her forearm and inspected the wound, then announced glumly, "I'm sweating like a pig. I won't find a thing; it'll all be washed away or degraded by now."

A vivid red weal had spread along her arm. Prabir said, "Forget about DNA. Drown the whole area in disinfectant, and take whatever antibiotics you can get your hands on. You should have seen what happened to my mother's leg once from an insect bite. You don't want to take any chances."

"Yeah." Grant rubbed her eyes, and smiled at him ruefully. "What a farce. That bird just flew down to me, like a gift, and I didn't even get an image of it."

Prabir gave up on the idea of waiting to be asked. He said, "If you want a guide, I'll do it for nothing. I'll even pay for my own food. The only downside is, I might have to leave you at some point to meet up with my sister. But you've got maps, you've got translation software. It's not as if you'd be lost without me." It was hard saying the last part with a straight face; he'd be relying on maps and software himself. But he wasn't seeking money under false pretences, or endangering this woman's life. She was the one whose skills would have the most bearing on their safety.

Grant regarded him with a mixture of sympathy and skepticism. "Wouldn't it be easier just to call your sister? I can't guarantee that we'll even get close to the expedition."

That was true. But though Madhusree had promised him that she wouldn't disclose anything about their parents' work, Prabir had no doubt that she'd still do her best to steer the expedition in the right direction. If he could do the same, not only would that lead him to Madhusree, but he'd end up being far more use to

Grant than the most experienced guide Ambon had to offer.

He shrugged. "I'm willing to take that risk. I mean, it's not as if I have much hope of reaching her any other way."

Grant still seemed to be uneasy about something. Prabir said, "You don't have to decide right away. Think it over. Sleep on it." He reached for his notepad to give her his number.

She said, "Can you tell me why your sister doesn't want you to find her?"

Prabir gave her a long, hard look, trying to decide how to take this. *What exactly did you have in mind, memsahib? You think I've come to drag her off to an arranged marriage? Doing my bit for the international conspiracy to throw all women into purdah?* That was unfair, though. Grant didn't know the first thing about him; she didn't need to be a racist to have qualms about helping him pursue an unwilling quarry.

He tried to think of a way to put her at ease. "Do you have any children?"

"Yes. I have a son."

"How old is he?"

"Fourteen."

"Where is he now?"

"At home with his father, in Cardiff."

"Suppose he was camping out in the countryside with friends, and you saw the weather changing, but you knew he wouldn't understand what that meant in the same way you did. How do you think he'd react if you called him up and suggested that you join him at the campsite, just to keep an eye on things? Just to give him the benefit of your experience?"

Grant said gently, "OK, I get the point. But why do you think the weather's changing? Why are you so afraid for her?"

"I don't know," Prabir confessed. "I'm probably wrong.

I'm probably mistaken. But that doesn't change the way I feel."

Grant did not appear entirely reassured by this answer. But there was no obvious next question, no simple way to pursue the matter. Finally she said, "All right, I'll stop prying. Meet me here tomorrow at eight, and I'll show you the boat."

Chapter 8

At dinner, Prabir managed to avoid Lowe and company, but he found himself sharing a table with Paul Sutton, an English science journalist who'd come to write a book about the Moluccan mutants. These were proof, Sutton insisted, of a "cosmic imperative for biodiversity built into the laws of physics" which was compensating for the loss of species caused by human activities. The distinctly nonrandom nature of the mutations showed that "the nineteenth-century science of entropy" had finally been overtaken by "the twenty-first-century science of *ecotropy*."

"I just can't decide on the title," he fretted. "It's the title that will sell it. Which do you think sounds best: *The Genesis Gene*, *The Eighth Day of Creation*, or *The Seventh Miracle*?"

Prabir mulled it over. "How about *God's Third Testicle*?" That summed up the book's three themes concisely: religiosity, superabundance, and enormous bollocks.

Sutton seemed quite taken by this, but then he shook his head regretfully. "I want to evoke a separate act of creation, but that's a bit too . . . genitally focused." He stared into the distance, frowning intently. Suddenly his eyes lit up. "*Gaia's Bastards*. That's it! That's perfect! Ecology with an edge. Nature breaking all the rules, walking on the wild side to keep the Earth in balance! It's got best-seller written all over it!"

In the morning Prabir met Grant, and they walked down to the marina where her boat was docked. It was a twenty-meter magneto-hydrodynamic craft, with a single large cabin sunk partly below deck. Most of the cabin space was taken up with equipment; Grant showed him the bunk where he'd be sleeping, in a narrow slot behind a row of storage lockers. "You won't have much privacy, I'm afraid. You can see why I didn't want six deck-hands and a cook on board."

"Yeah. I was expecting to travel in crowded conditions, though. This is one step up from my wildest dreams of luxury." He turned away from his "quarters" and eyed a rack full of spec-trometers and chromatographs; there was a whole analytical chemistry lab packed onto half a dozen chips here. "I have no idea what a freelance biologist does, but it must pay well."

Grant made an amused choking sound. "I don't own any of this; it's all on loan from my sponsor."

"Can I ask who that is?"

"A pharmaceuticals company."

"And what do they get out of it?"

"That remains to be seen. But there's no such thing as a use-less discovery in molecular biology. At the very least they can always play pass-the-patents, so someone else is left holding them when it finally becomes obvious that they have no commer-cial value whatsoever."

They sat on the deck and talked for a while, looking out across the harbor. It was humid, but still quite cool; the fishing boats had all left long ago, and the marina was almost deserted. When Grant asked about his childhood Prabir spoke of the family's rare trips to Ambon, and tried to create the impression, without actually lying, that they'd traveled all over the region. But when she came right out and asked him what his parents had done, he said they'd been involved in seafood exports.

"So they made a fortune and retired to Toronto?"

"No. They both died here."

"I'm sorry." She quickly changed the subject. "Do you have anything you want to ask me? Before you decide to trust me not to run us into the nearest reef?"

Prabir hesitated, wary of offending her. "Do you use alcohol much?"

Grant was scandalized. "Not *at sea*!"

Prabir smiled. "No, of course not. How could I forget the long nautical tradition of sobriety?"

"There is one, actually. Dating back to the Industrial Health and Safety Laws of nineteen . . . something-or-other." She was treating it as a joke, but she did seem slightly wounded. "Was I very drunk yesterday?"

Prabir replied diplomatically, "You were a lot more lucid than anyone else in the bar."

Grant stood up abruptly, stretching her shoulders. "Well, you have a deal, if you're still interested. And if you're willing to do the cooking, you can forget about paying for food."

"That sounds fair." He rose to his feet beside her.

"When would you be able to leave?"

"Whenever you like. I just have to get my things and check out of the hotel."

"If you can be back in an hour, we can go this morning."

"An hour?" Prabir was taken aback, but he had no reason to object. "OK. I'd better get moving then." He raised a hand in farewell and headed for the pier.

Grant called after him, "See you soon."

Replaying parts of their conversation in his head as he walked along the marina, Prabir felt a belated sense of panic. If he'd hitched a ride on a crowded fishing boat, he could have sat in a corner and disappeared amid the bustle, wrapped in the shield of his imperfect Indonesian. He and Grant could be stuck with each other's company for weeks, and there'd be no easy way to retreat into silence.

But this was the best opportunity he'd have of reaching Madhusree. And Grant would have far more important things to do than probe his story every waking moment. They'd probably get along well enough, but he could still keep her at arm's length. He'd worked harmoniously for nearly ten years with people at the bank to whom he'd never said a word about the war, or his parents, or the island. He really had nothing to fear.

Before checking out of the hotel, Prabir sat on his bed and called Felix. It was eight P.M. in Toronto, but he decided to leave a message rather than talking live. He'd promised to keep Felix informed of his plans, but the prospect of exchanging small talk held no attraction for him. They were twenty thousand kilometers apart, he was on his own, and he didn't want to forget that for a second.

Back at the marina, Grant was in high spirits, eager to depart after being delayed for so long. Prabir threw his backpack under his bunk and watched over her shoulder as she programmed the boat.

Ambon Harbor was as automated as any airport. Grant lodged a request for a southbound route into the Banda Sea, and the harbormaster's software fed it to the autopilot. The engines started up, with a sound like water flowing through plumbing, and they began backing out of the dock immediately. There were several large cargo ships moored farther along the wharves, but there was no traffic in sight other than the tiny water taxis and a few pleasure craft.

It was ten kilometers to the harbor entrance, and the speed

limit made it a leisurely trip. Grant had pointed out the visible parts of the boat's machinery earlier, but at Prabir's request she summoned up schematics on the console and had the software deliver its full technospiel.

The boat's fuel cells doubled as batteries which could be charged either by solar electricity, from the deck and cabin roof, or by pouring in methanol which was split into water and carbon dioxide. A single elaborate polymer contained both catalytic sites which "burned" the methanol, and embedded vanadium ions which stored and released the energy by toggling between oxidation states. All the chemicals involved were bound firmly in place; the water emerged pure enough to drink.

The engines were polymer, too, corrosion-resistant electrodes and superconducting coils that accelerated seawater through any of the six channels that ran through a streamlined hub on the underside of the hull. With no moving parts, the only routine problem the engines could suffer was seaweed fouling the sievelike filters guarding the channels, and even that was usually cleared automatically with a few pulses of reverse thrust.

Prabir said, "This is elegant. This is how a boat should be."

Grant appeared noncommittal. "You don't long for the romance of sail?"

"Ha. Did you ever long to spend your time fighting ropes and canvas in the middle of a storm on the North Sea?"

Grant smiled. "No, but—" She gestured at the cloudless blue sky. "As a boy, you must have been on praus all the time."

He shook his head. "Everything was diesel. We never lived in the kind of small villages where people built their own traditional fishing boats." He wasn't even lying, but as soon as he began talking about the past he could feel muscles in his face growing tense from the effort of concealment.

"Well, MHD certainly outclasses diesel," Grant conceded.

"Though I wouldn't use the word 'elegant' myself. On that score, an eel leaves a boat like this for dead." She leaned back against the bench beside the console; she was teasing him, but Prabir couldn't resist the bait.

He said, "That's professional bias talking. An eel isn't optimized for swimming, just because it's done no better for the past few million years. It fritters away half its energy on just being alive: every cell in its body needs to be fed, whether or not it's working. Like the crew you didn't want to hire. Evolution does a lot of things very nicely: shark skin minimizes turbulence, crustacean shells are strong for their weight. But we can always do better by copying those tricks and refining them, single-mindedly. For a living creature, everything like that is just a means to an end. Show me an eel without gonads, and *then* I'll concede that nature builds the perfect swimming machine."

Grant laughed, but she admitted begrudgingly, "You're right, in a sense: it costs us a lot of energy to build each new boat, but it's still convenient to segregate that from ordinary fuel use. I wouldn't want to travel in a pregnant ship, let alone one that had to prove itself to prospective mates in a ramming contest. And even marine engineers can get by without children; they just need good designs that will propagate memetically. But none of this is truly divorced from biology, is it? Someone, somewhere has to survive and have offspring, or who inherits the designs, and improves upon them, and builds the next boat?"

"Obviously. All I'm saying is, technology can potentially do better than nature because of the very fact that it's *not* always a matter of life or death. If an organism has been fine-tuned to maximize its overall reproductive success, that's not the same thing as embodying the ideal solution to every individual problem it faces. Evolution appears inventive to us because it's had time to try so many possibilities, but it has no margin at all for real risks, let alone anything truly whimsical. We can celebrate our own beautiful mistakes. All evolution can do is murder them."

Grant gave him a curious look, as if she was wondering what kind of nerve she might have touched. She said, "I don't think we really disagree. I suppose I'm just ready to take beauty where I can find it. The average mammalian genome would make the ink-stained notebooks of a syphilitic eighteenth-century poet look positively coherent in comparison: all the layers of recycled genes, and redundant genes, and duplicated genes that have gone divergent ways. But when I see how it manages to work in spite of that—every convoluted regulatory pathway fitting together seamlessly—it still makes hair stand up on the back of my neck."

Prabir protested, "But if the pathways didn't fit together, they wouldn't be there for you to study, would they? Would you marvel the same way at the botched job in the thirty percent of human embryos that have too much chromosomal damage even to implant in the uterine wall? Every survivor has a complicated history that makes it look miraculous. My idea of beauty has nothing to do with survival: of all the things evolution has created, the ones I value most are the ones it could just as easily crush out of existence the next time it rolls over in its sleep. If I see something I admire in nature, I want to take it and run: copy it, improve upon it, make it my own. Because I'm the one who values it for its own sake. Nature doesn't give a fuck."

Grant said reasonably, "Evolution takes a long time to roll over in its sleep. I'm a lot more worried that the things I admire are going to get crushed out of existence by people who don't give a fuck."

"Yeah." There was no arguing with that. Prabir felt foolish; he'd let himself rant. He said, "I could make lunch now, if you're as hungry as I am. What do you think?"

•   •   •

The sight of the open sea made Prabir feel strangely calm. It wasn't that it brought back fewer, or less painful memories than Darwin or Ambon; quite the reverse. But there was something almost reassuring about finally making literal the state he'd imagined himself in for so long. He'd never reached the destination he'd promised Madhusree: the island where their parents were waiting. After eighteen years he still hadn't struck land.

Grant joined him on the deck, beaming madly. She must have caught a trace of bemusement on his face; she said, "I *know*, but I can't help it. A sky like this makes my poor heart sing. Sunlight deprivation as a child, I suppose; when I finally get a good dose of it, my brain just wants to condition me to come back for more."

Prabir said, "Don't apologize for being happy." He hesitated, then added obliquely, "Everyone else I met in Ambon who'd arrived from temperate regions seemed to have suffered rather less beneficial effects."

Grant feigned puzzlement. "I can't think who you could mean. Mind you, some people really do go a bit psychotic when they hit the tropics for the first time. That's the downside. But you must have encountered that before, surely?"

"The British raj was a bit before my time."

Grant smiled, then closed her eyes and raised her face to the sky. Prabir glanced back toward Ambon, but the gray smudge on the horizon had vanished. He'd have happily stood in silence like this for hours, but that was too much to hope for; what he really needed was a topic of conversation that wouldn't keep leading them back to his supposedly boundless familiarity with everything in sight. Grant was hardly going to throw him overboard if she caught him out on some minor inconsistency, but if the whole mess of half-truths unraveled and he was forced to confess just how limited and rusty his grasp of the region's language, customs, and geography really were, he wouldn't put it past her to abandon him on the nearest inhabited island.

He said, "What do you think's going on here? With the animals?"

"I have absolutely no idea."

Prabir laughed. "That's refreshing."

"I do have a few vague hypotheses," Grant admitted, opening her eyes. "But nothing I'd reveal except under extreme duress."

"Oh, come on! You're not talking to a fellow biologist here. I'm much too ill-informed to recognize heresy, and my opinion has no bearing on your reputation anyway. What have you got to lose?"

Grant smiled and leaned on the railing. "You might blab to your sister, and then where would I be?"

Prabir was affronted. "Madhusree can keep a secret."

"Ha! Her, not you! That shows how far I can trust you."

Prabir said, "What if some kind of toxin, some kind of mutagenic poison had been dumped on one of the uninhabited islands here, decades ago? A few dozen drums of industrial waste, chemically related to the kind of stuff they use to induce mutations in fruit flies?" It seemed far-fetched that anyone would go to the trouble of doing that, rather than just dumping it at sea, but it wasn't impossible. He wouldn't necessarily have stumbled across the site; he hadn't explored every last crevice on the island. The shift from the butterflies to all the other species could be due to a dramatic change in exposure levels: the drums might have split open after a few more years of weathering, or the land where they were buried might have subsided in a storm. Or maybe the poison had simply worked its way up the food chain. "The successful mutants thrive and breed, and some of the healthiest ones manage to cross to other islands. The only reason we're not seeing any unfavorable mutations is because the afflicted animals are dying on the spot."

Grant regarded him with undisguised irritation; she seemed genuinely reluctant to be drawn on the subject. But she wasn't prepared to let this scenario go unchallenged. "Maybe you could explain the sheer number of genetic changes with a strong enough chemical mutagen, but the pattern still doesn't make sense. Given everything else we've seen, some proportion of the animals who escaped from this hypothetical island should have had at least a couple of neutral alterations: changes to their anatomy or biochemistry that wouldn't kill them or significantly disadvantage them, but which served no useful function at all. So far no one's seen anything of the kind."

"Yes, but even the most 'insignificant' disadvantage could be serious dead weight if you have to travel hundreds of kilometers just to be noticed. Maybe we're only seeing mutants with changes that have been positively beneficial. I mean, you'd have to be pretty fit to fly all the way to Ambon from any of the remote islands in the south."

Grant gave him an odd look. "They found a mutant tree frog in Ceram. That couldn't have come from too far south—assuming it wasn't hatched on the spot, which it might well have been." Ceram was a large island just ten kilometers north of Ambon. It was heavily populated around the coast, and parts of the interior had been logged and mined, but a considerable amount of rain forest remained intact. If Grant got it into her head to veer north and start traipsing through the jungles of Ceram, he'd never get anywhere near Madhusree's expedition.

"There are ferries running between the major islands," Prabir reminded her. "Something like a tree frog could have hidden in a crate of fruit, or even got on board a plane. Human transport can always complicate things to some degree."

"That's true. But what makes you so sure that these animals have traveled at all?"

Prabir thought carefully before replying. Even if he'd known nothing about Teranesia, wouldn't it be reasonable to suppose that there was an epicenter somewhere? He said, "If they haven't, their parents or grandparents must have. If you follow the mutations back to their source, every animal must have had at least one ancestor exposed to the same mutagen at some point. I mean, whatever the cause, isn't it stretching things to think that the same conditions could be repeated in half a dozen different locations?"

Grant shrugged. "You're probably right." But she didn't sound as if she meant it.

Prabir tried to read her face. If the animals weren't traveling, what was? Any chemical spill severe enough to retain its potency across thousands of square kilometers could hardly have gone undetected this long. A hushed-up nuclear accident was even less plausible.

He said, "You think it's a virus? But if it's spreading all over the Moluccas, doesn't that make it a thousand times harder to explain why we're not seeing any unhealthy mutants? And isn't it a bit far-fetched to think that it could infect so many different species?"

Grant gave him her sphinx impression. Prabir folded his arms and glowered at her. He wasn't just killing time now: he was genuinely curious. He'd kept pushing the question aside as a distraction, but what Felix had called his cover story wasn't entirely false: this was Radha and Rajendra's life's work, and part of him really did want to know what they would have discovered if they'd had the chance to complete it.

He said, "Unless the two mysteries are one and the same? Unless whatever makes the animals so impossibly successful makes the virus successful, too?"

Grant said firmly, "We'll gather some data, and we'll see what we find. End of discussion. OK?"

• • •

Prabir lay on his bunk with his notepad's headset on, brushing up on his Indonesian vocabulary. It was after midnight, but Grant was apparently still awake and busy. Most of the cabin was hidden from view by the row of lockers alongside the bunk, and the faint glow that diffused around them might have come from nothing but the phosphorescent exit sign, but whenever he took a break from his lessons he could hear the distinctive metallic squeaks of the "captain's chair." He had no idea what she was doing; with the collision-avoidance radar and sonar switched on there was no pressing need for anyone to keep watch.

His concentration was faltering. He froze the audio and took off the headset. The humidity had become almost unbearable; the sleeping bag he was using as a mattress was soaked, and the air was so heavy that it felt as if he were drawing every breath through a straw. Maybe he'd be better off sleeping on deck, now that they were far enough out to sea not to worry about insects. The genetic quirk that had required him to be a walking mosquito killer as a child had no effect on the modern vaccine—another triumph for biotechnology, though when they reached some of the islands with undrained swamps he'd probably wish he still sweated repellent.

He rolled up his sleeping bag and headed for the cabin door. Grant was seated at the console, examining a chart of the Banda Sea stretching all the way down to Timor. Prabir explained what he was doing. "Is that OK with you?"

"Yeah, of course. Go ahead." She turned back to the chart. Prabir wondered belatedly if he was eroding her privacy; the cabin windows had no blinds, so the two of them would no longer be as manifestly out of each other's sight as when he'd been tucked away behind the lockers. But she hadn't raised any objection, and once she switched off the console she'd be all but invisible anyway.

As he unrolled his sleeping bag on the deck, he tried to decide whether or not he owed it to Grant to tell her he was gay. On one level it seemed like an insult to both of them to suggest that it mattered; unless he'd misread her completely, she was the kind of person who'd start from the assumption that he wouldn't try to exploit their situation, and she'd certainly shown no sign of wanting to exploit it herself. But he knew that his judgments were sometimes skewed; he was so accustomed to ruling out by fiat the whole idea of sex that he forgot that other people weren't necessarily viewing him through the same filter. A few years after he'd started at the bank, he'd been assigned two graduate trainees to supervise while they were on a month's rotation in his department: a man and a woman, both about his own age. He'd done his best to put them at ease, remembering how nervous he'd been in his own first weeks on the job, and as far as he could tell he'd been equally hospitable to both of them. But after they'd moved on, the news had got back to him that the woman had found his behavior positively oppressive. *He'd been too nice. He must have wanted something.*

There was a gentle breeze moving across the water; for a minute or two Prabir was almost chilly, until his skin reached a kind of clammy equilibrium. The boat was pitching slightly as it crossed the waves, but that bothered him even less than it had in the confined space of the cabin.

He'd brought his notepad with him, but he was too tired to continue with the language lessons. He stared up at the equatorial sky, the sky he'd seen from the kampong at night: obsidian black, with stars between the stars. He could fix his eyes on one spot and try to map it, but his mind stopped taking in information long before he hit the limits of vision.

A few hours before he'd almost welcomed being back on the Banda Sea, but the connection seemed a thousand times more immediate now, the details of his memory sharper by starlight. He could feel the years melting away in the face of the accumulating evidence: the musical sound of the half-familiar language ringing in his ears, the struggle to sleep on a humid night. That was how memory worked, after all: placing like moments side by side. There was no linear tape inside his head, no date stamp on every mental image. It didn't matter what had happened since. Nothing could stop the days and nights of eighteen years before becoming like yesterday.

He picked up his notepad and scrolled to the address book. Felix would be at work, but they could still talk for a few minutes. Though he'd never admit to it, he'd probably been offended that Prabir had only left a message when he'd called from the hotel. He'd probably welcome a civilized conversation to make up for the slight.

Prabir put down the notepad. He was sure it would work, he was sure it would help: watching the face of his lover in Toronto painted before him in a fine grid of light. That would banish the night terrors. But it still felt like the kind of crutch he didn't want to lean on.

Prabir woke at dawn to the sight of Gunung Api, a black volcanic mountain rising out of verdant hills to tower over the Banda Islands. White mist—he hoped it was just mist—swirled around the peak. Gunung Api was still active, and though it hadn't done serious harm for fifteen years, a recent report had said that clouds of hot gas and ash were being vented every month or so.

Api, Bandaneira, and Lontar, the three main islands of the group, were about as close to each other as they could be without merging like Ambon's Siamese twins. Lontar, to the south, was the largest, and Prabir could just make out the tips of it protruding on either side of the smaller northern pair.

He glanced toward the cabin. Grant didn't seem to be up, so he urinated overboard to save disturbing her. He wondered if the boat would stop for him if he dived in for a swim to clear his head; the autopilot would certainly detect the event, but exactly how it responded would depend on the settings Grant had chosen. He decided not to risk it.

He sat on the deck and watched the volcano. Birdsong carried across the water, a faint, distorted version of the chorus that had woken him as a child. He laughed wearily. *He'd sailed this sea before, he'd seen these stars before, he'd heard these birds before . . . but so what?* Most people lived on in the very same town where their parents had died, some in the very same house. It was only because he'd left the whole country behind that it had come to seem so charged with significance. This was just a place like any other; it couldn't drag him back into the past.

Grant emerged from the cabin and stood beside him, yawning and groggy, but smiling at the spectacle in front of them.

She said, "I don't know about you, but quite frankly I stink. I'm going swimming."

They sailed into the gently curved channel between Lontar and the other islands, past a moss-encrusted Dutch fort, toward the main town of Bandaneira. A vast coral garden lay beneath them, clearly visible through the water. Grant almost swooned with delight, crying out excitedly every now and then when she recognized yet another species of fish or sponge or anemone. Prabir stood beside her trying to be blasé; even if he couldn't put a name to every one of these creatures, he *had* seen this all before, when the ferry had passed through on the way to Ambon. The Bandas had been a major tourist destination then, the harbor full of thirty-something Beijing honeymooners snorkeling and—rather more bafflingly, and a great deal less benignly—jet-skiing. But between the war, the 2016 eruption, and a number of subsequent minor earthquakes, the tourist industry seemed to have gone the way of the spice trade.

They found a mooring and set out into town. Apart from one abandoned modern hotel the buildings were in good repair, and Prabir felt no sense of poverty or decay; Bandaneira seemed to have shrunk back into obscurity gracefully. People moved unhurriedly on foot or on bicycles. The volcano loomed over the main street, barely three kilometers away; it was impossible to tell from here that it was on another island altogether.

After a while a swarm of children surrounded them: not beggars, just curious, exuberant kids, born long after the last tourists had departed. When they asked where the visitors were from, and Prabir said "Canada and Wales" they dissolved into fits of laughter; maybe they were too young to have heard of either place and thought these were unlikely sounding made-up names. When Prabir managed to get a question of his own in, the answer was disappointing but no great surprise: the biologists' expedition hadn't stopped here.

One of the older boys told him earnestly, "Your wife is very beautiful. Tell her she is very beautiful." Prabir translated the compliment but left out the presumption of matrimony. It had occurred to him back in Ambon that it might simplify things if they agreed to let people assume this as a matter of course, but he hadn't had a chance to discuss it with Grant, and he didn't want to argue the point in public.

Grant consulted her notepad and they turned down a side road. The children fell away. Prabir said, "Do you want to tell me where we're going?"

"Up into the nutmeg plantations."

"They're hardly plantations anymore. They've been abandoned for decades."

"Forests, plantations, call them what you like. We haven't come here to negotiate a shipment of mace."

Prabir couldn't imagine what she was hoping to find; centuries of cultivation had left the islands with little in the way of wildlife. He'd assumed that they'd only dropped anchor here to ask the locals for news from travelers passing through from farther south, or to scour the market for curiosities that might not have been shipped up to Ambon.

As they left the town behind, the dirt road became increasingly overgrown; they trudged through the heat, encountering no one. Grant had a license from the government in Ambon to collect specimens for research purposes throughout the RMS, but Prabir suspected that they should still have asked for permission from the Bandanese themselves before heading out into the countryside. Under *adat*, customary law, all visitors to the island would be seen as guests of the raja—an honor that carried an obligation to inform him of their movements—but short of requesting an audience with His Whateverness, they might at least have checked with the nearest villagers that they wouldn't be disturbing any ancestral shrines. The trouble was, if they went back into town so Prabir could sound people out about the correct protocol, Grant would soon realize that he was playing it by ear and start asking herself why she couldn't have done the same without him.

The narrow, unkempt path that the road had become led them into the plantation, then abandoned them completely. They picked their way slowly through the undergrowth. Even at the height of the spice trade the plantations had never been a monoculture, and the tall, white-blossomed kanari almond trees interspersed with the nutmeg—planted to give shade to the saplings—seemed to have retained their share of the light long after the withdrawal of human intervention. It was the space between the trees that had reverted to jungle: rattan and lianas snaked from trunk to trunk,

153

some of them unpleasantly spiked, and there were waist-high ferns everywhere. Prabir was glad he was in boots and jeans; he'd wandered Teranesia barefoot as a child, but his soft city feet wouldn't have lasted five minutes here. Grant had gone so far as to wear a long-sleeved shirt, and after half an hour his own arms were so scratched that, despite the heat, he envied her.

He stopped to catch his breath. "If you tell me what you're looking for, we might find it a little faster."

"Fruit pigeons," Grant replied curtly.

Prabir almost responded with an acerbic remark about the difficulty of doing fieldwork with such limited powers of observation, but he stopped himself in time. Fruit pigeons might easily have been classed as vermin and hunted to extinction by the plantation owners, but they'd been spared for the sake of their convenient habit of shitting out the nutmeg seed, sowing it naturally. They weren't exactly overwhelmed by competition or predators on any of the islands, but here they'd be in paradise.

So why hadn't he seen one yet?

The pigeons he remembered had all been large, noisy, and brightly colored, but he knew there were smaller species, too, some of them quite well camouflaged. They hardly needed to be silent and invisible, though, here of all places. And there had to be thousands of them.

He said, "Can we stop here for a while? Maybe we're scaring them away with all the noise."

Grant nodded. "That's worth a try."

Prabir stood motionless for ten minutes, staring up into the branches. He could hear other birds in the distance, and a constant hum of insects, but nothing like the discordant clacking he remembered.

Grant couldn't resist needling him. "So where are they, eagle-eyes? You have my advantage in both youth and experience; if you can't see them, we might as well go back to the boat."

"Don't tempt me." He had a better idea, though. "Have you got a camera on you?"

"Yeah, of course."

"Can I borrow it?"

Grant hesitated, then handed it to him.

He examined it carefully. "How much did this cost?"

"Five hundred euros. Which is well above my personal definition of 'disposable.' Why? What are you planning to do with it?"

Prabir commanded her loftily, "Be patient." Five hundred euros meant that the lens would give a much sharper image than his notepad's camera, and the stabilizer would be a laser-ring system, not a trashy micro-mechanical accelerometer.

Grant brushed the debris off a fallen trunk and sat down. Prabir set the camera to the widest possible angle, aimed it at a tree twenty meters away, and recorded sixty seconds of vision. Then he passed the data to his notepad through the infrared link.

The program he needed was three lines in Rembrandt, his favorite image-processing language. As he watched the result on the notepad's screen, Grant saw the expression of delight on his face and came over to see what he'd found.

Outlined in fluorescent blue by the software, half a dozen small green-and-brown birds moved along the branches. Prabir glanced up from the screen to the tree, but even now that he knew exactly what to look for, he couldn't see the birds for himself. The software was only identifying them in retrospect by comparing hundreds of consecutive frames, and even then it sometimes lost track of their edges against the pattern of leaves.

Grant complained indignantly, "You don't know how galling this is. I grew up on smug biologists' jokes about pathetic computerized attempts at vision."

Prabir smiled. "Things change." Grant was probably only

ten years older than he was, but the idea seemed as quaint to him as jokes about heavier-than-air flight.

"Can you replay it?"

"Sure."

As she watched the scene again, she mused, "I've seen stick insects with that level of camouflage. And some predatory fish. But this is extraordinary." She laughed and swatted something on her neck. Prabir had expected her to be elated by their find, but the birds' proficiency seemed to unnerve her.

He struggled to recall the images Madhusree had shown him back in Toronto. "You think this is the pigeon that turned up in Ambon nine months ago?"

Grant nodded. "We'll need specimens to be sure, but it looks like it."

"But how did you know it would be here? I thought no one had traced it back from the bird dealer."

"They hadn't, but this seemed the most likely spot. I can't think why no one else looked here. Maybe it was just prejudice: the Bandas aren't wild, they aren't pristine, they aren't havens of biodiversity. How could a new species possibly be born in a place that was so 'barren'?"

"You tell me."

"I will, when I know."

Grant had brought a tranquilizer gun. Prabir improvized software to display the outlines with the minimum possible time lag, but it still took them three hours to hit their first target. As he picked the sleeping bird out of the undergrowth, he reflected uneasily on the possible source of its mutations. He still believed it was more than likely that he was looking at a recent descendant of a Teranesian migrant, but if it had brought along a mutagenic virus that could cross between species, tens of thousands of people were potentially at risk. The virus might have taken eighteen years to leap the biochemical gulf between butterflies and birds, but birds were notorious for harboring potential human diseases. He wished he could get some straight answers out of Grant; it was one thing to avoid starting groundless rumors, but she owed him an informed opinion on whatever it was she thought they were dealing with.

They returned to the boat at dusk, grimy and exhausted, with blood from four pigeons. Prabir looked on as Grant prepared the samples for analysis; the preservative that had kept them stable in the heat had transformed them into blobs of puce jelly.

He said, "Do you know anything about the species that used to be here? I don't mean prior to the Dutch; just ten or twenty years ago."

"There's a 2018 report that mentions half a dozen sympatric species of *Treron*, *Ptilinopus*, and *Ducula*."

"*'Ducula'*? You're making that up."

"No, they're the big ones. Imperial pigeons."

"So what does 'sympatric' mean?"

"Sorry. Coexisting, sharing territory."

Prabir nodded, ashamed at his laziness; the child who'd named Teranesia wouldn't have needed to ask. He'd never studied European classical languages, but everyday English had inherited all the clues: just hybridize "symmetry" and "repatriate."

Grant said, "*Treron* are green, but the others are usually brightly colored, presumably for the sake of mate recognition. The theory is, that's how they formed separate species in the first place: runaway sexual selection based on plumage, overriding any need for camouflage in the absence of predators."

"So where have they all gone?"

She shrugged. "Maybe the bird trade wiped them out. The

prettiest fetch the highest prices, and they're also the easiest to catch."

Prabir wasn't so sure; fruit pigeons weren't exactly birds of paradise. Still, times must have been hard after the war, and maybe there'd been enough of a market to make it worth hunting them down.

Grant pulled open a panel on the rack of analytic equipment, and pushed one of the tubes of blood onto a spike. "Now we wait."

Prabir went for a swim in the deserted harbor, staying in the water until it was so dark that he began to wonder what he might be sharing it with. He'd forgotten to bring a towel out with him, so he sat on the deck for a while to avoid dripping all over the cabin. When he walked back in, Grant glanced up from her workbench, taken unaware. He went over to his bunk to put on a T-shirt.

He called out, "Any news?"

"I've got all the sequences."

"And?" He approached her. "Is it the same species as the one they found in Ambon?"

Grant replied hesitantly, "One of our sequences is almost identical to the Ambon data. And all four have the same novel blood proteins as the Ambon bird."

Prabir cheered. "So you were right: you found it in the wild. Congratulations!" Grant didn't look particularly pleased, though. He said, "What else?"

She glanced down at her notepad. Prabir could see strings of base-pair codes and a cladogram. "They also have genetic markers in common with some of the uncamouflaged species we assumed were gone."

Prabir tried to make sense of this. "You mean, they weren't wiped out, they started breeding with each other?"

"No, there's no evidence of that. Each individual specimen we collected shows signs of a distinct recent ancestry. I'm not even sure that they're not still separate species."

"Now I'm confused." He laughed. "They look identical, they share exotic blood proteins, but you think they have completely different lineages?"

Grant spread her hands on the bench. "I can't be certain, but it looks to me as if they've all converged on the same set of traits, within a couple of generations, without interbreeding. Something has given rise to the same genes for the blood proteins and the camouflage, independently, in at least four different species."

Prabir sat on the stool beside her. "Something?" This was absurd, she had to be mistaken, but he was hardly equipped to tell her where she'd gone wrong in her analysis. "What are you suggesting? There's a retrovirus on the loose that splices a set of *fruit pigeon genes* into anything it infects—including some genes that happen to be exactly what fruit pigeons need to vanish into the foliage?"

Grant scowled. "I haven't taken leave of my senses completely. And I don't have viruses on the brain like you do."

"OK, I'll shut up about viruses. But what's doing it then? Where did these genes come from?"

She stared down at the bench, still angry with him. He was sure she had an answer, though; she just wasn't willing to commit it to words.

Prabir said gently, "I know how important it is for you to be cautious. But I'm not going to leak your theory to *Nature*, or sell your data to some rival pharmaceuticals company. And if I'm at risk of fathering children with bright green feathers, don't you think I deserve to be told?"

He regretted the words as soon as they were out, but Grant's expression softened. She said, "If these pigeons haven't interbred for hundreds of thousands of years, what do they still have in common?"

Prabir shrugged. "They share the same habitat."

"And?"

"I don't know. I suppose they'd still share most of their genes, dating back to their last common ancestor."

Grant said, "Exactly. But not just working genes: whole stretches of inactive DNA as well. Don't you see? That has to be the source of all these 'innovations'—they're not innovations at all! You can't get functional genes appearing out of nowhere in two or three generations. You just can't! A random sequence of amino acids doesn't merely form a useless protein, it forms an ill-conditioned one: a molecule that doesn't even fold predictably into a well-defined shape. These blood proteins are perfectly conditioned: they have conformations with energy troughs as sharp as hemoglobin's. The same with the pigmentation morphogenesis proteins that produce the camouflage. The odds of that happening by chance—de novo, in the time frame we're talking about—are nil.

"Somehow, these birds must have repaired and reactivated genes from an old common ancestor. They've reached back into the archives and dusted off blueprints that haven't been used for a million years." She shook her head, smiling slightly, shocked at her own audacity but triumphant, too. "That's what I half suspected all along, but *this* makes the case a whole lot clearer."

Prabir was still catching up. "You're saying that all these different species of pigeon have found a way to resurrect fossil genes buried in their DNA, and because they have so much old baggage in common, the same traits have emerged in all of them?"

"That's right."

"So they've all reverted to the appearance of an ancestral species that needed camouflage to hide from some ferocious predator? And presumably they've not only lost their flashy plumage, they've lost the need for their mates to have it as a pre-requisite for sex, or they would have all died out by now?"

"Presumably, yes."

"And when a tree frog or a bat does the same thing with its DNA, the result is different, but still useful, because they're getting back something that was useful a few million years ago to some frog or bat then?"

"Yes. That's the theory."

Prabir ran a hand over his face; he'd forgotten how tired he was, but after nine hours slogging through the plantation his brain had turned to mush. "That much I follow. Now explain the next part to me, slowly: Why is this happening in all these different species? And how?"

Grant hesitated, as if she was about to draw the line here, but then she must have decided that she had nothing more to lose. She said, "The only reason I can think of for an innate capacity to do this would be as a response to genetic damage. No one's ever seen a repair mechanism that operates like this before, but it's been known for years that functioning genes are vulnerable to certain kinds of damage that leave other parts of the chromosome untouched. Cleaning up old sequences that have fallen into disuse could be a repair strategy of last resort, because even the random copying errors they've suffered over time might have done less harm than whatever's afflicting the modern genes."

Prabir didn't dare say it, but this sounded so much like restoring a computer in extremis from moth-balled backups that it was uncanny. It also sounded so far beyond any conventional notion of how genomes were organized that Grant's initial refusal to discuss her hypothesis, which he'd taken as verging on paranoia, now looked like mere self-preservation.

"And that might be handy in somatic cells, to stop certain

kinds of cancer?" he suggested. "If some growth regulator gene has been damaged in a cell in my intestine, say, the cell might reactivate a copy of the gene that was duplicated accidentally thousands of generations ago, and fell into disuse?"

"Exactly. So normally there'd be no visible effects: if an adult starts producing an archaic protein in a few intestinal cells, or skin cells, that's not going to change its gross anatomy. And even if the process was activated in an early embryo, it would generally produce just one altered individual, who'd bear perfectly normal offspring. To produce heritable changes, it has to be turned on in the germ cells; that must be what's happening here, but don't ask me why, because I have no idea yet."

"OK. But if this is a response to genetic damage, what's triggering it? Doesn't there still need to be some kind of powerful mutagen, even if what we're seeing is the result of the animals conquering it, rather than succumbing to it?"

"Maybe. Unless it's being triggered inappropriately; unless they're overreacting to some other kind of stress." Grant lifted her notepad off the bench and thumbed through the sequence of codons. "I don't have all the answers; I'm not even close. The only way to understand this will be to unravel the whole mechanism: identify the genes that are being switched on in every affected species, then see what proteins they encode, what functions they perform, and what activates them in the first place."

Prabir groaned. "'Every affected species'? Why don't I like the sound of that part?"

Grant regarded him with sergeant-majorly contempt. "A bit more fieldwork isn't going to kill you. You've got nothing to complain about; just wait until you get to my age."

"You wait until you've spent ten years behind a desk."

She shuddered. "All the more reason to want to be here instead. Besides, these are the creatures you grew up with, aren't they? Think of it as a chance to be reunited with all your old childhood friends."

"'Childhood friends'?" Prabir climbed off the stool and limped across the cabin to the galley. "Do you mean Bambi and Godzilla? Or their mutual great-great-grandparents?"

Chapter 9

Prabir slept on deck again, untroubled by insomnia. He woke at first light, aching all over, but unaccountably happier than he'd felt in months.

He dived into the harbor and swam slow laps to a navigation buoy and back, just to loosen the muscles in his shoulders. People heading out in rickety fishing boats shouted greetings, and in the water the close heat of dawn didn't feel oppressive at all. He'd taken up swimming in Toronto for a while, doing laps before work in a pool full of fanatics with scalp-to-toe anti-turbulence depilation and sports watches with faux-AI plug-ins to coach them on their stroke. But it had made him feel twice as tense as doing nothing, so he'd stopped.

Thinking back on the evening's revelations, his sunny mood seemed less of a mystery. Even if Grant's theory turned out to be misguided, one way or another the data they collected would help shed light on what was happening. That wasn't exactly what had brought him here, but the more he thought about it, the more it seemed like the key to all his anxieties. Ever since Madhusree had told him about the expedition, he'd been treating the spread of the mutations as some kind of vague malevolent force, reaching out from Teranesia to drag her back into its clutches, mocking the very idea that they'd ever escaped. That was every bit as deranged as anything the cranks in Ambon had spouted, but the clearer the real, molecular basis for the effect became, the harder it would be to sustain that kind of delusion. A complete answer might be decades away, but playing some small part in getting there would make him feel less helpless, less overwhelmed. That was what his parents had spent their lives fighting for: not just explaining the butterflies, but puncturing the whole deeply corrupting illusion that nature—or some surrogate deity—ever had designs on anyone, malevolent or otherwise.

Halfway through his fifth lap, he spotted Grant approaching. She called out to him jokingly, "I thought you'd been kidnapped."

"Sorry. I got carried away."

"I don't blame you. It's unbelievable." They trod water over an outcrop of branched red coral, festooned with anemones and swarming with tiny bright fish—all at least six meters below them, but the details were so sharp that they might have been looking down through air.

Prabir felt a sudden urge to come clean with her; whatever the significance of the butterflies turned out to be, he was tired of having the deception between them. He'd proved himself useful to have around, even if it was more as ad hoc technical assistant and general dogsbody than cultural liaison. And surely she'd understand his reluctance to reveal the whole family history to a stranger.

He struggled to find a place to start. "Were your family excited by the news last night?" He hadn't eavesdropped; she'd been talking to her son right in front of him as he'd gone out onto the deck to sleep.

Grant frowned. "News? You mean the pigeon sequences? I couldn't tell them about that; there's a confidentiality clause in my contract."

Prabir was shocked. "But you—"

"And you mustn't mention it to anyone, either. Especially not your sister."

Prabir was about to retort that he wasn't bound by any contract, but it didn't seem like a good idea to drive home the point that she'd been unwise to confide in him.

He said, "Whatever happened to scientists sharing data?"

"Welcome to the real world."

"And you're happy with this?"

"Delirious. I love being gagged." Grant plucked irritably at something crawling up the arm of her T-shirt.

"Then why did you do it? Why did you sign the contract? Couldn't you have joined the university expedition instead?"

"I'm not an academic. Everyone on that boat is being paid a salary from somewhere—student slave labor like your sister excepted. In the unlikely event that they'd let me on at all, I would have had to pay them for the privilege. I enjoy what I do, but I'm not in it for charity. I have a family to support."

Prabir wasn't about to do a postmortem on anyone's career choices. "How long does it apply? The gag?"

"That depends. Some things might be cleared for publication by the lawyers in a couple of months. Others might take years."

It came to him suddenly that his parents had published nothing in all their years on the island. They'd taken money from Silk Rainbow. They must have made the same kind of deal.

Grant frowned. "Are you OK?"

"Just a stitch."

"You're not planning to quit on me in disgust?"

"Hardly." It shouldn't have stung so much. They'd made one small compromise in order to do something that otherwise would not have been done at all. *When had he started thinking of them as flawless, immaculate?*

Grant started back toward the boat. Prabir called after her, "New rules, though. First one out of the water cooks breakfast."

Grant had chosen six small islands from which to gather samples, lying in an arc that ran southeast from the Bandas to the Kai Islands. All were uninhabited, unless they had settlements so small that they'd escaped the notice of the official cartographers. The third was just seventy kilometers northeast of Teranesia, slightly closer than the Tanimbar Islands to the south; if it had been on the maps when Prabir was a child, he and Madhusree might have ended up stranded there.

When he'd joined Grant in Ambon, he'd imagined himself somehow "steering" her toward the source of the mutations; fat chance of that, but the route she'd picked would already take them about as close as he wanted to get. He could only hope that whatever the biologists' expedition had discovered was drawing them in the same direction; it seemed naive now to think that Madhusree—lowest of the low in the academic pecking order— could have swayed a boatload full of experts with their own theories and agendas.

They sailed out of Banda harbor early in the afternoon, and it was close to sunset when they arrived at the first of the islands. They dropped anchor a hundred meters from shore and spent the evening recuperating, drawing entertainment off the net. To Prabir's amazement, Grant turned out to like Madagascan music as much as he did, and she knew all the esoterica better. After a while he stopped trying to compete with her at naming performers and recordings, and just let her dazzle him with her erudition.

Grant winced suddenly. "Quarter to ten! I promised Michael I'd call him in his lunch hour."

Prabir went out on deck to give her some privacy. He sat perched on the guardrail at the stern of the boat, swaying slightly to keep himself upright, the sound of the *valiha* still playing in his head.

If he agonized about it, he knew he'd never do it. He pulled out his notepad and hit three buttons in rapid succession.

Felix grinned up at him from the screen. "How's it going?"

Prabir shrugged. "It was strange being back at first, but I'm getting used to it. How's work?"

"Dull beyond words. I'm disgusted that you'd even ask. Any sign of Madhusree?"

"Not yet. I think we're both heading in the same direction, but it's going to be a matter of luck whether I catch up with her or not."

Felix said tentatively, "I could always call her and tell her you're on your way. It's not as if she could really pressure you into turning back now, even if she wanted to. And she might take the whole thing better if she was forewarned."

"I don't think that would be a good idea."

"Compared to what? Arriving unannounced?"

Prabir thought seriously about the suggestion. But why risk alienating her, when there was still no guarantee that their paths would actually cross? He said, "Don't worry about it. If we meet, we'll sort it out. If we don't, I'll confess everything once we're back in Toronto, and she'll just laugh and forgive me on the spot."

He recounted as much as he could about the Bandanese pigeons; Felix seemed neither surprised nor offended that he couldn't be let in on the sequencing results. They talked for almost half an hour, until Felix had to go and refill his pipetting robot's reagent tanks.

When the window closed and Prabir looked up, his eyes still adapted to the brightness of the screen, he felt unspeakably strange. It wasn't just a pang of loneliness; he wasn't sure that it had much to do with Felix at all. It was the connection breaking, the image fading, the whole illusion collapsing in front of him, leaving him with nothing but darkness and the mechanical rocking of the sea.

He sat on the railing, watching Grant smiling and laughing in the cabin, and waited for the feeling to pass.

They circumnavigated the island, probing its fringing reef with sonar until they found a safe approach to a small sandy beach. Grant anchored the boat in a meter of water, and they waded ashore. Prabir looked down at the fine, bone-white sand with a jolt of recognition, but he let the feeling wash over him, neither fighting it nor pursuing it to its source.

He found some shade and sat to pull his boots on, squinting back at the sunlit water. Silver on turquoise, the view was indistinguishable from one he'd seen a thousand times before. The memory went deeper than vision: as he tightened his laces he grew aware of a disconcerting ease in his limbs, an assured and unselfconscious physicality beneath the fading ache from the plantation. A few laps in Banda Harbor could hardly have restored him to childlike resilience, but on some level his body still carried a trace of what it had once felt like to swim in this sea every day.

Grant said, "Are you ready?" She gestured at the mine detector clipped to her belt. Prabir hit the self-test button on his own device; it chimed reassuringly and flashed a green light, whatever that was worth.

The whole island was low jungle, with soil trapped by dead coral that must have grown on a submerged volcanic peak. They'd barely passed the first palm tree when a cloud of small flies descended on them, biting them relentlessly.

They retreated to the beach. Grant shielded her eyes with one hand as Prabir circled her with the insect repellent. She seemed tense out of all proportion to the inconvenience; he couldn't even smell the stuff. "You're not allergic to this, are you?" He checked the can for warnings; if she went into shock he'd have to dash for the medicine cabinet.

"No. It's just cold."

They swapped places, and Prabir discovered that she wasn't joking; the solvent evaporated so quickly that it was like being doused with a fine spray of ice. He mused, "If we engineered ourselves to sweat isopropyl alcohol, humidity would have no effect on the efficiency of the process. What do you think?" *Come the revolution.* But the revolution was taking its time.

"I think you're completely unhinged."

They tried the jungle again. The insects retreated, but the undergrowth was even more impenetrable than Bandaneira's, with a dense, thorned shrub that Prabir had never seen before crammed into the gaps between the familiar ferns. He tore off a spiked, leathery branch and held it up to Grant. "What are the thorns for? I know there are plenty of birds that eat fresh shoots, but what is there here that would try to eat something this old and tough?"

Grant frowned. "Beats me. As far as I know, all the lizards here are insectivores. You can find deer this far east, but only where they've been introduced by humans. If you want to hang on to that I'll try and identify it later."

Prabir dropped it in his backpack. "You think plants could be affected, too?"

"It probably just blew in on the wind from somewhere." Suddenly she grabbed his shoulder. "Look!"

Ten meters away, a jet-black cockatoo exactly like the one they'd seen in Ambon sat perched on a branch, watching them.

Prabir said, "That's one for the migration theory."

Grant was conceding nothing. "If four different species on

Bandaneira can converge to the point of being indistinguishable, I don't see why the same thing can't happen independently here and on Ambon."

Prabir scrutinized the bird uneasily. The teeth embedded in the bill not only meshed with uncanny precision, they were limited to the sides of the jaw, where the upper and lower halves met; the great curved hook in the center had none. Even if they offered no particular advantage, they certainly weren't present at any point where they'd be utterly useless, for want of a matching surface to cut or grind against. But the specialized bill shape that suited the diet of an ordinary black cockatoo would have evolved long after its ancestors had given up on the whole idea of teeth, so how had the ancient reptilian genes supposedly responsible for their reappearance come to be switched on and off in exactly the right places? Why should two sets of genes that had never been expressed in the same animal before turn out to interact so harmoniously?

Grant took aim with the tranquilizer gun. The dart hit its target and stuck, but didn't take effect as rapidly as it had with the much lighter pigeons. The cockatoo rose from its perch with an outraged squawk, featherless red cheeks flushing blue, and swooped straight toward them, almost reaching them before it fell.

Prabir pushed forward to try to find it in the undergrowth while the arc of its descent was still fresh in his mind. Grant joined him. They combed through the shrubs together for five minutes without success; the bird must have been heavy enough to sink through the vegetation right to the ground.

Grant swore suddenly.

Prabir looked up. "What?"

She was forcing branches and leaves aside with both arms; maybe she was annoyed because she couldn't pick up what she'd found. She said, "Come and have a look at this."

Prabir complied. Tiny black ants were swarming over the

motionless creature, which was more pink now than black. It was already half-eaten.

"Did that look like carrion to you when it hit the ground?"

"Hardly." Prabir reached down gingerly; he didn't particularly want to fight the ants for their meal, but it would be too much hard work to give up and go looking for another specimen every time something like this happened.

"Be careful," Grant advised him redundantly.

He grabbed one bedraggled wing between thumb and forefinger and tried shaking the carcass clean. Ants swarmed onto his hand immediately; he dropped the dead bird and started swatting them. He crushed most of them in a matter of seconds, but the survivors continued doing something extremely painful—stinging or biting, they were too small for him to tell.

Grant fished out the repellent and sprayed his hand; they'd never thought before to be so thorough. The solvent itself smarted; his skin was broken in a hundred places.

"Are you OK?"

"Yeah, yeah." His hand was throbbing, but if he'd been stung he didn't seem to be suffering any systemic reaction.

Grant sprayed her own right hand, and the carcass, then broke a branch off a shrub and used it as a hook. There wasn't much flesh left on the bird, but it would be more than enough for DNA analysis.

"At least they weren't army ants," she joked. "We'd be lucky to have salvaged anything."

Prabir eyed the ground nervously. "No, but I didn't think we were in Guatemala." His old implant might have given him a rose-colored view of Teranesia's insects, but he was sure there'd been nothing as aggressive as this.

He said, "If this whole thing is a response to genetic damage, wouldn't it have shown up in some experiment by now? They've been irradiating fruit flies for a hundred years, at every conceivable dosage."

Grant was way ahead of him. "Maybe it has shown up. But one or two individual recovered traits wouldn't necessarily stand out clearly from genuinely fortuitous mutations. It's not as if the entire organism would regress to an archaic form that any competent paleo-entomologist would recognize instantly. I think what's happening with the displaced organs in some of the mutants is that part of the embryology has been modified out of step with the rest; the result isn't harmful, because there's so much conserved across the gap, but it leads to some detailed anatomy that's neither modern *nor* archaic."

"Right." Prabir still couldn't see how the cockatoo's teeth had come to be placed so efficiently, but he didn't know enough about the subject to argue the point with any confidence. "But when you look at the original DNA of the pigeons that used to live on Bandaneira, can you see where the recovered traits have come from? Can you pin down the sequences that have been cleaned up and switched on in the birds we saw?"

Grant shook her head. "But I don't expect to be able to do that until I understand how the repair process works. The original sequence might be cut out and spliced into a new location, and even hunting through the whole genome for partial matches wouldn't necessarily find it."

Prabir thought this over. "So what you really need to do is catch it in the act? Instead of just seeing the 'before' and 'after' genomes, if we could find an animal where the process was still going on—"

"Ideally, yes," Grant agreed. "Though I don't know how we'd recognize it. I don't know what we'd look for."

Nor did he. But it might still be happening most often, and most visibly, on the island where it had happened first.

Any lingering fear of retribution from Grant was absurd; they were friends now, weren't they? And however annoyed she might be that he'd lied to her, she was hardly going to abandon him here.

But Madhusree had promised to say nothing. How would she feel if he broke the silence first, without consulting her? And if Grant scooped the expedition with his help, the discovery wouldn't become public knowledge, it would be the property of her sponsor.

He said, "So all we can do is gather as many samples as we can, and hope to get lucky?"

Grant squared her shoulders stoically. "That's right. When you don't know what you're looking for, there's no substitute for overkill."

They stayed on the island for six days. Prabir didn't exactly grow inured to the drudgery, but there was some consolation in being so tired every night that he could fall asleep the moment he was horizontal. They found twenty-three species of animals and plants that appeared to be novel, though Grant pointed out that the odds were good that one or two had simply failed to make it into the taxonomic databases.

The second island was another half-day's sailing away. Within an hour of coming ashore, they'd seen what appeared to be the same thorny shrubs, the same flies, the same vicious ants.

They worked their way deeper into the jungle, staying within sight of each other but collecting samples independently. Prabir had rigged up software that took images from his notepad's camera and searched the major databases for a visual match to any previously described species. Grant scorned this approach; she had no encyclopedic knowledge of the region's original wildlife, but she seemed to have acquired the knack of recognizing subtle clues in body plan and coloration. At the end of the day, judged against the sequencing results, their hit rates had turned out to be virtually identical.

Prabir stopped beside a white orchid, a single bell-shaped flower almost half a meter wide. Its thick green stem wound around a tree trunk and ended in a skein of white roots that clung to the bark, wreathed in fungus but otherwise naked to the air. There was an insect sitting in the maw of the flower, a beetle with iridescent green wings. He crouched down for a closer look; he was almost certain that this was a species Grant had found on the previous island that had turned out to be modified. If so, it was worth taking for comparison.

He sprayed the beetle with insecticide and waited a few seconds. There was no death dance, none of the usual convulsions. He gripped it by the sides and tried to dislodge it, but it seemed to be anchored to the petal.

The flower began to close, the petals sliding smoothly together. Prabir drew his hand back, but the flower came with it; the sticky secretion that had trapped the beetle had also glued his fingers to its carapace. He laughed. "Feed me! Feed me!" He grabbed hold of the stem of the orchid and tried to extricate himself by yanking his hands apart, but he wasn't strong enough to break the adhesion, or tear the plant. It was like being superglued to a heavy-duty rope wound around the tree trunk.

The flower now loosely enclosed his forearm, and the reflex action hadn't stopped. He tried to stay calm: pitcher plants and sundews took days or weeks to digest a few flies; he wasn't likely to get doused in anything that would strip his flesh to the bone. He fumbled for his pocketknife and attacked the petal. It was tough and fibrous as a palm leaf, but once he'd punctured it he managed to saw through it easily enough, hacking out a piece around the beetle. The orchid began to unfurl immediately, maybe because he'd taken away the source of the attachment signal. But why hadn't it closed on the beetle itself?

Grant must have seen him struggling; she approached with a look of concern that turned into an inquiring smile as she realized that he was uninjured.

Using the knife blade, he managed to lever one finger free of the beetle. Grant took his hand and peered at what was still glued to his thumb. "That's extraordinary."

"Do you mind?" Prabir pulled his hand back. "If you want to wait five seconds, you can have a proper look." He forced the tip of the blade between skin and carapace, and finally dislodged the beetle, with orchid fragment attached.

Grant picked it up and examined it. "I was right. It's a lure."

"You're joking." Prabir took it from her and held it up to the light, examining the petal edge-on. What he'd taken for an insect was an elaborately colored nodule growing out of the plant itself. He said, "So a beetle comes along and tries to mate with this?"

"A beetle to mate with it, or maybe something else that thinks it's going to eat the 'beetle.' It's quite common for orchids to have one entire petal that looks like a female wasp or bee, as a pollination lure. But with an adhesive like that, I have a feeling the end result wouldn't be a light dusting with pollen."

Prabir reexamined the damaged orchid. There was no pool of digestive juices waiting at the bottom of the flower, but perhaps it would have secreted something if it had been able to close fully.

He passed the lure back to Grant. "Don't you think it looks like that modified species you found a few days ago?"

"Dark green shiny wing cases, about two centimeters long? Do you know how many beetles would fit that description?"

"I think it looks identical." Prabir waited for her to contradict him, but she remained silent. "If it is, isn't that stretching concidence? For a process that wakens old genes in this orchid to synchronize so perfectly with the same process in the beetle—"

Grant said defensively, "They might have been here together for millions of years. It's not inconceivable that two independently recovered traits could reveal an archaic act of mimicry."

"But I thought the beetle wouldn't look exactly like any of its ancestors. I thought you said the mixed embryology produced distorted body plans."

"The lure could be distorted, too."

"Sure. But in the same way? When its morphogenesis is completely different?"

Grant regarded him irritably. "I really don't think they look that similar."

They'd been photographing everything; they didn't need to wait until they were back on the boat to make a comparison. Prabir summoned up the image and offered her his notepad.

After almost a minute Grant conceded, "You're right. They're very close." She looked up from the screen. "I can't explain that."

Prabir nodded soberly. "Don't worry; you'll figure it out. Your hypothesis is still the only one I've heard that makes the slightest sense."

Grant said dryly, "You mean compared to Paul Sutton's highly esteemed theory of Divine Cosmic Ecotropy?"

"I didn't mean it that way. The last I heard from Madhusree, all her university colleagues were completely stumped, so you still have the advantage on them."

Grant gave him a weary smile. "Thanks for the vote of confidence. But remember how long it took me to confess to the idea. Do you really expect that these people would have been any more forthcoming with your sister?"

• • •

The third island was the largest of the six Grant had chosen, almost three kilometers across. Two weeks before, that had sounded like nothing to Prabir's urbanized ear; he'd often walked that far and back across Toronto in his lunch hour. But the area was eight times greater than the total of the two islands they'd toiled on for six days each, and when he saw the dense jungle stretching back from the beach into low, wooded hills, he finally felt the scale of it. It was a far more visceral reaction than anything he'd experienced flying over an ocean or a continent. Probably because Grant would want to gather samples from every last square meter.

They found a gap in the reef almost straight ahead as they approached. It was early afternoon, but Prabir begged for a full day off before they went ashore. They ended up spending three hours snorkeling along the reef, taking pictures but collecting no samples: Grant's license didn't extend to the marine life, and so far there'd been no sign that the mutations did either.

Prabir couldn't help feeling tranquil in the sunlit water; it was impossible to remain uncharmed by the colors of the reef fish, or the weird anatomy of the invertebrates clinging to the coral. Everything here was beautiful and alien, dazzling and remote. A thousand delicate, translucent fish larvae could die in front of him without evoking the slightest twinge of compassion, the kind of thing a chick or a rat pup in the beak of a hawk would have produced. It was this distance that made the spectacle seem so much purer than anything on land: the same vicious struggle looked like nothing but a metaphorical ballet. If his roots were here, he had no sense of it; his body had built its own tamed sea and escaped to another world, as surely as if it had ascended into interstellar space, too long ago to remember.

Sitting on the deck beside Grant in silence, the salt water drying on his skin, Prabir felt calm, lucid, hopeful. The past was not an immovable anchor. What evolution had done, design could do better. There would always be a chance to take what you needed, take what was good, then cut yourself free and move on.

The jungle was as lush as anything Prabir had seen, but without quantifying the impression with a count of species, it also struck him as impoverished. The thorned shrubs and the giant orchids were evident in abundance, but there was nothing at all in sight that merely resembled them. No close relatives, only the things themselves. Whatever else Grant's theory had trouble explaining, you couldn't wind the clock back on a set of surviving lineages and expect to maintain the diversity you started with, and here you could practically see the ancestral bottlenecks everywhere you looked.

Grant called him over. She'd found an orchid clamped shut around the corpse of a small bird, bright blue tail feathers protruding.

Prabir said, "I wish you hadn't shown me this."

"Forewarned is forearmed. What I really want to know is—" Grant sank her knife into the white petals and tore the shroud open.

Ants poured from the gash. As she pulled the knife away, the skeleton of the bird sagged down from the flower, swarming with them.

She inhaled sharply. "OK. But is that just opportunism?" She cut the flower again, then extended the incision down into the stem.

There was a hollow core, full of ants. Grant handed Prabir the camera, and he recorded everything as she continued the dissection, following the stem around the trunk five times until she'd laid the whole internal city bare. There were chambers full of foamy white eggs, and a bloated queen the size of a human thumb.

Prabir said, "What does the orchid get out of it?"

"Maybe just food scraps and excrement; that could be more than enough. Or maybe the ants are feeding it something specific, some secretion tailor-made to keep it happy and fit." Grant was clearly elated, but then she added wistfully, "Someone's going to spend a lifetime on this."

"Why not do it yourself?"

She shrugged. "Not my style. Begging to foundations for charity to do something beautiful and useless."

Prabir felt like grabbing her by the shoulders and shaking her; this sounded so defeatist. He said, "Maybe in a few years you'll feel differently. Once you're not facing the same financial pressures—"

Grant pulled a face. "Don't organize me; I hate that. No wonder your sister ran away from home."

Prabir crouched down beside the orchid. "First mimicry, now symbiosis. These gene-recovery enzymes of yours can hit a bull's-eye at fifty million years."

"And don't gloat, it doesn't suit you. I admit it, freely: there's something going on here that I don't understand."

Prabir said, "I still think your basic idea must be right. Functional genes take thousands of years to develop. If they appear overnight, the organism has to be cheating. 'Here's one I prepared earlier.' What else can it be?"

Grant seemed ready to accept this, but then she shook her head. "I can't answer that, but it's starting to look as if I'm missing something fundamental. Perfectly camouflaged birds with no predators. Thorned plants with nothing even trying to munch on them. There are misses as well as bull's-eyes. But even the misses are too *precise*."

She squatted beside Prabir. The ants were methodically crisscrossing the tear in the stem, secreting a papier-mâchélike scaffolding a thousand times faster than any plant could have grown new tissue. She said, "Don't you wish you could just ask them for the whole story? When did they get together and sort this all out? Why did they stop? Why did they start again? What is it we don't understand?"

It was late in the morning on the second day when they reached the mangrove swamp. They were at least a kilometer inland, but there was a narrow valley running from the heart of the jungle to the coast, its floor a would-be riverbed with too little runoff feeding it to prevent seawater flooding in at high tide. At low tide, the halophytic trees would stand naked in an expanse of salty mud, but that was still hours away; for now, the way ahead was inundated.

Grant peered into the tangle of branches and aerial roots. "It's only a few hundred meters across. We should be able to wade through without too much trouble."

"And then time it so we can cross back at low tide?"

"Yeah."

Prabir found that part appealing; if they had to do this at all, he'd rather do it while he still had the energy.

He double-checked that all the sample tubes he was carrying were sealed; his watch and notepad were fully waterproof. There didn't seem much point taking any of his clothes off; they'd get coated in slime however he carried them, and the more protection he had against scrapes and splinters from the roots, the better.

Grant waded in up to her knees. Prabir followed her, every step like an exaggerated mime of walking as his boots stuck afresh in the mud. The water was turbid with silt, almost opaque where it could be seen at all, but most of the surface was covered with a layer of algae and dead leaves. The odor of salt and decay was insistent—like breathing over a garden compost heap with seaweed added for effect—but not overpowering or stomach-turning. Other parts of the forest had smelled worse.

The protruding brown roots of the mangroves were dotted with snails, but Prabir spotted small brown crabs as well. Clouds of mites and mosquitos approached them and then backed away; at least their repellent was holding out. The trees were twenty or thirty meters tall; it was eerie to look up into the branches, decorated with small white blossoms and tiny green fruit, then down into what was essentially dirty seawater, as if a forest had sprouted in the middle of the ocean.

The mud was annoying, but it wasn't treacherous; the hidden mangrove roots were far more pernicious. Every time Prabir thought he'd learned to judge where a clear stretch of ground might lie between two trunks, he walked into a root at shin height. The water was above his waist now, and the clues from the visible roots were getting harder to read. He'd started out following directly behind Grant, unashamedly letting her blaze the trail, but then his concentration had lapsed, and he'd skirted a submerged obstacle on his own to find that they'd been shunted to either side of it. Since then, they'd been moving farther apart, following entirely separate paths through the drowned maze.

Grant called out to him, "Hey, watch out!" Prabir looked around; a black snake about a meter long with narrow yellow stripes was swimming toward him. He scanned the tangle of litter around the nearest trunk, looking for a forked stick he could use to persuade the snake to keep its distance, but it veered away of its own accord, blinking elliptical green eyes like a cat's.

The water grew deeper, reaching high on his chest; the trees thinned slightly, but not enough to compensate for the loss of visibility. Grant was a few centimeters shorter than he was, and she was submerged almost up to her chin. Prabir shouted, "Next time, we cheat and take the boat around the coast."

"Amen to that."

"I don't want to come back this way, even when the tide's

out. We'd be better off walking along the beach, and swimming across the inlet if we have to."

Grant swore suddenly; Prabir assumed she'd just been bruised twice in the same spot in rapid succession, which was particularly painful. She shouted, "This is ridiculous! I'm going to try swimming, here and now." She leaned forward into the water and began a slow breaststroke.

Prabir observed the experiment with interest. She was scooping aside some of the surface muck as she went, but it was still piling up around her face and shoulders. "What's it like?"

"Not too bad. The current's pretty strong, though." She wasn't exaggerating; as the water carried her sideways she almost collided with a trunk, but she managed to swim clear of it. It looked no more dangerous than tripping through the roots, and a whole lot faster.

Grant was wearing light canvas shoes; he'd have to take his boots off to swim. He hesitated, wondering if it was worth the trouble. He crouched down, submerging his head to reach the laces, but they were too slippery and waterlogged to untie; his fingernails slid uselessly over the knots he'd made to secure the bows.

He stood up, scraping mulch off his face. Grant was no longer in sight.

He shouted after her, "Wait for me at the shore!"

A faint reply came back, "Yes!"

Prabir trudged on, occasionally making a halfhearted attempt to swim over obstacles. He'd grown fitter over the last two weeks, and reached the point where their normal day-long excursions were bearable, but just stepping over the endless, unpredictable succession of mangrove roots was turning the muscles in his legs to jelly. Once he was out of this shit-hole, he had no intention of spending three hours gathering samples for Grant;

he'd walk down to the ocean, wash the slime off his body, and curl up under a palm tree. How had she managed to stretch his unpaid duties so far beyond bad translations, bad cultural advice, and surprisingly reasonable cooking?

He could see a grassy clearing ahead, with ordinary trees behind it. The water was still up to his chest, but dry land was just ten or fifteen meters away. He shouted, "Grant? I've had enough! I'm going on strike!" If she was in earshot she didn't deign to reply.

The ground climbed abruptly, the water dropped to waist height; the shore was within reach, no longer an unattainable mirage. Prabir's shins collided with an obstacle that felt like a large fallen branch; wearily, he stepped back in order to step over it, but then his calves hit something behind him, just as high, that felt much the same.

For a moment he was simply bemused. Could he have sleep-walked right over the first branch, without even noticing it?

Then the gap between the two obstacles tightened, and he realized that they were parts of the same thing.

He quickly pulled his right foot out of the enclosing coil, and probed forward for a safe place to put it. As his foot touched mud, the snake shifted, dragging his left leg back, overbalancing him. He hit the water with his hands over his face, cringing with fear— terrified of coming eye-to-eye with the thing, though he knew that was the least of his problems. He swam forward clumsily, fighting both the instinct to right himself and the weight of his boots dragging his feet down. Then he felt something pass by swiftly and smoothly in the water ahead of him, and his arms came down against the body of the snake, blocking his way again.

He backed away, staggering to his feet, shifting the tightening noose from his lungs to his abdomen just in time. He still couldn't see any part of the snake, but he'd felt its girth. This wasn't one of the placid four-meter pythons he'd seen feeding on birds as a child, merely adapted to salt water. It was half as thick as his torso. It would be more than capable of swallowing him.

He opened his mouth to cry for help, but the sound died in his throat. What could Grant do? Tranquilizer darts wouldn't penetrate the water, and even if she could pump her whole supply into the snake, its body weight would be hundreds of times greater than the largest of the birds they'd used the darts to subdue. She'd end up standing helplessly on the shore watching him die, or getting killed herself trying to rescue him. He couldn't do that to her. He couldn't sentence her to either fate.

Prabir groped for his pocketknife, shivering with fear. He scanned the water desperately; if he plunged the knife into the snake's head with enough force, the blade might just penetrate its skull. The coil of its body slid smoothly over his hips, tightening its hold. He followed his sense of where the motion was coming from, and saw a ripple in the water, a faint wake disturbing the surface.

It was six meters away. He'd be wrapped all the way up to his shoulders before the head came within reach.

He started stabbing wildly at the snake's body, bringing the knife down from high above his head. The blade bounced off its skin. He collected himself; he was wasting his energy splashing up water. He put both hands underwater and drew the knife up toward his belly with all the strength in his arms and back, seppuku in self-defense. The knife burst through the leathery hide and sank up to the hilt. He tried to drag it along, to make a cut, giddy for a moment with triumphant visions of flaying the snake from head to tail. The knife wouldn't budge; he might as well have tried to split a tree trunk this way. He pulled it out, and repeated the thrust that had proved successful. As the blade made contact, the snake shifted again, and the knife went spinning out of his hands.

He bent down and fumbled for it. The snake jerked him off balance, immersing him completely. He groped across the mud, but he couldn't find the knife. He lifted his face up, arching his back to get his mouth out of the water, spluttering for breath. The telltale wake was passing in front of him again; the snake had almost completed a second coil. *Grant might be able to reach its head. She might find a way to attack it without risking her own life.*

And if she couldn't?

She wouldn't martyr herself. And if there was nothing she could do, and he died in front of her, she wouldn't be crippled by the experience. She wasn't a child.

He filled his lungs and bellowed, "Gra-a-a-ant! *Help me!*" The snake had finally worked out how to drown a biped: Prabir could feel it change the tension in its muscles, skewing the angle of the coils, forcing him down. He tried to fill his lungs again while he still had the chance, but the constriction around the bottom of his rib cage stopped him dead halfway through; it was like hitting a brick wall.

Then he went under.

Prabir lay beneath the water, no longer struggling, faint lights dancing in front of his eyes. This was all wrong: he should have died in the minefield of the garden instead. The first blast would have been enough to kill him instantly; no one would have had to follow him in. His parents would have grieved for the rest of their lives, but they would have had Madhusree, she would have had them.

Suddenly he heard a loud, rhythmic splashing noise. It wasn't the snake turning hyperactive: someone was beating the water with a heavy object. The timbre gradually changed, as if the water was being struck in successively shallower locations. Then there was a resounding thwack, wood against wood.

The snake's muscles slackened perceptibly. Prabir fought to

raise his head. He caught a shallow breath, and then a glimpse of the lower half of someone standing on the shore. Not Grant: a woman with bare dark legs. The snake twitched back to life and jerked him down again. The beating sound resumed, ten, fifteen powerful blows.

As he struggled to snatch another mouthful of air, Prabir heard the woman slip into the water. He didn't question his sanity: he knew he wasn't hallucinating. As he turned the strange miracle over in his head, he felt no fear for her. Everything would be all right, now that they'd been reunited.

The woman said urgently, in bad Indonesian, "You need to work, you need to help me! It's only stunned. And I can't pull you out on my own." Prabir forced himself upright, fighting the passive weight of the snake. The woman wasn't Madhusree.

She helped him loosen the coils enough for him to climb up onto her back. He didn't seem to have any broken bones, but he was even weaker from the ordeal than he'd realized; she carried him like a child to the water's edge, then maneuvered him onto the ground before she clambered out of the water herself. She picked up the heavy branch she'd used to bash the python senseless, then reached down and hauled him to his feet. "Come on. Back from the water before we rest. It won't be out cold much longer."

Prabir staggered after her, still holding her hand. His teeth were chattering. He said in English, "You're a biologist, aren't you? You're with the expedition?"

She frowned at him, and replied in English. "You're not Moluccan? I knew there were no villages here, but—are you a scientist?"

Prabir laughed. "I must be, mustn't I?" *Stick to the cover story.* His legs collapsed.

She crouched beside him. "OK. We'll rest for a bit, then I'll get you back to base camp."

"What were you doing here?"

She nodded toward the snake; its head was still lying exposed on the mangrove roots where she'd cornered it, but it was showing signs of regaining consciousness. "Observing them, among other things. Though I prefer not to get quite as close as you did." She smiled uncertainly, then added, "You're lucky; given that it already had prey secured, I wasn't sure that even the most frantic imitation of an animal in distress would catch its attention. There's a paper in there somewhere, on supernormal stimuli versus inhibition signals."

The snake slid drunkenly off the mangroves, its body rising to the surface in a horizontal sine wave as it swam away. It had to be at least twenty meters long.

Prabir asked numbly, "What do they live off? There can't be that many tourists."

"I think they eat wild pigs, mostly. But I've seen one take a saltwater crocodile."

He blinked at her, then jumped to his feet. "There are crocodiles? My friend's back there!" He started running frantically toward the shore. "Martha? *Martha!*"

Grant appeared suddenly out of the jungle behind him. She seemed about to berate him jokingly for his tardiness, then she saw his rescuer. She hesitated, as if waiting for introductions, then made her own. "I'm Martha Grant. I'm with Prabir, we got separated."

"Seli Ojany." They walked up to each other and shook hands. Grant turned to Prabir expectantly, clearly aware that she was missing something significant, but he didn't know how to begin. If the python hadn't fled, he would have just pointed at it and mimed the rest.

Ojany was staring at him, too, with an expression of disbelief. "You're not Prabir Suresh? Madhusree's brother?"

"That's right."

"You followed her here, all the way from Toronto?"

"Yes."

Ojany broke into a wide, delighted grin.

She said, "You're in trouble!"

Chapter 10

The expedition's ship was anchored outside the reef; the biologists had landed in small boats and set up camp in half a dozen tents on a grassy plain not far from the beach. It was mid-afternoon, and the camp was almost deserted; nearly everyone was still out in the field. But one of the expedition members taking a day off was a woman with medical training; she examined Prabir to confirm that he had no broken bones, and gave him glucose and a sedative.

The three of them were covered in swamp matter; they washed themselves in the ocean, and Ojany found them clean clothes. Prabir was still shaky; he was being led through everything like an infant. Ojany said, "Come on, champ, you can use my bed for now, and we'll organize something later for tonight."

Prabir lay down on the rectangle of foam and stared up at the roof of the tent. He had a sudden, vivid memory of lying exhausted in his hammock, the day he'd walked halfway up Teranesia's dead volcano to try to measure the distance to the nearest island. There was nothing especially poignant about the memory itself, but the sharpness of the recollection was enough to make him want to bash his head against the ground. He was tired of having to think about that idiot child, tired of having been him, but every attempt to get rid of him was like trying to slough off dead skin, only to find that it was still full of living nerves and blood vessels.

Grant shook him gently. It was dusk. She said, "Everyone's eating now. Do you want to come join us?"

At least thirty people were gathered in the space between the tents. There were hurricane lamps set up, and a man was serving food from a butane stove. Grant said, "This isn't just the expedition. A fishing boat turned up while you were asleep. Word seems to have leaked back to Ambon; a few people hitched a ride down."

Prabir followed her into the serving line, looking around for Madhusree. He spotted several of the barflies from Ambon; Cole was wandering about delivering Delphic pronouncements to anyone who'd listen, his eyes glistening in the lamplight. "I have pursued the black sun across the salt flats of millennium, into the heart of the primeval calenture!"

Grant whispered to Prabir, "For God's sake, someone give that man an antipyretic."

When his turn came, Prabir gratefully accepted a steaming plate of stew, though he was unable to determine its exact nature even after he'd taken a mouthful. He walked to the edge of the gathering to eat; he could see Grant talking shop with Ojany, but he wasn't in the mood to join in. As some of the diners began to improvise seats out of packing crates or rolled-up sleeping bags, he saw Madhusree standing with two other women, talking and laughing as they ate. She saw him watching her, and stared back for a moment with an utterly neutral expression, neither welcoming nor angry, before rejoining the conversation. Someone would have broken the news of his arrival to her as soon as she'd returned to the camp, but perhaps she still hadn't decided whether or not to forgive him.

Cole's student, Mike Carpenter, wandered over from the

serving line. He stood beside Prabir, eating in silence for a while, then said, "You know Sandra Lamont?"

"Not personally."

"I saw her once, in real life," Carpenter boasted. "She's got terrible skin. Pores, wrinkles. They just smooth it all out with software."

"Gosh. How scandalous. Would you excuse me?"

Prabir made his way across the camp. A man with a Philippines accent in a Hawaiian shirt and a Stetson was saying to a similarly attired companion, "—welcomed by an animatronic dinosaur! Full marina facilities! And the hook-line is, '*Earth* is the alien planet!'" Two biologists were arguing heatedly about transposons; one of them seemed to have independently reached an idea similar to Grant's: "—shuffles back in the sequence for a *complete functional protein domain* that was cut out and shelved eons ago—"

He walked up to Madhusree and touched her arm.

"Hi, Maddy."

She turned to him, and smiled impassively. "Hi."

Her friends smiled, too, but they appeared distinctly uncomfortable. Madhusree said, "This is Deborah, and Laila. This is my brother Prabir, who narrowly avoided becoming one of Seli's stomach content samples." Prabir nodded in acknowledgment; they were all holding plates, it was too awkward to try to shake hands.

He said, "How's the work going?"

"Good, good," Madhusree replied smoothly. "We've gathered lots of data: behavioral, anatomical, DNA. No conclusions yet, but we've started posting it all on the net, so everyone can take a look for themselves."

"Yeah? I should tell Felix about that."

Madhusree frowned. "Don't you think he'd already know that he could follow everything from back in Toronto? I would have thought it would be obvious to anyone, how easy and convenient that would be."

Prabir was impressed by her self-control. The message wasn't exactly subtle, but she hadn't let the slightest hint of anger spoil her innocent delivery: there was no flash in her eyes, no tension in her voice. He said, "I'm not sure. I'll have to ask him."

Madhusree glanced at her watch. "You could do that right now. It would be the perfect time to catch him."

"Yeah. Thanks. That's a good idea."

He nodded again to her friends, and turned away. As he hunted for a place where he could stand and finish his meal alone, he felt an overwhelming sense of relief. He'd done what he'd done, and she'd told him how she felt, and now that it was over it was insignificant. He'd no more seriously undermined her dignity than those embarrassing parents who'd turned up with forgotten box lunches and sent his sixth-grade classmates into paroxysms of humiliation. And unlike schoolchildren, most of her colleagues would surely sympathize with her, rather than ridicule her, for having to go through life with such a cross.

He could see now that she'd be safe here, his own close call notwithstanding; she had ten times as many people looking out for her. He'd leave in the morning with Grant; the sting of resentment would wear off in a day or two, and when they met again in Toronto she'd punch him in the shoulder and call him a shit and laugh without malice, and the whole thing would be transmuted into a joke forever.

"Come out of the tent. I want to talk to you."

Madhusree was standing over him in the darkness, prodding his chest with her foot.

Ojany shared the tent with two other postdocs, but they'd found some spare bedding, and agreed to let him stay for the night. The tents all had insect-proof groundsheets; though it was unbearably hot, Prabir wouldn't have liked to have tried sleeping outside, tempting the ants.

"What time is it?" he whispered.

"Just after two," she hissed. "Now come out of the tent."

Prabir grinned up at her. "When they ask me back at work what I did on my vacation, do you think I should admit to having spent a night with three beautiful women on a tropical island?"

Madhusree was infuriated. "Don't waste your breath trying to make a joke of this. Just get up!"

"All right. It might help if you take some of your weight off me."

He followed her out, into the deserted center of the camp.

She said, "How dare you! How dare you come here!"

Prabir had never seen her so enraged, but he was having trouble adjusting; in his mind it had all been resolved, she'd already punished him.

He said gently, "I'm sorry if I've embarrassed you. I just wanted to see for myself how you were. I wanted to see what it was really like here."

Madhusree stared at him, almost weeping with frustration. "I don't care if you *embarrass me*! Just how shallow do you think I am? What do you think I used to say to my friends at school? Do you think I renounced you every day? Do you think I made up pretend parents? I don't give a fuck what anyone here thinks about either of us. If they don't like my family, they can screw themselves."

Prabir ran his hand through his hair, touched by her passionate declaration, but a great deal more afraid now.

He said haltingly, "What then? Treat me like an idiot. Spell it out."

She wiped her eyes angrily. "All right. How's this for a start? You couldn't trust me to make this *one decision*, and live with it.

You couldn't trust me to look into the risks myself: the mines, the border skirmishes, the diseases, the wildlife. They're not trivial. I never *said* they were trivial. But I'm nineteen years old. I'm not retarded. I had access to people who could give me good advice. But you still couldn't trust my judgment."

Prabir protested, "I never stopped you doing anything in your life! What have I ever done, before this? Did I interrogate your doped-up boyfriends? Did I stop you going to nightclubs when you were fourteen years old? Name one thing I did that showed I didn't trust you."

She bit her lip, breathing hard. Finally she said, "That's all true, but it's not good enough. You didn't treat me like a child then. Why do you have to treat me like one now?"

"I'm not treating you like a child. And you know why this is different."

Madhusree's face contorted with pain. "That's the worst part! That's the worst insult! Different for you, but not for me? You think it isn't hard for me, too, coming back to where they died? Just because I don't remember them the way you do?"

She started sobbing dryly. Prabir wanted to embrace her, but he was afraid he'd only anger her. He looked around helplessly. "I know you miss them, too. I know that."

"I'm *sick* of having to go through you to reach them!"

That was unfair. He'd told her every detail of their lives that he'd remembered, and a few he'd invented to fill in the gaps. But what else could he have done? Offered her a Ouija board?

He said, "I never wanted it to be like that. But if that's how it felt to you, then I'm sorry."

Madhusree shook her head wearily; she wasn't forgiving him, but she didn't have the energy to resolve the matter now. Prabir could see her putting aside all her grief and anger, steeling herself for something more pressing.

"I made a promise in that note I left you," she said. "And I've kept it: I haven't told anyone about the butterflies. But tomorrow, I'm going to the head of the expedition and explaining everything. Our parents' work was important. What they did was important. Everyone should know about it."

Prabir bowed his head. "All right. I have no problem with that. Just promise me you won't go to the island yourself. Leave it to someone else. There must be plenty of work to be done right here."

"I have to go. I'll check the huts for records while the others are gathering samples. And if I can find the remains, I'll have them taken back to Calcutta for the proper ceremonies."

He looked up at her, stunned. "'Proper ceremonies'? What the fuck does *that* mean?"

Madhusree said calmly, "Just because they weren't religious, it doesn't mean we have to leave them lying where they fell. Like animals."

Prabir's skin went cold. She was saying this just to wound him. The implication was that if he'd loved them enough, he would have done this himself long ago, instead of cowering on the other side of the world like a scared little boy for eighteen years. But it was all right now: an adult had come along, with the strength to do what needed to be done.

He turned away, unable to look at her.

She said, "It's the right thing to do. You know that. I wanted to talk to you about it, but you just shut me out."

Prabir said nothing. He knew that if he opened his mouth and spoke now, he'd pour out so much contempt for her that they'd never be reconciled.

"You should be happy. We'll finally put them to rest."

He stared at the ground, refusing to reply, refusing to acknowledge her. She stood there for a while, repeating his name, pleading with him. Then she gave up and walked away.

. . .

Prabir found Grant in the third tent he entered; she woke instantly when he whispered her name, and followed him out without a word.

She must have sensed the seriousness of his purpose; once they were beyond earshot of anyone who might have been awake, she asked without a trace of irritation, "What's going on?"

Prabir said, "I know where this all began. Do you want me to take you there?"

"What are you talking about?" But he could already see her reassessing their old conversations. "Are you telling me you saw something as a child? When you were traveling with your parents?"

"Not traveling. My parents knew exactly where they wanted to go, long before we left Calcutta. We spent three years there. They were biologists, not seafood exporters. They came here to study the very first mutant, back in 2010."

Grant didn't waste time contesting this possibility; she just demanded, "What species? Where?"

Prabir shook his head. "Not yet. This is the deal: you post all the data you've gathered on the net, so everyone has access to it. Just like the expedition scientists. If you agree to that, I'll take you there, and I'll tell you everything I know."

Grant smiled wearily. "Be reasonable. You know I can't do that."

"Fine. It's your loss." He turned and started walking away.

"Hey!" She grabbed him by the shoulder. "I could always ask your sister."

He laughed. "*My sister?* You're a complete stranger to her, a rival scientist and a data burier, and you think she's going to give you a better deal?"

Grant scowled, more baffled than angry. "Why are you being such a prick? You might as well have kept me in the dark completely; at least I wouldn't have known what I was missing. *I can't do what you're asking.* I've signed a contract; they'd cut my hands off."

"Would you go to prison?"

"I doubt it, but that's hardly—"

"So it's just money? They'd just need to be bought off?"

"Yeah, that's all. Is this the point where you reveal that you're also Bill Gates's love child?"

Prabir said, "If this is important enough, and you crack it wide open, do you really think there'll be no opportunities to make money out of that fact? Face it: none of the real cash is likely to be in biotech applications anyway. Whatever's happening here isn't going to solve any medical problems—and even if your theory's right, it's not going to give people pet dinosaurs any more easily than standard genetic methods. But if you handle this properly, you can be a celebrity scientist with a nine-figure media deal for your story."

Grant was amused. "That's pure fantasy. Is that why you're doing this? You think you'll get an eight-figure deal as costar?"

Prabir didn't dignify that with an answer. "Maybe the rights wouldn't be that much. But I don't believe that you couldn't find a way to make money from this, if you put your mind to it."

"I never realized you had such a high opinion of me."

"I could always lead the expedition there, instead. Madhusree's decided not to tell them anything; she wants to leave our parents undisturbed. The only reason I'm even asking *you* is to avoid putting her through the ordeal of going back there."

Grant hesitated, reevaluating old clues again. "Your parents died there? In the war? And the two of you were left alone?"

"Yes." Prabir hadn't meant to reveal so much; he could see the sympathy it evoked eating away at Grant's natural cynicism, and it made him feel much worse than when he'd merely lied to her. But he pushed the advantage for all it was worth. "They were gagged by their sponsor, just like you. That's why nothing they did was ever published. I want what they began to be completed, properly, with everyone sharing the information. The way it should have been all along."

Grant shook her head regretfully. "I can't risk it. It could bankrupt me."

"So your sponsor will bury you in obscurity instead, just like Silk Rainbow buried my parents? You had the best theory, first. You've worked as hard as any of these people." He gestured at the tents around them. "If I lead them to the source, and some prat from Harvard beats you to the answer, you won't even get a footnote."

Prabir watched her uneasily, wondering if he'd put his case too bluntly. But if she couldn't conform to the strictures of academic life, she'd also resent every curtailment of freedom her sponsor had forced upon her. If there was a way to shaft both sides and survive the experience—and a chance to emerge covered in glory—she'd have to be tempted.

She whispered angrily, "I can't decide this now. I have to think about it, I have to talk to Michael—"

"I'll give you until dawn. I'll wait for you down on the beach."

Grant looked at her watch, horrified. "Three hours?"

"That's three times as long as you gave me in Ambon."

"That was time to pack! You weren't gambling with your life."

"I didn't think I was. But you didn't mention anything then about leaving me behind as snake food."

Grant opened her mouth to protest.

Prabir said, "I'm joking. *I'm joking!* It's been a long day."

● ● ●

Prabir lay unsleeping on his borrowed bed. He'd told his watch to wake him at a quarter to six, but by five o'clock he was too restless to stay in the tent. He dressed in his own clothes—he'd rinsed them in fresh water and hung them out to dry—and headed down to the beach.

He sat and watched the stars fade, listening to the first birdcalls. Broken sleep had left a foul taste in his mouth, and there was a rawness to all his perceptions, as if his senses had been doused in paint-stripper; even the faint brightening of the sky hurt his eyes. He was aching all over, from something more than exertion; he could remember the pain in his calves as he'd trekked through the swamp, but now every muscle in his body seemed equally wrecked. *It was the way he'd felt at dawn on the Tanimbar Islands, after the long boat ride. After the dying soldier had let him in on the big secret.*

He heard a sound from farther down the beach. One of the men from the fishing boat was performing *salat al-fajr*, the Muslim dawn prayers. Prabir's skin crawled, but the sense of being haunted only lasted a split second; the fisherman was a young Melanesian who looked nothing like the soldier.

When he'd finished praying, the man approached and greeted Prabir amiably, introducing himself as Subhi and offering a hand-rolled cigarette. Prabir declined, but they sat together while he smoked. The tobacco was scented with cloves; the potential this recipe offered as a fumigant had definitely been underexploited.

It was a struggle making conversation; Indonesian was still being taught in schools throughout the RMS, but as far as Prabir could judge the two of them were equally bad at it. He gestured at Subhi's prayer rug and asked, jokingly, if he was the only devout man on the boat.

This slur horrified Subhi. "The other men are all pious, but they're Christians."

"I understand. Forgive me. I didn't think of that possibility."

Subhi generously conceded that it was an understandable mistake, and launched into a long account of the virtues of his fellow crew members. Prabir listened and nodded, only making sense of half of what he heard. It was several minutes into the story before he realized that he was being told something more. Subhi's village in the Kai Islands had been destroyed during the war. His family had all been killed; he was the sole survivor out of more than two hundred people. The Christian village with *pela* obligations to his own had sheltered him and raised him, and he'd continued to live there, though when he wasn't at sea he attended Friday prayers at the mosque in another village. This was a very satisfactory arrangement, at least until he married, because he could continue to uphold the faith of his parents without moving away from his friends.

When he'd finished, Prabir was unable to speak. *How could anyone lose so much, and emerge with so little bitterness?* Religion had nothing to do with it; *pela* did not derive from either Islam or Christianity, it was a conscious strategy developed to detoxify the unavoidable mixture of the two. But some combination of personal resilience and an accommodating culture had pulled this man out of the conflagration of his childhood, apparently intact.

Prabir felt a need to reciprocate, to relate some of his own history. He asked Subhi if he knew of an island with a dead volcano, seventy kilometers southwest.

Subhi's face became grim. "That's not a good place, there are spirits there." He looked at Prabir anew. "Are you the son of the Indian scientists who went there before the war?"

"Yes." Prabir was amazed to be identified this way, but then he remembered the laborers from the Kai Islands who'd helped his parents set up the kampong. If Teranesia had since gained a supernatural reputation, its whole recent history might have become widely known.

He said, "What kind of spirits? Spirits in the form of animals?" Any advance intelligence about the modified fauna could help them prepare.

Subhi nodded uneasily. "There are many kinds of spirits there, released as punishment for the crimes of the war. Visible and invisible. Possessing animals, and men."

"Possessing men?" Prabir wondered if this was merely a formulaic recitation of metaphysical possibilities. "Who? No one lives there now, do they?"

"No." Subhi looked at the ground, discomforted.

"So who did the spirits harm? Did a boat stop there?"

He nodded.

"When?"

"Three months ago. To make repairs."

"And the men on board became sick?"

"Sick? In a way," Subhi agreed reluctantly.

"Did they eat something on the island? Did they catch some of the animals? How were they sick?"

Subhi shook his head, pained. "It's not respectful to talk about this."

Prabir didn't want to offend him, but if there was any evidence of effects on human DNA, nothing could be more important than tracking it down. "Could I meet these men? If I went to their village?"

"That's not possible." Subhi rose to his feet abruptly, brushing sand from his clothes. "It's time I joined my friends." He reached down and shook Prabir's hand, then started walking away along the beach.

Prabir called after him, "The men who visited the island? Are they alive, or dead?"

There was a long silence, then Subhi replied without turning. "God willing, they're at peace."

Grant arrived at twenty past six. Prabir said, "I'd almost given up on you. Have you decided?"

She held up her notepad. Prabir took out his own and cloned the page she was displaying, then reread it independently via a randomly chosen proxy, to verify that it really was publically available.

He flipped through the sequence data; there was no way he could tell whether or not it was correct, he'd simply have to trust her. Then he noticed the sponsorship logo: Borromean rings built of rotating plasmids. The logo detected his gaze and said proudly, "This information is brought to you by PharmoNucleic, as a service to the scientific community."

He looked up at Grant, amazed. "You're rubbing their face in it? Isn't that begging to be sued?"

Grant said matter-of-factly, "They're not going to sue anyone. I told them the choice you'd offered me, and they agreed to release all the data. They don't see any serious patent prospects, given that the expedition has collected so much data of their own. Instead of wasting all the money they've invested so far, they'd rather have some good PR. Oh, and an eighty percent share of any media rights."

Prabir was delighted. "You're a genius! Why didn't I think of that?"

"Misdirected hostility toward authority?"

"Ha! You're the one who told me how much you hated being gagged. I thought you'd be dying for an excuse to bite their hand off."

Grant said dryly, "I'm the one who still has a family to support."

Prabir hefted his backpack. He was still aching all over, but the oppressive mood he'd felt at dawn had lifted. Even if Madhusree's colleagues took her belated revelations seriously, the expedition would be saddled with enough logistical inertia to keep them from doing anything about it immediately. If he and Grant could return in a day or two with samples from the island—and all their findings were in the public domain—there'd be no urgent need for a second visit. Maybe their results would merit a comprehensive follow-up, eventually, but the expedition had a finite budget and a limited timetable. Madhusree would be back in Toronto long before anyone went near Teranesia again.

He said, "Are you ready?"

"Yeah. Are you sure you're up to this?"

"I'm up to anything that doesn't involve mangroves."

Grant put an arm across his shoulders and said solemnly, "I shouldn't have left you behind. It was a stupid thing to do, and I'm truly sorry. We won't get separated again."

The route back along the coast was infinitely less arduous than the jungle. They swam past the inlet to the mangrove swamp through crystalline water at the reef's inner edge, where at least they'd have a chance to see any predators approaching. But they made the crossing unmolested; despite the multitude of fish, the swamp and the forest were apparently considered better hunting grounds.

As they trudged along the beach again, Prabir told Grant about Subhi's story of the fishermen.

She said, "That could mean anything. They might have cooked a plant they were accustomed to eating safely, and it turned out to have acquired some extra protective toxins."

"Yeah." That did sound like the simplest explanation, and if the men had died badly, psychotic and hallucinating, it would have been enough to confirm the presence of spirits. Prabir wished he could have questioned someone else about the incident, but they didn't have time to go off to the Kai Islands to hunt for reliable witnesses to an event nobody wanted to talk about.

Grant said, "Tell me about your parents' work."

Prabir sketched the sequence of events that had led Radha and Rajendra to the island. It was a long time since he'd discussed this with anyone but Madhusree, and as he listened to himself betraying her—handing over the family history to this stranger, to keep Madhusree from making use of it herself—he felt far worse than he'd anticipated. But Grant had kept her side of the deal, and he had no reason to believe that his parents would have wanted him to keep any of this secret.

"Can you describe the butterflies?"

"They were green and black. Emerald green. There was a pattern, a sort of concentric striping; not quite eye spots, but a bit like that. They were pretty large; each wing was about the size of an adult's hand. There was something about the veins in the wings, and the position of the genitals, that my parents made a big deal about. But I've forgotten the details."

"Would you recognize the other stages? The eggs, the larvae, the pupae?"

Prabir pictured the sequence laid out in front of him. *He'd been inside the butterfly hut, just once: at night, in the dark.* In his memory, though, he could see the contents of all the cages. Spiked, hissing larvae. Orange and green pupae like rotten fruit.

"I'm not sure." The words came out like an angry denial.

Grant turned to look at him, surprised by his tone. "They might be easier to collect than the adults, that's all. But if you can't remember, it's not the end of the world."

They reached the boat just after noon. Prabir unpacked the samples he'd collected before entering the swamp; the python had crushed half his tubes of gelled blood, but even so, the morning hadn't been a complete loss.

Grant had no trouble finding the island on her chart from his description, but she asked Prabir to confirm it. He ran his finger over the bland set of contour lines on the screen, some satellite's radar echo blindly cranked through a billion computations to spit out a shape that would have taken a human surveyor a month of hardship to map.

He said, "That's it. That's Teranesia."

Grant smiled. "Is that really what you called it?"

"Yeah. Well, it was the name I came up with, and my parents went along with it. But it was nothing to do with the butterflies; after about a week I was bored to tears with them. I didn't pay much attention to any of the real animals; I used to make up my own. Child-eating monsters that chased us around the island, but never quite caught up."

"Ah, everyone has those."

"Do they? I never had them in Calcutta. There was no room."

Grant said, "I packed a pretty good bestiary into the stairwell of a twelve-story block of flats. Not that I didn't have competition: one of my idiot brothers tried to give the whole building a kind of layered metaphysical structure—full of ethereal beings on different spiritual levels, like some lame cosmology out of Doris Lessing or C.S. Lewis—but even when his friends went along with it, I knew it was crap. All his little demons and angels had endless wars and political intrigues, but apparently no time for either food or sex."

"You had trouble attracting as many believers to a world of rutting carnivores?"

She nodded forlornly. "I even had hermaphroditic dung beetles, but no one cared. It was so unfair."

Grant programmed the autopilot, and the engines started up smoothly. The boat circled around to face the reef, then retraced the safe path it had found on arrival.

As they rounded the coast and headed out to sea, Prabir stood on deck near the bow, waiting for the tip of the volcano to appear on the horizon. It was still too far away, though, too small to stand out from the haze.

Grant joined him. "So who do you want to play your character in the movie?"

Prabir cringed. "Did I really suggest going for the movie rights? I thought I must have dreamed that part. Can't you just bring out a cologne, like the physicists do?"

"Only because they have nothing worth filming. And I think they make more from donor gametes." She eyed him appraisingly. "One of the Kapoor brothers might just be dashing enough."

"That's very flattering, but I doubt that any of them would be willing to take the role."

Grant laughed, baffled. "Why on Earth not?"

"Never mind. What about you?"

"Oh, Lara Croft, definitely."

She'd brought a pair of binoculars; she lifted them to the horizon. After a few seconds she announced, "I can see it now. Do you want a look?"

Prabir's throat filled with acid. *He still wasn't ready.* But everyone went back: to battlefields, to death camps, to places ten thousand times worse than this. Subhi to his lost village, no doubt. Every piece of land, every stretch of sea, was a graveyard to someone. He wasn't special.

He took the binoculars and turned his head until the red azimuth needle was centered; the autopilot was providing the correct bearing. At first the image was nothing but a dark triangular smudge, blurred by turbulence. Then the processing chip recalibrated its atmospheric model and the scene leaped into focus: a cone of black igneous rock rising above the forest canopy. The distortion of the lowest light paths was impossible to correct; the image broke down into blobs of gray and green before the sea blocked the view completely.

He said, "That's the place."

We're going to the island of butterflies.

Chapter 11

Prabir was hoping that they'd find a previously undetected passage through the reef, but as they inched their way around the island watching the sonar display, the chance of that diminished, then vanished altogether. The old southern approach was narrow, and twenty years before no one would have attempted to pass through it in such a large craft, but the autopilot confidently declared that there was sufficient clearance.

They dropped anchor just inside the reef. It was too late to go ashore, with less than an hour of light remaining. The beach appeared smaller than Prabir remembered it, though whether the jungle had encroached, a storm had gouged sand away, or he was just misjudging the tide it was impossible to say. There were still coconut palms standing at the edge of the sand, but he could see the strange thorned shrubs choking out everything else in the undergrowth. There was no sign at all of the path that had once led from the beach to the kampong.

After they'd eaten, Grant made her nightly call home. Prabir sat out on deck, stupefied by the heat. He couldn't call Felix; he didn't want to be forced to justify what he'd done to Madhusree, let alone risk some kind of mediated confrontation if the two of them had been in contact.

He lay down and tried to sleep.

Just after midnight, he heard Grant come out on deck. She stood beside him. "Prabir? Are you still awake?"

As he rolled over, he saw her gazing down at him with the kind of unguarded fascination that he'd learned never to betray on his own face by the time he was about fifteen. But then her eyes shifted to a neutral point behind his shoulder, and he doubted the significance of whatever he'd seen.

"I just thought you ought to know that your extortion has borne its first fruit." She handed him her notepad. He glanced at the banner at the top of the page, then sat up cross-legged on his sleeping bag and read through the whole thing.

A molecular modeling team in São Paulo had examined the sequence data from the two expeditions, and identified a novel gene common to all the altered organisms; they'd sent Grant a copy of their results, as well as submitting them to a refereed netzine. Preliminary models of the protein the gene encoded suggested that it would bind to DNA.

Prabir said, "You think this is it? Your mythical gene-repair-and-resurrection machine?"

"Maybe." Grant seemed pleased, but she was a long way from claiming victory. "Part of what they've found makes sense: this gene has a promoter that causes it to be switched on in meiosis—germ cell formation—which explains why there's no need for a mutagen to activate it in these organisms. But there's no evidence of a similar gene in any of the original genomes, let alone one that would only be switched on when it was needed to repair mutations."

Prabir thought it over. "Could we be seeing the gene that the original version resurrected in place of itself? Once it went hyper-active, it not only substituted old versions of other genes, it substituted a completely unrecognizable version of itself?"

Grant laughed, through gritted teeth. "That's possible, and it would make things very tricky. These modeling people might be able to determine the current protein's function, but I wouldn't count on them to be able to work backward and determine the structure of an unknown protein that changed its own sequence into the current one. What we really need is DNA from two consecutive generations of the same organism, for comparison." She hesitated. "And if possible, DNA from two early consecutive generations of the butterflies."

Prabir said, "You mean samples my parents took? They didn't have your magic gelling agent. And I think the refrigeration would have failed by now."

Grant looked uncomfortable, unsure whether to pursue the matter.

"It's OK," he said. "I don't mind talking about this." They'd come here for the butterflies; he couldn't afford to clam up every time the subject was raised.

She said, "They might have preserved whole specimens for storage under tropical conditions; there were treatments available twenty years ago that would have protected against bacteria and mold, without damaging the DNA. You said they bred the butterflies in captivity. One or two well-documented samples could tell us a lot."

"I appreciate that. But don't get your hopes up. With all the vegetation changed and the old paths gone, I'm not even sure that I could find my way back to the kampong. And if I can, who knows what state the buildings would be in?"

Grant nodded. "Yeah. It was just a thought. We'll go ashore tomorrow, and we'll find what we find." She stood up. "And we'd both better get some sleep now."

Prabir woke badly, to another Tanimbar dawn. When he opened his eyes there was a message in the sunlight: *His parents were*

*dead. Everyone alive would follow them. The world he'd once
seen as safe and solid—a vast, intricately beautiful maze that he
could explore from end to end, without risk, without punishment—had proved itself to be a sheer cliff face, to which he'd
cling for a moment before falling.*

He rose from the deck and stood by the guardrail, shielding
his eyes. He was tired of the pendulum swings, tired of finding
that all the carefully reasoned arguments and deliberate optimism
that shored him up well enough, on the good days, could still
count for nothing when he needed it the most.

But this could be the last cycle, the downswing deep enough
to carry him through to the other side. Wasn't this the day he'd
step ashore and demonstrate once and for all that Teranesia was
powerless to harm him, like an IRA debunker striding tri-
umphantly across a bed of hot coals? He might yet return to
Toronto at peace, as infuriatingly tranquil as Felix, free of his parents, free of Madhusree, every useless fear banished, every obligation to his past, real or imagined, finally discharged.

And he'd told Grant not to set her hopes too high.

They brought the boat closer to shore, then waded onto the
beach. Grant was carrying a rifle now, as well as the tranquilizer
gun. They went through the rituals of the insect repellent and the
mine detector tests. As Prabir sat pulling his boots on, looking
back at the reef, he pictured a water man rising from the waves,
angry and ravenous, teeth shining like glassy steel. Then he punctured the illusion, scattering the figure into random spray. That
was the trouble with the demons dreamed up by children and reli-
gions: you made the rules, and they obeyed them. It wasn't much
of a rehearsal for life. Once you started believing that any real
danger in the world worked that way, you were lost.

They penetrated the jungle slowly; the thorned shrubs were

even denser and more tangled than the species they'd seen before, with long, narrow involuted branches like coils of barbed wire. Prabir cut off a sample, tearing his thumb on a barely visible down of tiny hooks that coated the vines between the large thorns. He sucked the ragged wound. "Nice as it would be to solve the mystery, I'm beginning to hope we don't stumble across a herbivore that needs this much discouragement."

"It'd probably be no worse than a rhinoceros or a hippo," Grant suggested. "But apparently it has no descendants here, to give birth to something similar."

Prabir fished in his backpack for a Band-Aid. "OK, I can accept that: seeds get blown about, continents drift, animal lineages die out locally. But why is it always the most extreme trait that gets resurrected? Why couldn't these shrubs just grow something *mildly* inappropriate, like flowers optimized for a long-vanished pollinating insect?"

Grant mused, "There's no evidence of the São Paulo protein ever having been used for mutation repair. So maybe that was never the case; maybe I've been clinging to that idea too stubbornly. It could be that the protein's role has *always* been to reactivate old traits, to bring old inventions back into the gene pool from a dormant state."

Prabir considered this. "A bit like a natural version of those conservation programs where they cross endangered animals with frozen sperm from twenty years ago, to reinvigorate the species when the population becomes too inbred?"

"Yeah. And sometimes they use a closely related species, not the thing itself. If this protein manages a kind of 'frozen gene bank,' it would be even less purist about it: it wouldn't have any qualms about creating a hybrid with a distant ancestor."

To Prabir this sounded both simpler and far more radical

than the mutation repair hypothesis: shifting the mechanism from an esoteric emergency response to a major factor in genetic change. Most of the same problems remained, though.

He said, "That still doesn't explain how particular traits get frozen and thawed. Are you saying that this plant's ancestors *knew* that they'd evolved a spectacularly effective set of defenses, and deliberately tucked away a copy of the genes for the next eon when they'd come in handy?"

Grant smiled, refusing to be provoked. "More likely it's just a matter of the genes that persist the longest having the greatest chance of being duplicated at some point, which then increases their chance of surviving in an inactive form."

"And the mimicry? The symbiosis? How does something like that get synchronized?"

"That, I don't know."

They pressed on. Prabir kept waiting for a flash of recognition, for the sight of an old gnarled tree or an outcrop of rock to awaken memories more strongly than the beach. He'd explored this side of the island completely; every step he was taking here was one he must have taken before. But too much had changed. Though the trees themselves appeared unaltered, there were no ferns, there were no small flowers on the ground, just the carnivorous orchids they'd seen on the other islands, and the ubiquitous barbed-wire shrubs. Even the scent of the forest was alien to him. It was like returning to a city to find it repaved and repainted, emptied of its old inhabitants and repopulated by strangers with new customs and new cooking smells. Ambon with its nouveau-colonial refurbishment had seemed more familiar than this.

The black cockatoos were here, too. Prabir stood and watched one for half an hour, waiting for Grant to finish dissecting an orchid.

The bird was sitting in a kanari tree. Using its teeth, it

chewed straight through a slender branch that sprouted twigs bearing half a dozen white blossoms swollen with fruit. The cluster of twigs and fruit fell at the bird's feet, landing on the large, solid branch where it was perched. It proceeded to attack one of the fruits, chewing through the leathery hull, which had not quite ripened to the point where it would split open and spill the seeds, the almonds, onto the ground.

Grant came over to see what he was looking at. Prabir described what he'd observed so far. The bird had extracted one of the almonds from the fruit, and was performing an even more elaborate routine to penetrate the hard shell.

She said, "This part's old hat: it's a famous case of specialization for a food source." The bird had broken away part of the shell, and was now holding the nut with one foot while it used the sharp, hooked part of its upper beak to tear out fragments of the kernel; a tongue like a long-handled pink-and-black rubber stamp darted out to pick up the pieces and take them into the bird's mouth. "Going for the unripe fruit is new, though."

"So it doesn't have to wait for the nuts to fall. Which means the teeth are there to help it stay off the ground?"

"I suppose so," Grant conceded. "But there might have been any number of reasons in the past why that was a good idea. It doesn't require coevolution with the ants."

Prabir turned to her. "If you'd come to this island knowing nothing about its history, nothing about the ordinary fauna of the region—if you'd dropped in out of the sky in a state of complete ignorance about this entire hemisphere—what would you think was going on here?"

"That's a stupid question."

"Humor me."

"Why? What point is there in ignoring the facts?"

Prabir shook his head earnestly. "I'm not asking you to do

that. I just want you to look at this afresh. If you'd just arrived from the insular British Isles with an immaculate, theoretical training in evolutionary biology, but no contact for a thousand years with anyone east of Calais, what would you conclude about the plants and animals here?"

Grant folded her arms.

Prabir said, "I'm withdrawing my labor until you answer me. Forgetting all the history you know, what does this really look like to you?"

She replied irritably, "It looks to me as if the affected species originally shared territory with all the others, then became isolated on some remote island and coevolved separately for a few million years . . . and now they're being progressively reintroduced. OK? That's what it *looks like*. But on what island is this meant to have happened?" She spread her arms. "It didn't happen here: you can vouch for that yourself. There's no island in the whole archipelago sufficiently isolated, and sufficiently unexplored."

"Probably not."

"Certainly not."

Prabir laughed. "OK. There's no such island! All I'm saying is, when the account you've just given sounds *so much* simpler than a hundred separate genes in a hundred separate species marching back from the past in perfect lockstep . . . I have a lot of trouble seeing how it can't be telling us *something* about the truth."

Grant's expression softened, her curiosity getting the better of her defensiveness. "Such as what?"

"That, I don't know."

Prabir had rewritten the image-processing software to run directly on Grant's camera. In the afternoon, she found the camouflaged fruit pigeons all around them.

Fluttering across the viewfinder between the pigeons were

the butterflies. The wing patterns had changed dramatically—the dappled imitation of foliage and shadows they'd acquired was far less striking, far less symmetric, and far more variable from insect to insect than the old concentric bands of green and black—but when Grant finally captured one and Prabir saw the body, he knew they were the descendants of the insect he'd first seen pinned to a board in his father's office at the university.

The tranquilizer darts were useless for insects, but Grant had a spray based on wasp venom that could temporarily paralyze the butterflies without killing them. Using a net to keep their victims from falling to the ants, they managed to collect half a dozen live specimens of both the pigeons and the butterflies.

Back on the boat, Grant killed and dissected one of the male pigeons, removing the testes and then working under a microscope to extract stem cells and various stages of maturing spermatocytes. She was hoping to catch the São Paulo protein in the act, though given the uniformity of the pigeons it seemed unlikely that it was still producing radical changes in their genome.

Prabir left her to it and stood out on the deck, staring back into the harmless shadows of the jungle, numb with relief as he realized how painlessly the day had passed. Between the distracting riddle of the altered species and the sheer physical effort of gathering samples, he'd had little time or reason to dwell on the significance of the place. And that was how it should be. He'd already mourned his parents, in the camp, in Toronto, and he'd recounted their triumphs a thousand times for Madhusrce. There was nothing to be done here, nothing to be remembered, nothing to be learned but the secret of the butterflies. He refused to imagine them trapped on the island. In the only sense that they survived at all, they'd left in the very same boat as he had.

And though Teranesia had proved to be no more dangerous than the other islands, he was still glad that he'd kept Madhusree away. She might resent his intervention for years to come. She might accuse him of standing between her and the memory of her parents. But the alien jungle would have meant even less to her than it did to him, and he'd spared her the pointless anguish of digging through the ruins of the kampong. *His mother had told him, "Take her away! She mustn't see!"* He'd completed what he'd begun when they'd set out on the boat. It had been a long trip, but now it was over.

Grant emerged from the cabin frowning, carrying her notepad.

"More news from São Paulo," she said. "They've refined their model."

"And?"

She propped the notepad on the guardrail in front of Prabir; it was displaying a graphic of a couple of large molecules bound to strands of DNA. "I don't know what to make of this. I was hoping they'd find evidence that some part of the protein resembled a transcription factor, and recognized disabled promoters—"

Prabir stopped her. "I used to know all these terms when I was a kid, but I'm pretty hazy now. Can you—?"

Grant nodded apologetically. "Promoters are sequences of DNA that sit next to the coding region of a gene, which is the part that actually describes the protein. Transcription factors bind to promoters to initiate the copying of the gene into RNA, which is then used to make the protein: to 'express the gene.'

"If a gene is accidentally duplicated, mutations that build up in the promoter of one copy might eventually stop that copy from being expressed. To identify a gene that's become inactive like that, you'd need something that was capable of binding to a damaged promoter—something roughly the same shape as a transcription factor, but a little less fussy. And then to reactivate the gene, there'd be a number of possible strategies, either working base by base to repair point mutations in the promoter, or snipping the whole thing out and splicing in an intact version."

Prabir said, "OK, that all makes sense. Now what have the modelers found?"

Grant hit a button on the notepad and animated the graphic. "*This* bloody thing just crawls along causing havoc during DNA replication. What normally happens is: the double helix unwinds, the two strands separate, and DNA polymerase comes along and stitches together a new complementary strand for each of them, from free-floating bases. What the São Paulo protein does is slide along each single strand, cutting it up into individual bases, while splicing together a whole new strand of DNA to take its place. Then DNA polymerase comes along and duplicates *that*."

Prabir took the notepad from her and slowed down the animation so he could follow the steps. "But what's the relationship between the old sequence and the new sequence?"

"Basically, the new one is the old one, plus noise. SPP changes shape as it binds to each base of the original strand—it assumes a different conformation depending on whether it's cutting out adenine, guanine, cytosine, or thymine—and that in turn determines the base it adds to the new strand. But the correlation isn't perfect; there are some random errors introduced."

Prabir laughed, disbelieving. "So it's just an elaborate, self-inflicted mutagen? These creatures might as well be bathing their gonads in radiation or pesticide?"

Grant replied dejectedly, "That's what they're claiming."

He replayed the animation. "No. This is crazy. If you wanted to add a few extra random errors to your offspring's DNA, would you take the easy way out and just alter your DNA polymerase slightly, so it made occasional mistakes—or would you invent a whole new system like this for making deliberately flawed single-strand copies?"

"Well, exactly," Grant said. "And even if you had a good reason to take that approach, the whole protein's vastly overengineered. There are commercial enzymes that do something similar, and they're about one-hundredth the molecular weight."

"Maybe there's a bug in their software. Or maybe there's some logic to the changes, some pattern that they simply haven't noticed."

Grant shrugged morosely. "They've synthesized some of the protein for real now; they're doing test-tube experiments as we speak, to try to confirm all this."

She seemed to be taking it all too much to heart. Prabir said, "You *know* that the things we've seen here can't be explained by random mutations. Maybe there's still some way this can be compatible with your theory. But whatever's going on, at least we're closing in on it."

"That's true." She smiled. "They have synthesized protein in São Paulo, and I have cultured fruit pigeon spermatocytes. By morning they'll know what happens in a test tube, and we'll know what happens in a living cell."

When Prabir woke, this prediction had been fulfilled. Grant had been up since three o'clock trying to make sense of the results.

The experiments in São Paulo had confirmed the computer model: fed a few hundred different test strands of DNA, the protein had chopped them up and synthesized new strands of exactly the same length, copying the original sequence but introducing random errors. Another group, in Lausanne, had repeated the work and found the same thing.

Grant had detected RNA transcripts for the São Paulo protein in the pigeon spermatocytes, which implied that the protein itself was being made in the cells; she had no direct test for it. But when she compared sequence data for cells before and after meiosis, the error rate was about a thousand times less than for the two experiments in vitro.

She said, "There has to be a second protein, some kind of helper molecule that modifies the whole process."

"So they need to look harder at the sequence data?" Prabir suggested. "The gene for it must be in there somewhere."

"They're looking. SPP alone is a bit like a pantograph with a whole lot of superfluous hinges. So maybe this is something that binds to it and stabilizes it—not enough to produce perfect copies, but enough to allow its internal state to reflect the last few dozen bases to which it was bound."

Prabir opened his mouth to say, *Turing machine*, but he stopped himself. Most processes in molecular biology had analogies in computing, but it was rarely helpful to push them too far. "So it could recognize a sequence of something like a promoter, even though it only binds to one base at a time?"

"Maybe," Grant agreed cautiously. "They've also got hold of samples from the Ambon fruit pigeon, and they're going to see what pure, synthetic SPP does to an entire chromosome, in the presence of nothing but a supply of individual bases."

As they waded ashore, Prabir looked down into the warm, clear water where he'd swum with Madhusree, then across the dazzling white beach where they'd played. He wasn't just cheating her out of a role in the study of the butterflies, he was depriving her of the chance to demystify the island, to purge it of its horrors the way he was doing for himself.

But he could never have brought her back here. He could never have undone the one good thing.

Grant wanted to collect specimens of the butterfly's other stages, so they spent the morning doing nothing but searching appropriately succulent leaves for the spiked larvae, and the branches of the same trees for pupae. The original versions would not have been hard to spot: both had been covered in bright orange patches, warning colors to signal their toxicity. Grant found signs of leaf damage that looked promising, but there were no culprits nearby. If the larvae had switched strategy and opted for camouflage that was as efficient as the adults', their movements would be far too subtle for the image-processing software to detect.

They stopped and ate lunch in the middle of the forest, in a rare spot where the ground was rocky enough to keep the shrubs at bay. Prabir still didn't feel safe sitting down until he'd sprayed a cordon of insect repellent on the ground; the ants were never content to stay inside the orchids, waiting for easy prey. He wasn't sure why they didn't swarm up the trees and take nestlings; maybe they were lacking some crucial adaptation for the task, or maybe it just wasn't worth the energy.

Grant said, "So your whole family was here for three years, from 2010? Was your sister born on the island?"

He laughed. "We weren't quite that isolated. We went to Ambon on the ferry four times a year. And we flew down to Darwin for the birth."

"Still, it must have been a rough place to raise a young child." Grant added hastily, "I'm not criticizing your parents. I'm just impressed that they could cope."

Prabir shrugged. "I suppose I took that for granted. I mean, the people in small villages on the other islands had better access to transport, clinics they could get to, and so on. But we had a satellite link, which made it easy to forget the distance. I even had lessons from a school in Calcutta; they'd set up a net service for kids in remote villages, but I could join in just as easily."

"So at least you had some friends your own age through the net."

"Yeah." Prabir shifted his position on the rock, suddenly uncomfortable. "What about you? What were your school days like?"

"Mine? Very ordinary." Grant fell silent for a while, then she took out her camera and began scanning the branches around them.

She said, "The butterflies spend a lot of their time quite high in the canopy. Maybe they lay their eggs there." She lowered the camera and asked casually, "What are you like at climbing trees?"

"Seriously out of practice."

"It's like riding a bicycle. You never forget."

Prabir gave her a stony look. "You're the field biologist, remember? I'm the desk zombie. And I don't care how ancient you are: you're twice as fit as I am."

"You put that so gallantly."

Prabir said flatly, "I'm not doing it! The deal we made in Ambon—"

Grant nodded effusively. "OK, OK! I only asked because I'm not used to judging the strength of the branches of these species. I thought you might be more confident, since you must have climbed them as a kid. I'll go back to the boat and get a rope—"

"A *rope*? You're not serious?"

"I had a bad experience in Ecuador," she admitted. "I broke a lot of bones. So I'm ultracareful now."

Prabir's resentment faded. There was a principle at stake, but he didn't want to be petty and sadistic. "I'll do it, but you have to pay me. Ten dollars a tree."

Grant considered this. "Make it twenty. I'll feel better."

"With a conscience like that, who needs labor laws?"

Grant selected a nutmeg tree. Prabir took off his boots and rolled up his trouser legs. He hesitated, unsure how to begin. The lowest branch of this tree was just above his head; he must have been able to scale a sheer trunk once, gripping the bark with his arms and legs—he'd even climbed coconut palms—but he felt certain he'd make of fool of himself if he tried that now.

He grabbed the branch and raised himself up, then hooked his feet around it and hung slothlike for a while before figuring out how to right himself. It was a clumsy start, but once he was standing squarely on the branch, with a firm grip on the next one up, he was elated. The scent of the bark, the feel of it against his soles, was utterly familiar; even the view straight across into the other trees was far closer to anything he remembered than the view from the ground. He glanced down at Grant, not wanting to lose perspective, not wanting to be drawn back too strongly.

She shaded her eyes and looked up at him. "Be careful!"

He took a few steps along the branch, feeling it flex, trying to recalibrate his old instincts for his adult weight. He called down, "I promise you, I have no intention of breaking my neck for a caterpillar."

He scoured the clusters of leaves hanging around him for signs of larval feeding, but there was nothing. He climbed higher. Fruit pigeons fled as he approached, a rush of air and a blur of motion. There were foul-smelling beetles on the trunk, but they scurried away from the repellent. There'd been pythons in the trees once, but even the lowest branches wouldn't have taken the weight of anything remotely like the one he'd met in the mangrove swamp; as long as he didn't panic and fall to his death, he probably had nothing to fear from its tree-dwelling cousins. Assuming they hadn't acquired venom.

Twenty meters up, Prabir found something hanging from a slender side branch. At first glance he'd mistaken it for a nutmeg fruit, but then a hint of unexpected structure had made him look again. When he was close enough to examine it properly, he found a butterfly, wings folded, suspended from the branch. It had to be a pupa, but it looked more like a tiny sleeping bat than an insect about to emerge from metamorphosis—and it still looked more like a nutmeg fruit than anything else. He touched it warily; it even felt like a nutmeg fruit.

He took out his notepad and recorded some vision, to document the attachment method before he broke the pupa free. The silk girdle around the bulk of the insect was virtually undetectable, the color matched so well; the short length anchoring it to the branch looked exactly like a stalk. He sent the images down to Grant, and spoke to her through the notepad; it was easier than shouting.

"What do you make of that? Pretty good camouflage, at the risk of being eaten by mistake."

"Maybe they smell bad to the fruit pigeons," Grant suggested.

"Why not just—oh, forget it." *Whatever anything did, why not do it differently?* It was frozen history, not rational design. He broke the pupa free, and dropped it in his backpack. "I'll go up one more level, just to see if there are any larvae."

"Are you sure it'll take your weight?"

The next branch above him was barely chest high now. He wrapped his arms around it and lifted his feet off the one below. "Yes, I'm sure."

He clambered up. He had a firm hold and a secure footing, but he could feel the top of the tree swaying, and the branches around him had thinned enough to make him feel exposed. Looking sideways through the forest at this level, the distant branches appeared uncannily like the struts for some elaborate geodesic folly. Maybe the Stetsoned entrepeneurs who'd followed the expedition down from Ambon could anchor a Perspex roof to all this scaffolding, and turn the whole island into an exhibition center.

He looked down and saw the ruins of the kampong.

A wave of vertigo swept over him, but he kept his grip on the branch beside him. The center of the kampong had been reclaimed by the forest, but the trees couldn't quite obscure the roofs of the huts: the matte gray photovoltaic surface was still visible through a thin layer of creepers. The buildings had all become badly skewed, but none of them appeared to have collapsed completely. The six huts had been arranged in a regular hexagon, and in their current state he couldn't tell them apart; with the path from the beach erased there were no cues to enable him to orient the view.

He looked away, remembering his purpose. There wasn't much foliage around him, but he examined it dutifully. Then he spoke into his notepad.

"There's nothing else here. I'm coming down."

Three more trees yielded five more pupae, but still no sign of the larval stage. It was mid-afternoon; Grant decided there was no point looking further. Prabir was dripping with sweat, and itching from all the contact with bark and sap. When they reached the beach, he handed his samples to Grant and swam out to the reef and back. After the heat of the forest, the water was glorious beyond belief.

He collected his clothes from the beach and waded back to the boat. As he climbed up onto the deck, Grant met him with the latest news from Brazil. "They've copied whole, purified pigeon chromosomes, using just SPP," she said. "And the error rate was the same as mine, for the cultured cells."

It took Prabir a moment to interpret this result. "So there is no second protein after all?"

"Apparently not," Grant concurred. "SPP alone in a test tube does just as good a job as SPP in an intact cell, *if and only if* the sequence being copied is the same. Which shows that these changes aren't errors at all. Or at least, they're not just random copying mistakes. They must depend in some way on the sequence itself."

Prabir pondered this. "The pigeon genome has probably been copied in the presence of SPP dozens of times. So whatever transformation SPP causes must be convergent: the genome must change less and less with each iteration, until by now it's virtually stable under the process."

Grant nodded. "Whereas there's no reason at all why the test sequences they first tried copying would have been stable. Randomly chosen input sequences would have undergone apparently random changes."

Prabir had a minor epiphany. "And all the different fruit pigeons on Banda that ended up looking identical . . . the process must also be convergent for sufficiently similar genomes. Not only is there a stable endpoint for a given starting point, but similar starting points—closely related species—get dragged toward the same endpoint." He beamed with delight. "It all makes sense!"

Grant was pleased, but slightly less rapturous. "Except we still don't know what SPP actually does, or how it's doing it."

"But the Brazilians have all the information they need to crack this now, don't they? They just have to look more closely at their model."

"Maybe. For a molecule as large as a protein you can never solve the equations for its shape and binding properties exactly, and it can be hard to choose a set of approximations that only cause trivial discrepancies. They've already tried simulating the pigeon chromosome being copied by SPP, and the simulation produced exactly the same error rate as for any other sequence."

Prabir winced. "So their model has just proved that it's missing the most important subtlety of the real protein."

Grant didn't see it quite so bleakly. "Missing it now, but they might yet be able to capture it with a little fine tuning. At least they know what they're aiming for, what they need to get right."

Prabir said, "OK. So what do we do next?" Grant had been posting all their results on the net, stating precisely where they'd been collecting their samples; the expedition biologists would already know that there was no need for anyone else to come here. So long as Grant didn't cut corners.

She said, "I'll have a proper look at these pupae, see what that tells us. I don't know whether it's worth going back to hunt for the larvae; I mean, the life cycle is of interest in itself, but larvae don't make germ cells."

Prabir filled a bucket with seawater and set about washing his sap-stained clothes, while Grant went for a swim. The travel shop in Toronto had sold him a detergent with enzymes that worked in the presence of salt; as long as you applied it swiftly, you could remove almost anything with the stuff.

When he walked back into the cabin to get fresh water for rinsing, he glanced at the wire cage holding the adult butterflies they'd captured.

There was a pupa, similar to the ones he'd collected in the forest, hanging from the top of the cage. Except it couldn't be a pupa. The adults had only been there for a day; at most they might have laid eggs. Grant had been in the cabin twenty minutes before. This had happened since then.

Prabir counted the adults. One of them was missing.

He ran out on deck. "Martha! You have to see this!"

She was halfway to the reef. "See what?"

"The butterflies."

"What about them?"

"You won't believe me if I tell you. You have to see it for yourself."

Grant turned back toward the boat. She followed him into the cabin dripping. Prabir watched her expression go through several changes.

He said, "There's something I've been wanting to try, if you'll let me."

"I'm listening."

He picked up one of the dormant adults he'd taken from the forest. "This insect hangs there, looking like a nutmeg fruit, unable to fly away. So presumably it has some defense: it must smell bad, or taste bad, to the birds that would otherwise want to eat it on sight."

"Presumably."

Prabir approached the cage where they'd placed the fruit pigeons, and gave Grant a questioning look.

She said, "Go ahead, please. I want to see this, too."

He opened the door just wide enough to toss the dormant adult onto the floor of the cage. All of the fruit pigeons rushed forward; one of them managed to shoulder the rest aside and grab the insect. The bird stretched its jaws to their full extent and swallowed the sleeping butterfly whole.

Grant sat down heavily on one of the stools. After a long silence, she declared, "Maybe there's a parasitic larval stage. Maybe the adults don't lay their fertilized eggs; maybe they're incubated inside the pigeons, after the adults act as a lure."

"And that's why we've seen no larvae?"

"Maybe." Grant stretched her arms and leaned back on the stool. "I suppose it could burrow out through the skin, but I'm beginning to have visions of sifting through a large pile of pigeon shit."

Prabir walked over to the butterfly cage. They'd placed some foliage in the bottom, but there'd been no elevated twigs or branches from which the would-be martyr could hang itself. He squatted down to try to get a better view of it, and saw a long string of dark gray beads sticking to the underside of one of the leaves.

He said, "Was this foliage clean when you put it in the cage?"

"I believe so. Why?"

"I think I've just found some butterfly eggs."

Prabir lay awake, listening to the waves breaking on the reef. The eggs would allow them to observe every stage of the butterfly, but that still wouldn't be enough. The butterfly's genome would be stable now; only samples from the kampong could show the way the São Paulo protein had changed it, from generation to generation, twenty years before. They needed to extract every clue the island held; if they didn't finish the job properly, the expedition would follow them here.

He went into the cabin and woke Grant, calling out to her from the doorway. Her bunk was hidden in shadows, but he heard her sit up. "What is it?"

He explained what he'd seen from the treetops. "I know where it is now. I can get to it from the beach."

She hesitated. "Are you sure you want to do this? You could draw me a map, I could go by myself."

Prabir was tempted. The place meant nothing to her: she could walk in and take whatever she needed, ransacking the site unflinchingly, immune to its history.

But this was his job. He couldn't claim to be sparing Madhusree the pain of returning, only to hand the task over to a stranger.

"I'd rather go alone."

Grant said decisively, "We'll go together, first thing tomorrow. I promised you after the mangrove swamp: we won't get separated again."

Chapter 12

Prabir took comfort in the usual routine: wading to the beach, insect repellent, mine detector checks. Looking back at the reef as he pulled on his boots. They'd gather some samples and return to the boat. It would be a day like any other.

He'd estimated GPS coordinates for the kampong, from his notepad's log of its position the previous day and his recollection of the treetop view. They picked their way laboriously through the shrubs; this was the first time they'd had no choice about their destination, no option of taking an easier route. Grant had once tried clearing a path in the undergrowth using a parang she'd bought in Ambon, but it had been a waste of effort; the machete was perfect for chopping through occasional vines, but the knee-high thicket was too tangled, there were too many strands to sever.

Grant was unusually quiet; she might have done this easily enough alone, but his presence must have made her feel more like a trespasser. Prabir said, "You wouldn't believe it only took me half an hour a day to maintain this path."

"That was one of your jobs?"

"Yeah."

She smiled. "I thought I was hard done by having to clean

the bath. And at least I had somewhere to spend my pocket money. I suppose you got paid in net privileges?"

"I don't remember."

Prabir's eyes kept filling with sweat. As he wiped them clear, he could almost see the approach as it had once been. *He'd heard the thud of the mine and raced toward the kampung with Madhusree in his arms. Sailing past the trees ever faster, as if he was falling.*

Grant spotted one of the huts before he did: it was leaning precariously, covered in fungus and lianas. Unlike the roofing panels he'd seen from above, the walls were stained and encrusted to the point where they might as well have been deliberately camouflaged. Prabir was suddenly much less sure that they'd followed the old path; he didn't expect the hut to be recognizable, but its position was not where he'd imagined it. Maybe they'd taken a different route entirely, one that had always been uncleared jungle.

Even when they were standing at the edge of the kampong, it took him a while to find all six huts amid the trees. He said numbly, "I don't know where we are. I don't know where to start."

Grant put a hand on his shoulder. "There's no rush. I can look inside one of these buildings and describe it for you, if you like."

"No. It's all right." He turned and walked toward the hut on his right. The doorway facing the center of the kampong was hidden beneath a dense mat of creepers, but the walls had split apart at one corner, leaving a gap that made a much easier entrance.

Grant came after him. "You need a torch, and we need to do this slowly. We don't know what's in there."

Prabir accepted the flashlight from her. She unslung her rifle and followed behind him as he ducked down to enter the hut. Enough soil had blown in, and enough sunlight came through the gap in the walls and the vine-draped windows to cover the floor in pale weeds. There was a hook on one wall, and the cracked, shriveled remnants of a rectangle of canvas curled up beneath it.

He said, "This was mine." He gestured at the hammock. "That was where I slept."

"Right."

Termites must have devoured the packing crate where he'd kept his clothes, once the preservative had leached out of the wood. The hut looked barer than a prison cell now, but it had never been full of gadgets and ornamentation; all the possessions he'd valued most had been stored in his notepad.

He'd looked out at night from this hut, his stomach cramped with anxiety. And then he'd thought of an act that would justify everything he was feeling: a crime to match his sense of guilt, an alibi to explain it.

Guilt about what, though? Had he stolen something, broken something? What could be worse than sabotaging his parents' work?

"The butterfly hut." He backed out, then tried to orient himself. "It was straight across the kampong."

He threaded his way between the trees, with Grant walking beside him in silence. It was the most direct route, but he lost sight of the surrounding huts, lost count of their position in the circle.

The door had fallen off the hut he approached, leaving an entrance curtained with creepers. Grant handed him the parang and he slashed them away. Then he pointed the flashlight into the darkness.

Madhusree's plastic cot was covered in fungus, warped and discolored but still intact. Behind it, his parents' folding bunk was strewn with debris, the foam mattress rotted, the metal frame a shell of corrosion.

He'd been afraid for them. Afraid the war would reach them, in spite of the island's obscurity, in spite of his father's reassurances.

But why would he feel guilty? Why would he imagine that he'd be to blame if the war came to the island? Even if he'd fought with his parents and wanted them punished—even if he'd shouted from the slopes of the volcano that he'd wanted them dead—he'd never been superstitious enough to believe that his wishes would be granted.

Prabir said, "Wrong hut. It's the next one."

One wall of the butterfly hut had collapsed outward, leaving the two half-supported roofing panels to swing down almost to the ground. The result was a rickety triangular prism, with a narrow space between one standing wall and the tilted roof through which Prabir could just squeeze. Grant followed him.

The wall that had fallen had borne the hut's windows and door, and the soft forest light hit the gaps in the structure at the wrong angle to penetrate the darkness ahead. Prabir played the flashlight beam along the floor, looking for signs of the lab bench, but the wood had all gone to termites and fungus. The hut was knee deep in twigs and rotting leaves, debris that had blown in and never found its way out again.

In the far corner, two yellow eyes caught the beam. There was a python, maybe half the size of the one in the mangroves, coiled on top of a pile of litter. Prabir felt his legs turn to water at the sight of it, but he didn't want it killed unnecessarily.

"Maybe we can work around it," he suggested. "Or drive it out with sticks."

Grant shook her head. "Normally I'd agree, but right now we can do without the aggravation." She raised her rifle. "Stand aside and cover your ears." She dropped a pinprick of laser light between the snake's eyes, then blew its head off. Clumps of white fungus rained from the ceiling. The snake's decapitated body twitched and rose into a striking position, uncoiling enough to reveal a clutch of fist-sized blue-white eggs.

Grant held the flashlight while Prabir sifted through the mess on the floor. It was slow work, and the humid air above the decaying leaves was suffocating. When he found the metal stage of his father's microscope he gave up all pretense of being in control and let tears of grief and shame run down his face.

He knew what he'd done. He knew why he'd poisoned the chrysalis, he knew what he'd needed to hide.

He'd killed them. He'd brought the plane to the island, he'd brought the mines.

It was too much to face. He couldn't live, staring into that light—but he'd lost all power to avert his gaze, and every lie he'd held up as a shield was transparent now. He had to let it melt him, he had to let it burn him away.

He was determined to find the specimens first; they were the last things left that he could hope to salvage. Grant stopped asking him if he wanted to rest or swap positions. Beetles and pale spiders fled as he plunged his hands into the leaves, again and again.

He pulled out a slab of light, cool plastic, thirty centimeters wide, covered in filth. He wiped it on his jeans. It was an adult butterfly, embedded in something like lucite. An adult from twenty years ago, with the old concentric green-and-black stripes.

Grant said something encouraging. Prabir nodded dully. There was a bar code engraved in the plastic; any pigmentation it had once held was gone, but the ridges still felt sharp, the code could still be read. The numbers wouldn't mean a lot without matching computer records, but they'd probably be sequential. He delved around in the same spot, and his fingers hit another slab.

They left the hut with twelve preserved specimens: eight adults and four larvae. Prabir looked around, getting his bearings.

He turned to Grant. "You might as well go back to the boat now. I'll follow you in a little while." He handed her his backpack, in which they'd placed all the specimens. She accepted it, but remained beside him, waiting for an explanation.

He said, "I want to visit my parents' grave."

Grant nodded understandingly. "Can't I come with you? I don't want to intrude, but we should be careful."

Prabir pulled his shirt over his head, mopped his face with it, then held it bunched at his side to conceal his hand as he switched off the mine detector. He tried to compose his face into an appropriate mask.

He said, "Look, how many snakes that size can there be in this area? I'll be fine. You might as well start working on the samples. I just want to be alone here for a few minutes."

She hesitated.

"Is that too much to ask?" he demanded. "I've given you everything you wanted. Can't you show some respect for my feelings?"

Grant bowed her head, chastened. "All right. I'm sorry. I'll see you back there." She turned and headed across the kampong.

Prabir made his way around to what he thought was the storage hut. But he didn't trust his memory, he had to be sure. The door had fallen away; he squeezed through the vines. When his eyes had adjusted to the gloom, he saw the two life jackets hanging on the wall.

He walked out of the hut and headed for the garden.

Suddenly the device on his belt started chanting, "Mine at seventeen meters! Mine at seventeen meters!" He stared down at the machine: a red arrow was flashing on its upper surface, pointing to the hazard. He flicked the ON switch back and forth; it had no effect whatsoever. You couldn't turn the fucking thing off. All he'd done was stop it wasting power by showing its usual reassuring green light.

He heard Grant call his name from a distance.

Prabir backed away until the detector fell silent, then he shouted in a tone of light-hearted exasperation, "It's all right! I knew there'd be mines here! The detector's working, and I'll stay well clear of them! I'll be fine!"

There was a long pause, then she shouted back reluctantly, "OK. I'll see you on the boat."

He waited a couple of minutes to be sure that Grant was gone, then he unclipped the detector and tossed it away toward the center of the kampong. He'd noted the direction the arrow had pointed. He was very tired, but there was nothing left to do now. He turned and started walking.

Something sharp pierced his right shoulder. He felt the skin turn cold, then numb. He reached back and pulled it out. It was a tranquilizer dart.

He didn't know whether to laugh or to weep with frustration. He looked around for Grant, but he couldn't see her. He called out, "I weigh seventy kilograms. Do the arithmetic. You don't have enough."

She shouted back, "I can blow a hole in your knee if I have to."

"And what would that achieve? I'd probably bleed to death."

Grant showed herself. She was at least twenty meters away. Even if she was capable of tackling him to the ground, she wouldn't stop him with anything but a bullet before he could reach the mine.

She said, "Maybe I'll risk that."

He pleaded irritably, "Go back to the boat!"

"Why are you doing this?"

Prabir rubbed his eyes. Wasn't it obvious? Wasn't the evidence all around them?

He said, "I killed them. I killed my parents."

"I don't believe you. How?"

He stared at her despairingly; he was ready to confess everything, but it would be a slow torture to explain. "I sent a message to someone. A woman in New York, a historian I met on the net. But I was pretending to be my father, and what I said made him sound like an ABRMS supporter. The Indonesians must have read it. That's why they flew over and dropped the mines."

Grant absorbed this. "Why did you pretend to be your father?"

"He wouldn't let me tell anyone my real age. He was paranoid about it—maybe something happened to him as a child. But I didn't know how to pretend to be anyone else, and I didn't know how to say nothing at all."

"OK. But you don't know that the message was intercepted, do you? They might have dropped the mines anyway. It might have all been down to aerial surveillance, rebel activity in the area, deliberate misinformation from someone. *It might have had nothing to do with you!*"

Prabir shook his head. "Even if that's true: I heard the plane come over, and I didn't warn them. And it was my job to weed the garden, but I went swimming instead. If I didn't kill them three times, I killed them twice."

Grant said, "You were nine years old! You might have done something foolish, but it was the army who killed them. Do you really imagine that they'd blame you?"

"I was nine years old, but I wasn't stupid. After I'd sent the message, I knew what I'd done. But I was too afraid to tell them. I was so full of guilt I went and poisoned one of the butterflies, to try to fool myself. To make myself believe that was why I felt so bad."

Grant hesitated, searching for some escape route. But she had to see that there was none.

She said, "However much it hurts, if you've lived with this for eighteen years, you can keep on doing it."

He laughed. *"Why?* What's the point? Madhusree doesn't need me anymore. You know why I came after her? You know why I followed her here? *I was afraid she'd work it out.* I was afraid she'd find something here that would tell her what I'd done. I wasn't trying to protect her. I just wanted to keep her from discovering the truth."

"So how am I going to explain your death to her?"

"As an accident."

"I'm not going to perjure myself. There'll be an official inquiry, it'll all come out."

"Are you *blackmailing me* now?"

Grant shook her head calmly. "I'm telling you what will happen. That's not a threat, it's just the way it will be."

Prabir covered his face with his arms. The prospect seemed unbearable, but maybe it would help Madhusree put his death behind her if she understood that she owed him nothing. He hadn't acted out of love for her, or some sense of duty toward their parents. He hadn't even been protecting their shared genes. Everything he'd ever done for her had been to conceal his own crime.

He turned and started walking toward the minefield. Grant shouted something, but he ignored her. A rain of darts hit his upper back; he lost all feeling after the fourth or fifth, he could no longer count them. He began to feel slightly giddy, but it didn't slow him down. Grant still had no chance of catching up with him.

He felt a sting on the side of his right leg, like a hot sharp blade passing over the skin. He lost his footing, more from surprise than from the force of the bullet, and toppled sideways into the undergrowth. With his shoulders paralyzed he had no strength in his arms: he couldn't right himself, he couldn't even crawl.

A minute later, Grant knelt beside him and plucked out the darts, then helped him to his feet. He was bleeding almost as much from the barbed-wire shrubs as from the grazing wound she'd made in his leg.

She asked, "Are you coming back to the boat now?"

Prabir met her eyes. He wasn't angry with her, or grateful. But she'd robbed him of all momentum, and complicated things to the point where it would have been farcical to keep opposing her.

Farcical, and monumentally selfish.

He was silent for a while, trying to come to terms with this. Then he said, "There's something I want to do here, if you're willing. But we'll need some tools, and I'll have to wait until this shit wears off."

They returned to the kampong in the afternoon, with a chainsaw and a mallet. Grant cut branches into meter lengths and Prabir drove them into the ground, making a small fence all the way around the mined garden. He nailed warning signs to each side, in six languages, using his notepad to translate the message. There wasn't much chance of fishermen coming this far into the jungle, but when the next biologists arrived it would be one small extra safeguard.

Grant said, "Do you want to put up a plaque?"

Prabir shook his head. "No shrines. They'd have hated that."

Grant left him, trusting him now. Prabir stood by the fence and tried to picture them, arm-in-arm, middle-aged, with another half-century ahead of them. In love to the end, working to the end, living to see their great-great-grandchildren.

That was what he'd destroyed.

Grant had kept insisting: *They wouldn't have blamed you!* But what did that mean? The dead blamed no one. What if his mother had survived, crippled by grief, knowing he was responsible? She might have tried to shield him at first, when he was still a child. But now? And for the rest of his life?

And his father—

He had no right to test them like this, asking them to choose between rejection and forgiveness. And whatever excuses they might have made for him, however much compassion they might have shown, it made no difference in the end. He didn't want their imaginary blessing, he didn't want any kind of plausible solace. He only wanted the impossible: he wanted them back.

He sat on the ground and wept.

Prabir made his way back to the beach, before the light failed. He'd lost the will to die, to anesthetize himself out of existence.

But to live, he'd have to live with the pain of what he'd done, not the hope that it could be extinguished. That would never happen. He'd have to find another reason to go on.

Chapter 13

Grant spent the next morning extracting tissue from the pre-served butterflies, then sequencing their DNA. Even with the São Paulo protein scrambling parts of the genome, it was possible to construct a plausible family tree from genetic markers, using the serial numbers as a guide to chronology.

Prabir had guessed one thing correctly: the São Paulo gene had changed. Its own protein had gradually rewritten it, though the twenty-year-old protein seemed to have made much subtler changes from generation to generation than the modern version. This added a new twist to the convergence process: at least in the butterflies, the transformation itself had been subject to succes-sive refinements. Whatever SPP did to produce its strangely beneficent mutations, over time the mutations it had wrought in its own gene had enabled it to perform the whole process more efficiently.

Grant posted the historical data on the net, giving credit to Radha and Rajendra Suresh. Then she set to work on the dormant adults, taking samples for RNA transcript analysis. They weren't in any danger of running out of specimens: apart from the six Prabir had plucked from the trees, all their captive adults had now entered the same state.

Prabir sat and watched her work, helping where he could. Maybe it was just the realization of what she'd done for him in the kampong finally sinking in, but her face seemed kinder to him now, her whole demeanor warmer. It was as if he'd finally learned to read the dialect of her body language, in the same way as he'd adjusted to her unfamiliar accent.

In the evening, after they'd eaten, they sat on the deck, facing out to sea, listening to music and planning the voyage's end. Unless news from São Paulo or Lausanne reached them by morning to suggest otherwise, they'd conclude that they'd gathered all the data needed to fuel research into the mutants for the foreseeable future. They'd rejoin the expedition for a day or two, to compare notes face-to-face, then Grant would sail back to Sulawesi to return her hired boat. Prabir wasn't sure yet whether he'd hitch a ride with her to Ambon. It would depend on the reception he got from Madhusree.

"What are you going to say to her?" Grant asked.

Prabir shook his head. "I don't know. I can't tell her the things I told you. I'm not going to poison her life with that. But I don't want to lie to her anymore. I don't want to feed her some line about coming here to spare her from the trauma."

Grant shot him an exasperated look. "Doesn't it occur to you that that could still be true? You can have more than one reason for doing something."

"I know, but—"

She cut him off. "Don't let this blight everything. Don't let it rob you of the things you have a right to be proud of. Do you honestly believe that you've never once tried to protect her, just because she's your sister?"

Prabir replied fiercely, "If I haven't, then at least I'm not a slave to my genes."

Grant's eyes narrowed. "And that matters more to you?" For

a moment Prabir thought he'd lost her, that his words were unforgivable, but then she added dryly, "At least in a bad enough movie you could turn out to be adopted."

He said, "If that's your idea of a bad movie, you've had a very sheltered life."

He reached over and stroked her face with the back of his hand. She kept her eyes on his, but said nothing. He'd acted on a barely conscious sense of rightness, half expecting to have his instinct proved utterly mistaken, but she neither encouraged nor rebuffed him. He remembered her watching him, the night they'd arrived; at the time he'd doubted it meant anything at all, but now he felt as if scales had fallen from his eyes.

He bent down and kissed her; they were sitting propped up against the wall of the cabin, it was hard to face her squarely. For a moment she was perfectly still, but then she began to respond. He ran a hand along her arm. The scent of her skin was extraordinary; inhaling it sent warmth flooding through his body. The Canadian girls in high school had smelled as bland and sexless as infants.

He slipped his hand under the back of her shirt and stroked the base of her spine, pulling her toward him, aligning their bodies. He already had an erection; he could feel his pulse where it pressed against her leg. He moved his hand to her breast. He had to fight away any image of where they were heading; he was afraid that if he pictured it he'd come at once. But he didn't have to think, he didn't have to plan this: they'd be carried forward by the internal logic of the act.

Grant pulled away suddenly, disentangling herself. "This is a bad idea. You know that."

Prabir was confused. "I thought it was what you wanted!"

She opened her mouth as if to deny it, then stopped herself. She said, "It doesn't work like that. I've been faithful to Michael

247

for sixteen years. I'll sit up all night and talk if you want, but I'm not going to fuck you just to make you feel better."

Prabir stared down at the deck, his face burning with shame. *What had he just done?* Had it been some clumsy attempt at gratitude, which he'd imagined she'd accept without the slightest scruple?

She said gently, "Look, I'm not angry with you. I should have stopped you sooner. Can we just forget about it?"

"Yeah. Sure."

He looked up. Grant smiled ruefully and implored him, "Don't make a big deal out of this. We've been fine until now, and we can still be fine." She rose to her feet. "But I think we could both do with some rest." She reached down and squeezed his shoulder, then walked into the cabin.

After the lights had gone out, Prabir knelt at the edge of the deck and ejaculated into the water. He rested his head on the guardrail, suddenly cold in the breeze coming in off the sea. The images of her body faded instantly; it was obvious now that he'd never really wanted her. It had been nothing but a temporary confusion between the friendship she'd shown him in the kampong, and the fact that he hadn't touched Felix for what seemed like a lifetime. It had never occurred to him that he might have lost the knack for celibacy, that after nine years it could take any effort at all to get through a mere three or four weeks.

When he returned to his sleeping bag and closed his eyes, he saw Felix lying beside him, smiling and sated, dark stubble on the golden skin of his throat. *When had it become conceivable to betray him?* But instead of agonizing over one stupid, aberrant attempt at infidelity, better to think of the changes he could make back in Toronto to put an end to all the far greater risks he'd been courting ever since they'd met. Felix had been patient beyond belief, but that couldn't last forever. The simplest thing would be to let Madhusree have the apartment to herself; he'd keep paying the rent until she graduated. He'd move in with Felix, they'd have a life of their own, a mutual commitment without reservations.

It was not unimaginable anymore. Even if he'd had the power to imitate his father in every respect, it would not have brought Radha and Rajendra back to life. And he no longer cared that he couldn't read between the lines and extract some kind of unspoken blessing from his parents. There had to be an end to *what they would have wanted* and *what they would have done*.

He had to take what he believed was good, and run.

An hour after they'd left Teranesia behind, Grant emerged from the cabin looking bemused.

She said, "Strange news from São Paulo."

Prabir grimaced; it sounded like the title of one of Keith's Country-Dada albums. "Please tell me we're not turning back."

"We're not." Grant ran her hand through her hair distractedly. "I'd say the last thing they need is more data. We seem to have given them rather more than they can cope with."

"What do you mean?"

She handed him her notepad. "Joaquim Furtado, one of the physicists on the modeling team, has just posted a theory about the protein's function. The rest of the team have refused to endorse it. I'd be interested to hear what you think."

Prabir suspected that she was merely being polite, but he skimmed down the page. Furtado's analysis began with a statement no one could dispute: the discrepancies between the computer model and the test-tube experiments proved that there were crucial aspects of the molecule's behavior that the simulation was failing to capture. Various refinements to the model had been tried, but so far they'd all failed to improve the situation.

One of the many approximations made by the modelers

involved the quantum state of the protein, which was described mathematically in terms of eigenstates for the bonds between atoms: quantum states that possessed definite values for such things as the position of the bond and its vibrational energy. A completely accurate description of the protein would have allowed each of its bonds to exist in a complex superposition of several different eigenstates at once, a state that possessed no definite angles and energies, but only probabilities for a spectrum of different values. Ultimately, the protein as a whole would be seen as a superposition of many possible versions, each with a different shape and a different set of vibrational modes. However, to do this for a molecule with more than ten thousand atoms would have meant keeping track of an astronomical number of combinations of eigenstates, far beyond the capacity of any existing hardware to store, let alone manipulate. So it was routine practice for the most probable eigenstate for each bond to be computed, and from then on taken to be the only one worth considering.

The trouble was, when the São Paulo protein was bound to DNA, many of its bonds had two main eigenstates that were equally probable. This left no choice but to select the state of each bond at random: the software tossed several thousand dice, and singled out a particular conformation of the molecule to analyze. And in the first test-tube experiments, nature had appeared to be doing virtually the same thing: when the strands of DNA had been copied with random errors, SPP had seemed to be merely amplifying quantum noise when it chose a different base to add to the new strand. But the near perfect copying of the fruit pigeon chromosome, and the successive intergenerational changes in the DNA from the Suresh butterfly specimens, showed that something far subtler was going on.

The crucial subtlety, Furtado claimed, was that none of the probabilities that controlled the shape of the protein really were precisely equal. One or the other would always be favored, though the balance was so fine that the choice would depend, with exquisite precision, on the entire quantum state of the strand of DNA to which the protein was bound. Furtado conjectured that SPP was exploiting this sensitivity to count the numbers of various "counterfactual cousins" of the DNA: similar, but non-identical sequences that *might have been* produced in its place, if only its recent history of random mutations had been different. If the most numerous cousins dictated the sequence of the new copy of the DNA, that explained why the mutations weren't random, why they never killed or disadvantaged the organism. They'd been tested, and found to be successful: not in the past, as Grant had hypothesized, but in different quantum histories.

Prabir looked up from the notepad. "I don't know what to say. Nobel prize–winning physicists have been throwing rotten fruit at each other for a hundred years over interpretations of quantum mechanics, and as far as I know they're still at it. Nobody has ever resolved the issues. If Furtado thinks the Many Worlds Interpretation is right, there's a long list of famous physicists who'd back him up, so who am I to argue? But drawing information from other histories is something different. Even most believers would tell you it could never be done."

Grant said, "That's pretty much my own feeling." She leaned over to see how far he'd read. "There's some interesting speculation later on, suggesting the kind of data analysis the protein could be performing to extract the interference patterns between the DNA and its cousins from all the noise produced by thermal effects. If any of it's true, though, SPP must have evolved into a veritable quantum supercomputer."

Prabir scrolled down and glanced over the section she'd described; most of the equations were completely over his head, but there were passages of text he could follow.

Although the Hilbert space in which the pure states reside can not be reconstructed with certainty, it has been shown theoretically for simpler systems [Deutsch 2012, Bennett 2014] that an exhaustive search for global entropy minima over the unknown degrees of freedom can identify probable candidates in polynomial time by exploiting quantum parallelism.

Could a very bad quantum supercomputer have found a gene for a slightly better one? And so on? Furtado was claiming as much, but in the final section of the article he admitted that it was impossible to prove this directly; modeling any version of the São Paulo protein to the necessary level of precision was out of the question. He was, however, planning an experiment that could falsify his hypothesis: he was synthesizing a copy of one of the fruit pigeon chromosomes, right down to the methylation tags. This molecule would be identical to the biological chromosome in both its raw sequence of bases and every known "epigenetic" chemical subtlety, but its quantum state would not be correlated with that of the DNA in any living bird, real or counterfactual. If SPP copied this with the same low error rate as the natural version, Furtado's flamboyant theory would go down in flames.

"If this was true," Prabir mused, "it would explain a lot of things. You yourself admitted that Teranesia looked like a place where relatives of the locals, who'd parted company and co-evolved elsewhere, were being gradually reintroduced. If Furtado is right, that's exactly what's happened. Only they parted company when different mutations put them into different quantum histories, and they're being 'reintroduced' via a gene that goes out of its way to steal ideas from the most successful members of the family."

Grant smiled indulgently. "Explain the fruit pigeons, then. And the barbed-wire shrubs. What's going on with the camouflage, and the thorns?"

Prabir pondered this for a while. "It's a counterfactual defense. Once you have the São Paulo gene, you can block predators that have never even tried to prey on you, *in your own history*. And so long as you maintain the defense, they won't bother evolving in that direction, because they can see that there's no point. It's like a simple chess program: no elaborate strategies copied from grand masters, just the power to look ahead a few moves and assess the consequences. If brute force computation reveals a strategy—like castling, say—that gives a medium-term advantage over all possible moves by its opponent, the program will use it. And it will never reverse it, even if there's no immediate threat, because it can look far enough ahead to see that any back down would be exploited."

Grant was beginning to look slightly uncomfortable. "You don't seriously believe that's what's happening, though?"

"Absolutely not. He'll run the experiment on the synthetic chromosome, and prove himself wrong."

Grant made a halfhearted sound of agreement, as if she was afraid that excessive confidence might be tempting fate.

Prabir said, "I meant to ask you: did you get the results of the RNA analysis of the dormant adults?" The last he'd heard, it had been running overnight.

"Yeah. There's a peptide being produced that's virtually identical to a well-known hormone that puts the adults of certain temperate species of butterflies into diapause when they hibernate over winter. And the alteration in the texture and pigmentation of the wings seems to have followed from a cascade of gene activity very similar to one that happens in ordinary metamorphosis. It's all pretty much what I'd expected: just a few existing tricks redeployed."

"OK. But redeployed to what end? I know it's pointless now, because the adults have already laid their eggs externally, but could this be a throwback to a species that used to reproduce via parasitic larvae?" Maybe the gene resurrection idea could still be salvaged, after all.

Grant shook her head. "Not unless it's gone even more awry than that. The males are all doing it, too."

Prabir held the guardrail and pushed against it, trying to unknot his shoulders. "If the gene *didn't* start off as something every species has for mutation repair, we still have to account for its spread from the butterflies to everything else." He turned to Grant, smiling disarmingly, hoping she'd suffer a little more frivolous speculation. "Just for argument's sake: if Furtado was right, maybe the São Paulo gene saw this as an easy way to get copies of itself into the fruit pigeons."

Grant didn't respond immediately; Prabir assumed she was thinking up a suitably withering reply.

"I found something else in the RNA analysis," she said.

"Yeah?"

"Large amounts of an endonuclease—an enzyme for cutting and splicing DNA—being produced throughout the bodies of the dormant adults. I haven't characterized it any further yet—" She trailed off.

Prabir said, "But if it's the right kind of endonuclease, it might be perfect for the job of splicing the São Paulo gene into the genome of the fruit pigeons?"

Grant nodded, and continued reluctantly. "The fraction of DNA and endonuclease that survived digestion and entered the bloodstream would always be tiny, though I suppose it could be packaged in something like liposomes to protect it, and help it get absorbed by the wall of the gut. There's then another hurdle to get the gene into the ovaries or testes. This *might* be the transmission route, but the whole picture's not clear, by any means."

Prabir looked back across the water; he could still see Teranesia's volcanic cone in the distance. "Everything else could be a throwback, couldn't it? If mimicry was once used to get parasitic larvae into the fruit pigeons, then if the genes for that have been reactivated now, pointlessly, in egg-laying females, they might also have been reactivated in males—simply because the switch isn't functioning properly."

"I suppose so."

"And there are other uses for endonucleases, aren't there? It might be a coincidence that the endonuclease gene is switched on at the same time as the others?"

"It might."

Prabir laughed suddenly. "Listen to me. We've been to Teranesia, we've been to the source, and I expect everything to fall into place in a day. I've gone twenty-one years without an answer. I can wait a little longer."

He glanced down at the graphic of SPP in Furtado's article, which was cycling through sixteen of the conformations it could adopt, binding to each of the four bases in the old strand while adding each of the four to the new. Between them, these sixteen simple transformations could generate every conceivable change: as the old strand was broken apart and the new one constructed, the potential existed for the organism to become anything at all.

And from that limitless sea of possibilities, what marvelous inventions did the São Paulo gene pluck?

Those that made as many copies of the São Paulo gene as possible.

They reached the island of the mangroves and made use of the same approach as before, then sailed around the coast inside the reef. As they drew nearer to the point where the expedition had set up camp, Prabir saw that the fishing boat was gone, but another vessel had taken its place alongside the research ship.

They dropped anchor and waded ashore. They were halfway

to the camp when a young man appeared on the beach about fifty meters ahead of them, dressed in camouflage trousers, combat boots, and a Chicago Bulls T-shirt. He raised a rifle and aimed it at them, then barked out a series of commands in English.

"Halt! Put your hands on your heads! Squat down!"

They complied. The man walked up to Prabir and held the rifle to his temple. "What are you doing here? Where have you come from?" Prabir was too agitated to reply immediately, but as he struggled to relax his larynx sufficiently to speak he took some comfort from the realization that the man was probably not a pirate. Only a soldier would be so interested in their movements, and whatever misunderstanding was provoking his hostility would surely be easy enough to resolve.

Grant explained calmly, "I'm a biologist, this is my assistant. I have a permit from the government in Ambon."

The soldier's reaction to this last phrase was not encouraging. "Pig-fucking ecumenical heretics!" Prabir's heart sank. The man was not a Moluccan soldier: he was with the Lord's Army, West Papua's born-again Christian militia. Officially, they weren't even part of that country's armed forces, though it was widely assumed that they received clandestine government support. They'd been making trouble in Aru for years. But Aru was almost three hundred kilometers east.

"Where have you been?" the man demanded.

Prabir said, "On the other side of the island." If Teranesia's infamy had spread throughout the region, it might not be wise to admit to having visited the place.

"You're lying. Yesterday, there was no sign of your boat."

"You must have missed us. We were halfway into the mangroves."

The man snorted with derision. "You're lying. You come and see Colonel Aslan."

• • •

As they walked through the camp, Prabir saw three more armed men lounging around looking bored, and several of the expedition members standing nervously at the entrances to their tents. The biologists weren't exactly being guarded like hostages, but this was definitely not a guest/host relationship. There was no sign of Madhusree. Prabir kept telling himself that there was no reason for the soldiers to have harmed anyone, but nor was there any obvious reason for them to be here at all. Maybe there'd been a case that Aru should have joined West Papua at independence—even if that was now about as attractive a prospect as West Bengal being declared a part of Pakistan—but it was hard to imagine what kind of mileage the Lord's Army expected to gain for the cause by bullying foreigners deep in RMS territory.

The Colonel had taken up office in one of the expedition's supply tents; Prabir and Grant were made to stand and wait outside in the early afternoon sun. After twenty minutes, the soldier guarding them muttered something irritably in his native language and went and sat in the shade of a tree, his rifle propped up on one knee to keep it pointing vaguely in their direction.

Prabir whispered, "You do know who we're dealing with?"

"Yeah, yeah. I'll be on my best Sunday school behavior." Grant seemed more weary than afraid, as if this was just another tedious obstacle to get through, no different from slogging through the mangroves. But she'd traveled widely, so perhaps she'd grown accustomed to occasional periods of arbitrary detention.

"'Colonel Aslan'? Do you think he's a foreign mercenary? It sounds more like a name from central Asia than anything from around here."

Grant smiled, somewhat condescendingly. "I believe it's now a common choice upon conversion to Christianity all over the planet, at least when the evangelists get their hooks in early enough. Just don't admit to a fondness for Turkish delight, and you should be OK."

"Turkish delight?"

"Don't worry. It would take too long to explain."

A second young soldier emerged from the tent and shot a warning glance at their guard, who leaped to his feet. The two of them escorted Grant and Prabir into the tent, past drums of flour and boxes of toilet paper.

Colonel Aslan turned out to be a muscular Papuan man in his thirties, apparently devoted to the Dallas Cowboys. He was seated behind a desk improvised from crates. When Grant handed over her permit, he smiled graciously. "So you're the famous Martha Grant! I've been following your work on the net. You've been to the heart of the contagion, and returned to tell the tale."

Grant replied warily, "There's no evidence that the mutations are contagious."

"Yet these creatures turn up hundreds of kilometers away. How do you account for that?"

"I can't. It will take time to explain."

Aslan nodded sympathetically. "Meanwhile, my country and my people remain at risk from these abominations. What am I expected to do about that?"

Grant hesitated. "The impact on agriculture and health of flora and fauna transported across national borders by inadvertent human actions, or acts of nature, is the subject of a number of treaties. There are international bodies where these issues can be discussed, and any appropriate response coordinated."

"That's a very diplomatic answer. But there are boats weaving back and forth across the Banda Sea as we speak, without regard to anything some subcommittee of the World Health Organization might have to say on the matter in five years' time."

Grant said neutrally, "I can't advise you on this. It's beyond my expertise."

"I understand." Aslan nodded at the soldier from the beach, who led Grant out of the tent. Then he turned to Prabir.

"You accompanied her on this trip?"

"Yes."

"Did you fornicate with her, on the boat?"

Prabir was unsure for a moment that he'd heard correctly. Then he replied icily, "I'm not familiar with that dialect of English."

Aslan was indulgent. "Did you have sexual intercourse?"

"That's none of your business."

The soldier who'd remained took a step toward Prabir, holding up his rifle like a club.

Prabir stared down at the tent's mud-spattered ground sheet. *What was going on in these peoples' heads?* Were they looking for an excuse to brand Grant as promiscuous, so they could rape her with a clear conscience?

"No. We didn't have sex."

There was a long silence, then Aslan said calmly, "Look at me."

Prabir raised his eyes reluctantly.

"Are you a Muslim?"

"No."

Aslan seemed disappointed; maybe he'd been hoping to demonstrate his sophistication in the presence of the enemy. "Then I won't ask you to swear on the name of the Prophet. But you're a healthy young man, and she is a very charming woman."

"She is a *virtuous married woman*."

"But you took advantage of her? You raped her?"

Prabir was about to offer an outraged denial, when he realized that there'd be no end to this until Aslan had an explanation for his discomfort at the line of questioning. He looked him in the eye and said, "Why would I want to? I'm homosexual."

Aslan blinked bemusedly, and for a moment Prabir wondered if he only knew derogatory terms and Biblese. Then he spread his arms and proclaimed joyously, "Hallelujah! *That* can be cured!"

Prabir muttered, "Not half as easily as Christianity."

The soldier beside him swung the rifle butt into his temple. Prabir reeled, and fought to keep his balance. But the blow hadn't been heavy, he wasn't even bleeding.

"You can cut off a man's cock," Aslan declaimed, "but you can't cut out his soul."

Prabir was sorely tempted to improvise a maximally offensive rejoinder involving kuru and Communion wafers, but it didn't seem worth the risk of discovering that this homily was actually a recipe for surgical intervention.

Aslan said mildly, "Get him out of here."

Prabir was led to another tent, where the expedition member who'd examined him after the python attack—he thought he remembered Ojany calling her Lisa—took a blood sample from him. She was clearly acting under duress as much as he was, but he'd rather she stuck the hypodermic in his arm than have one of the Lord's Army do it.

Another soldier, closer to Aslan's age, took the sealed tube of blood from her and spiked it onto the input nozzle of a robust-looking machine that resembled nothing so much as a field radio in a World War II movie. Well, not quite: it had an LCD flatscreen in the lid, like an old laptop computer. The soldier hit some buttons, and the machine began to whir. Prabir glanced down at the markings on the case, and saw the acronyms NATO and PCR. NATO had been the U.S. imperial force in Europe, PCR was polymerase chain reaction. It was an old army surplus genetic analyzer, presumably designed to detect traces of DNA from biological weapons. But its current owners could have cut and pasted any sequence they liked into the software, and it would have happily purred away and spat out the necessary primers and probes.

They were testing his blood for the São Paulo gene.

Prabir felt a surge of panic—*What did they know that he didn't?*—then grew calm again almost immediately. A medical officer in the Lord's Army could grab a sequence of codons off a web page as easily as anyone; it didn't mean they'd found evidence of human effects. They were merely paranoid about contagion. And if passing this witchfinder's test meant ceasing to be of interest to them, so be it. Grant would pass, he would pass. Everyone in the expedition had surely passed already.

Prabir was allowed to join Grant and a dozen of the expeditioners, who were eating lunch under an awning. Cole and Carpenter were with them, but the businessmen seemed to have left with the fishing boat. A soldier sitting on a fuel drum in the corner looked on listlessly; compared to burning Muslim villagers out of their homes in Aru, this could hardly be a stimulating tour of duty.

Prabir approached Seli Ojany, who was standing with a small group of people beside a crate covered in plates of sandwiches. He caught her eye and whispered, "Do you know where my sister is?"

Ojany put a finger to her lips, then pretended she'd been wiping off bread crumbs. It occurred to Prabir belatedly that half the expedition could have been out in the field when the Lord's Army arrived, and some of them would have had the opportunity to see what was happening and stay away. It wasn't an entirely comforting thought; Madhusree would probably have been safer in the camp than in the jungle, unless there was some brutality going on here that he'd yet to observe.

Prabir glanced at the soldier, but he didn't seem to be paying them much attention. "So what's brought the Inquisition here?" he asked. "Are there really that many animals turning up in West Papua?"

Ojany gestured at a colleague beside her. "Mayumi heard the story closer to firsthand."

"Not animals in West Papua," Mayumi said, "but there were some fishermen who went to Suresh Island." Prabir did his best to accept this casual use of his parents' name; it seemed Madhusree had put them on the map forever, pinning their memories to the spot. "They came back to Kai and ran amok in their own village; most of them were captured, but one of them escaped and ended up on Aru. That seems to be why the LA got interested."

"What do you mean 'ran amok'? What exactly did they do?" Prabir was hoping for some solid evidence at last to write this off as the result of a psychotropic plant toxin.

Mayumi shrugged. "The Kai islanders who were here earlier wouldn't tell me. And the LA aren't exactly forthcoming either."

Deborah, one of Madhusree's friends whom Prabir had met earlier, responded impatiently, "Forget what the Lord's Army think: we *know* from the fruit pigeons and the butterflies that the São Paulo gene can cross between species. We can't assume that we're immune to that posibility, so we have to stop taking risks. At the very least, we should quarantine Suresh Island. Maybe even sterilize it, if it comes to that. You wouldn't need to use an atomic weapon: just enough herbicide to kill all the vegetation, so the whole food chain collapses."

Ojany said, "But what if that increases selection pressure for a version that can cross into marine species?"

"If Furtado is right—" Mayumi began, at which point almost everyone in earshot groaned. *"If Furtado is right,"* he persisted, "it would do a lot more than increase selection pressure. Any avoidable risk of extinction would only sharpen the contrast between favorable and unfavorable mutations: if every surviving counterfactual cousin would have moved into the sea, the strategy would become impossible to miss. It would be like herding the gene straight into a new ecosystem."

Deborah glanced at her watch and predicted, "In less than twenty-four hours, we'll be able to stop worrying about Furtado." Prabir looked at her inquiringly; she explained, "The Lausanne team have gone ahead and started the synthetic chromosome test themselves. The verdict will be out by about noon tomorrow, our time."

Cole, who'd been hovering at the edge of the group, interjected urbanely, "All this fear of 'contagion' would be put swiftly to rest, if you took the trouble to consult my seminal text on ambivalence toward the natural world, *M/Other*. My analysis of the relevant cultural indices across a time span of several centuries reveals that the predominant passion changes cyclically, from deep filial affection to pure xenophobia and back. Pastoralism, industrialism, romanticism, modernism, enviromentalism, transhumanism, and deep ecology are all products of the same dynamic. The anxiety in the midst of which we stand at this very moment is a stark validation of my thesis, whereby the nurturing, enfolding presence of the mother is radically reinterpreted, psychically transmuted into a threatening, disempowering, even alien force. But this perception will not endure. In due course, the pendulum will swing back again."

Prabir had been watching Carpenter while Cole spoke; there'd been an encouragingly troubled expression building on his face. Some of the biologists followed Prabir's gaze, until everyone in the group was looking at the student, waiting for his response.

Carpenter began tentatively, "If this gene *does* spread, wouldn't it be neat, though? All the animals would evolve: they'd grow hands, and opposable thumbs, and we could talk to them. And if it happened to us, too, we'd become telepathic. That's the next level, right? And why keep it out of the ocean? What's wrong with you people? Don't you want the reefs to dream? The super-dolphins won't stop us surfing. They'll be our friends!"

Prabir detected movement in the corner of his vision; he turned to see the medical officer and two junior soldiers approaching.

The medical officer addressed him. "Come with me, please."

"Why?" Prabir looked around for support. "You've taken a blood sample, what more do you want?"

"This is for your own protection," the man insisted blandly.

"*What* is for my own protection?" Prabir caught sight of Grant, who was watching with an expression of alarm. But she gave him a reassuring glance, as if to say that she hadn't abandoned him, that she'd be working to get him out of this.

The medical officer said, "You're infected. You're going into quarantine."

Chapter 14

Prabir had expected to be placed under guard in a tent at the edge of the camp, or perhaps imprisoned in a cage built from rough-hewn branches tied together with rattan—the kind of thing they always seemed to be able to construct at short notice in movies, whenever someone on a tropical island needed to be restrained. What the Lord's Army did instead was trash the control console of Grant's boat, dispose of all the pigeons, butterflies, and blood samples in a bonfire on the beach, steal Grant's rifle and tranquilizer gun, and lock Prabir in the cabin. They posted one sentry on deck and another on the beach.

Prabir sat in the captain's chair in front of the ruined console, swinging the seat slowly back and forth. The ancient PCR machine might have malfunctioned. Or it might have amplified nothing but a fragment of plant DNA that had entered his bloodstream through a scratch from a barbed-wire shrub. A foreign cell in the process of being taken apart by his immune system wouldn't even have been replicating, let alone creating germ cells through meiosis—the prerequisite for the São Paulo gene to be expressed. Whatever the powers of SPP in the right context, an inert copy of its gene was just another piece of junk to be scavenged, broken down, and recycled.

The gene *had* found ways to cross between other species,

though; he couldn't pretend it was unthinkable that it had breached his body's defenses. He'd been cut, scratched, bitten, and glued by half a dozen kinds of Teranesian plants and animals, and handled dozens more with broken skin. The gene might not have created a transmission route specifically for humans, but having been exposed to so many different mechanisms tailored for other animals, he could have been infected with a viable copy by sheer bad luck.

What did it do when it succeeded? Headed for the place where germ cells were made, carrying an endonuclease to incorporate itself into the genome. What was the worst possible scenario, then? His sperm would all carry the São Paulo gene, their DNA would be rewritten by the protein. But if there was any risk of transmission through sex, he could always learn to use condoms—and if he ever wanted a genetic child, that could be done almost as easily with another cell type in place of sperm. If it was warranted, he could even have new testes grown for transplant from a single uninfected skin cell.

That was not the worst scenario. *What had the fishermen done in their village?* And why had Aslan been so ready to accuse him of rape? Could a gene that was switched on only in the stem cells that manufactured sperm influence sexual behavior? Testosterone was made by other cells nearby; perhaps SPP could rewrite the genes of spermatocytes in such a way that they emitted chemical signals to enhance the secretion of testosterone by their neighbors. If the level in the blood had been cranked up sufficiently, could that alone have transformed the fishermen into rapists? It wasn't completely far-fetched; body builders had once gone psychotic from injecting similar hormones. The progression would not be inevitable, though: there were drugs that blocked testosterone. And again, in the longer term a transplant could dispose of the affected cells entirely.

Still not the worst. *Why had he tried to make love to Martha?*

Because she'd saved his life, and he'd imagined she'd welcome it? Because he'd wanted to be comforted any way he could, after facing the kampong? Because a surge of testosterone and a lack of alternatives had been enough to overwhelm both his nature and his judgment?

He had no end of rationalizations, no end of excuses. But the worst scenario was that none of them had really been enough. If the gene could gauge the reproductive consequences of everything it did, it might "sense" the fact that it was in a cul-de-sac, and find a way to change that. If Furtado was right, once the gene was active, whatever it was physically capable of doing to his brain or body that would lead to it counting more copies of itself *would be done*.

At dusk, they brought him a meal. The sentry ordered him to the far side of the cabin then left the plate inside the door. Prabir tried to think lustful thoughts as he ate, but the situation was not conducive. What was he hoping to do: assay his sexuality by introspection, hour by hour, like a diabetic monitoring blood sugar? What had happened with Grant proved nothing, except that strong emotions could breach a barrier that he'd come to think of as inviolable.

It did not prove that the São Paulo gene was in the process of tearing it down.

Later in the evening, as the sentries were changed, Colonel Aslan appeared on the moonlit beach. Prabir stood by the cabin window watching him. They both wanted the same thing: for the São Paulo gene to be contained, for the risks to humans to be minimized even if the gene itself could not be eliminated. The only problem was, Prabir was still hoping to fall on the right side of the line when the abominations were incinerated, but the Colonel might have some trouble with his criterion for judging that.

"We are praying for you," Aslan announced. "If you repent, you will be forgiven. You will be healed."

"Repent of *what*?" Prabir demanded angrily.

Aslan seemed to take pleasure in refuting the assumption that he had a one-track mind. "All your sins."

Skin crawled on Prabir's arms. What would it be like, to believe in a God as corrupt as that? But if his parents had been floating in fairy-floss heaven, there would have been a whole lot less to forgive. Lying about death was the only way these elaborate pathologies remained viable; all the milksop Christian sects that diverged from the dominant strain and embraced mortality with a modicum of honesty soon withered and vanished.

He called back, "What happened to the fishermen? Were they forgiven? *Were they healed?*"

Aslan replied, "That is between them, and God."

"I want to know what their crimes were, and how they died. I want to know what's in store for me. You owe me that much."

Aslan was silent, and too far away for Prabir to read anything from his face. After a moment, he turned and walked away along the beach.

Prabir shouted after him, "You can stop praying: I can already feel the power of the creator inside me! *That's who you're fighting, you idiot!* After four billion years, the old donkey's finally woken up, and he's not going to keep on carrying any of us the way he used to!"

By two A.M., Prabir felt tired enough to sleep. He had nothing to gain from vigilance, and he knew that if he didn't grab at least a couple of hours he'd lose whatever judgment he had left. He lay down on Grant's bunk; the air moved far more freely out in the cabin than in his allotted corner. He could still smell her sweat on the sheets, though, and the scent conjured up images of her, vivid memories of the night before.

He rolled off the bunk and stood in the darkness. He was

becoming paranoid. He'd never been repelled by the thought of sex with women, merely indifferent, and despite all his failed, dutiful attempts in adolescence, he might yet simply be bisexual. Either way: he loved Felix, and nothing would change that. Their history together, brief as it was, had to count for something. He was not a tabula rasa, he was not an embryo.

If his brain could be melted and rewired, though, anything could change. It wasn't just his sexuality at stake: the human species was riddled with far stranger compromises, any of which the São Paulo gene might find superfluous. Most of evolution had been down to luck; apart from the first few hundred thousand years of simple chemical replicators, there'd never been an opportunity for every physically possible variation to compete. At every step, chance and imperfection had created organisms with outlandish traits that would not have been favored by a comprehensive exploration of the alternatives. Complexity had ridden on the back of success, but if the efficiency of the process had been tightened a few more notches, single-celled organisms—still the most successful creatures on the planet—would never have bothered to become anything else. The São Paulo gene wasn't that farsighted, it hadn't dissolved every bird and butterfly into a swarm of free-living bacteria. But if it was allowed to reshape the evolutionary landscape for humans, many more things would vanish than the oxbow lakes.

Prabir heard a dull thud outside the cabin. He peered out onto the deck. The soldier had slumped to his knees; as Prabir watched, he keeled over onto his side.

The sentry on the beach was still standing, facing the jungle, oblivious to his comrade's fate. Prabir searched the moonlit water, but the cabin was so low that the deck hid most of the view near the boat. The sentry reached back as if to slap away an insect, then staggered. Prabir couldn't see the dart in his neck, but it

could not have been a bullet. Grant must have borrowed a tranquilizer gun, but what had she loaded it with to have such an
effect? *Strychnine?*

The man collapsed facedown in the sand. Grant would probably search him—and it seemed unwise to shout out to warn her
not to bother—but neither sentry had the key to the boat: Prabir
had seen it passed from hand to hand when his meal had been
delivered, it had been brought from the camp and taken back
again. There was no point both of them wasting time; he tried his
strength against the door of the cabin, but neither the lock nor the
hinges gave any sign of yielding. He picked up a stool and
bounced it repeatedly against a window, hoping to flex the pane
enough to snap the rivets that held it to the frame; the assault was
gratifyingly silent, but completely ineffectual.

Someone tapped a staccato rhythm on the window on the
other side of the cabin. He put down the stool and turned.
Madhusree called out softly, "I'm told you can slide this one open
from the inside."

Prabir approached her. She was dripping wet, her hair tied
back, long bare limbs catching the moonlight. She hadn't seemed
so beautiful to him since the day she was born, and all the reasons
were reversed now: her vulnerability, her ungainliness, her bewil-
derment, had all been replaced by their opposites. His parents
should have seen this transformation, not him, but he savored the
sweet kick in the chest, unearned or not.

He said, "I don't want to infect you. You'd better get off the
boat."

Madhusree sighed. "Are you sneezing? Are you covered in
pustules? What's it going to do, launch missiles? It's a molecule,
not a voodoo curse. If you want to be careful you can stand away
from me, but I need to come into the cabin and check out the
equipment."

Prabir was mystified. "Why?"

"So I don't waste time bringing things from the other boat."

"What are you talking about?"

Madhusree grimaced with impatience. "I don't know what we'll need. Martha said I could take whatever's working from here, so it will help if I know what that is. Now open the window."

Prabir complied, then retreated to the far corner as she climbed into the cabin and began inspecting the rack of biochemical instruments. The soldiers had attacked the autopilot with a crowbar, and taken away everything organic to be burned, but they seemed to have left these machines untouched.

"You've spoken with Martha?"

"Yeah, through the wall of a tent. She couldn't get away herself, but it's not exactly maximum security back there. They've got poor Dr. Sukardi tied up somewhere and guarded round the clock, but they seem to think that's all that matters, as if he's our own little tinpot Colonel and we're all helpless drones without him."

Madhusree had a tranquilizer gun tucked into the back of her shorts. Prabir asked nervously, "What was in the darts?"

She replied almost absentmindedly, "The normal sedative, but I added something to wreck the catalytic portion. It's a self-degrading molecule, that's why it's safe to use on so many species: half of it forms an enzyme that lyses the whole thing into harmless junk in the presence of ATP, so it doesn't require anything fancy in the organism to detoxify it. But it breaks itself down so quickly once it enters the bloodstream that if you disable the enzyme, it makes a huge difference: the potency goes up a thousandfold." She turned to him and added pointedly, as if she'd finally realized what he'd been fearing, "We have enzymes in the liver that can deal with it, though. It's still not toxic to humans."

She finished her inventory. "OK, this is great. You start

unmounting these and stacking them on the deck. I'll go and get the inflatables. I should be back in about ten minutes."

Prabir said, "I must be slow, but I think I'm missing something. Where are we going with all this? What's the plan?"

Madhusree smiled, proud and conspiratorial, as if Amita might walk in at any moment and ask why they were whispering.

"What do you think? We're heading south."

Prabir followed his instructions while Madhusree swam out to the expedition's ship. Then he checked the sentry curled up on the deck; the man was still breathing, slowly and deeply.

He stood and waited for Madhusree to return. Simply by traveling with her, he'd endanger her to some degree. But Grant had remained uninfected, after handling every Teranesian species he'd touched himself, after they'd kissed. With no one to keep him grounded he'd let his imagination run wild: the only hard facts were that a trace of the gene had been found in his bloodstream, and the fishermen had changed in some way that nobody wanted to talk about.

Madhusree appeared from behind the ship, rowing a bright orange inflatable dinghy toward him, with a second one in tow, loaded with cargo. For one awful moment, Prabir wondered if she planned to get to safety under human power alone, but both dinghies had outboard motors, she was just minimizing noise. He looked back toward the camp; the sentries had been changed around ten P.M., and it was now nearly twenty to three. In the moonlight, the orange polymer might as well have been fluorescent. Would they have until dawn, or just till the hour, to vanish over the horizon?

Madhusree brought the dinghies up against the boat. "Hand those down to me, one at a time."

Prabir passed her the first of the machines. "What's this all for?" There were already half a dozen identical silver boxes in the second dinghy, as well as bottles of reagents, and four large fuel cans.

"To monitor you, of course. And treat you, if necessary."

"Are you serious?"

"I hope it won't be necessary. I'm hoping nothing will happen before we reach Darwin."

"*Darwin?* If the Australians get the slightest idea of what I'm carrying, they'll lock me in a hut in the middle of the desert on top of their nuclear waste dump."

"No, they'll deport you back to Canada in a military jet with biohazard containment facilities, then send you the bill. I can think of worse fates if we head in other directions."

Prabir said, "What exactly is it you're hoping won't happen en route?"

"If I knew that, we'd be traveling lighter." She slid the last machine into place between the others and tested the whole pile for stability. Then she tossed him a life jacket; she was already wearing one herself. "OK. Get in."

"I'll ride in the back."

"You just don't want to help me row."

Prabir climbed over the guardrail and lowered himself into the second dinghy. He was afraid it would sink perilously low, but the air-filled walls gave it a lot of buoyancy and his weight barely made a difference. The tide was high, and Madhusree seemed to have crossed right over the submerged reef on her way in, without bothering to steer any special course.

She began rowing them laboriously toward the open sea. "Remember Orr, in *Catch 22*?" she asked cheerfully. "He rowed a lifeboat all the way to Sweden."

"I remember." He'd given her the book for her eleventh birthday. "But I take it we're going to stop at Yamdena and hitch a ride in something more seaworthy?"

"That's the plan. I wouldn't want to cross the Arafura Sea in these things."

Prabir was silent for a while, then he said, "Are you angry with me?"

Madhusree laughed. "How can I be angry? Not only do I have the first authenticated specimen of a Teranesian mammal, I have exclusive access to all his biochemical data. I'll be able to spin this into a Ph.D., for sure." She turned to him without missing a stroke and said, "We should have done all of this differently. You should have come along as part of the expedition. We should have been open about everything from the start. But it doesn't matter now. Their work's been acknowledged, and someone will complete it. That's good enough for me."

They were well past the reef, but still in easy sight from the beach. Madhusree's arms were trembling from fatigue; she'd swum several hundred meters before picking up the oars. Prabir said, "Swap places, I'll do some rowing."

"OK."

They swam between the dinghies; it was easier than trying to leap across the gap without landing on something. Prabir took the oars and settled into a rhythm. The emptiness ahead of them, the useless stars, the circle of moonlit water that followed the boat, were all the same as they'd been eighteen years before.

He struggled to stay in the present. "How many people are hiding in the jungle?"

"Ten, now."

"So what are they going to live on?"

"It's not that hard to smuggle out food. Anyway, we've already sent word up to Ambon; the situation should be resolved in a couple of days. I gather that it's all a matter of diplomats calling in favors, until one of West Papua's major aid donors agrees to apply some muscle. I know that sounds horribly convoluted, but it's probably a lot safer than Ambon sending in a warship."

"Yeah. Can you see anything happening back on the beach?"

Madhusree had brought a pair of binoculars. "That guy's still lying where he fell." She added teasingly, "Still glowing at body temperature."

"I never thought you'd killed them," Prabir protested.

"You're a bad liar."

"Martha might have. Not you."

"You don't think I'm commando material?" Madhusree sounded disappointed.

"I certainly hope not." He glanced over his shoulder at her; she was grinning. She didn't remember the soldier in the grass, bleeding slowly to death. He joked, "I knew I should have never let you take up *muay thai*. All that brutality. You've been scarred for life."

After a while they swapped places again. Prabir looked back with the binoculars in IR mode, waiting not only for the prone soldier to vanish, but for the haze of distortion above the water to swallow the entire beach.

"You can start the motor."

Madhusree hit the ignition and her dinghy shot forward, pulling the connecting rope taut. The motor was running on diesel, but it was so quiet that Prabir almost wept. They could have fired it up half an hour ago; they'd been making more noise just by talking.

"Do you think they'll come after us?" she asked. "It might not be hard to guess the right direction."

Prabir said, "I don't know if I'm worth the trouble to them. As long as I'm not heading for their country, I'm someone else's problem now."

• • • •

The dinghy's outboard motor had its own GPS, its own inertial navigation, its own autopilot. Madhusree zeroed in on their chosen destination on a map displayed on a small panel, confirmed the choice, then left the machine to steer. The only thing not automated was obstacle avoidance; they'd have to take over manually if they ran into shipping, and with any luck that would mean cutting the motor and waiting to be rescued, not swerving wildly to avoid getting mowed down.

As dawn approached, she tossed Prabir a plastic-wrapped hypodermic. "If you're going to be paranoid, you'll have to take your own blood samples."

"Urgh. This should be fun." He tore open the packet; there was a disinfectant swab enclosed, like an airline's miniature scented towel. He pulled off his belt and tightened it around his left arm. "I feel like a drug addict."

Madhusree shook her head despairingly. "Junkies use sonics now: transdermal acoustic delivery systems that make the skin permeable to small molecules like opiates. There's no risk of infection, because viruses are too large to get through. How do you think hepatitis C got wiped out?"

"I knew all that," he lied. He applied the swab then slid the needle carefully into the crook of his elbow, but the dinghy lurched just as he was applying pressure, and the needle transected the vein. "Fuck." He steeled himself, then tried again at a different point; this time the blood spurted satisfyingly into the low-pressure sample tube. "How often do we have to do this?"

"Every couple of hours at first, just to see what's going on."

Prabir left the hypodermic in place and flung the tube of blood across to Madhusree. A valve had shut off the flow automatically, but it was awkward trying to stop the needle slipping out. "Have you got some tape or something? I might as well keep this in."

"Good idea. There's an anticoagulant coating on the needle,

so it won't clog up. But you knew that, of course." She tossed him a packet of Band-Aids.

"What are you looking for? In the samples?"

"Levels of the gene, tissue types affected." Madhusree tinkered with one of Grant's silver boxes until it emitted an encouraging boot-up chime.

"Tissue types?"

She fed the blood to the machine. "If the gene is being incorporated into various kinds of cells in your body, occasionally one will break free and end up in your bloodstream. If I sort the cells with flow cytometry before bursting them and probing the DNA, I can track what's happening."

Prabir said, "It should only be in my testes, though, shouldn't it? I mean, it has a promoter that will only switch it on during meiosis, so why bother incorporating anywhere else?"

The machine began whirring. Madhusree looked up and said encouragingly, "I hope it hasn't even got a hold there. We'll probably never know how it got into your bloodstream, but it certainly hasn't come to you via another mammal, so its past experience is of limited relevance. Nothing works the first time in a new environment."

"You don't believe in Furtado's theory, then?"

She laughed and said flatly, *"No."*

Prabir didn't challenge her to provide her own explanation; he didn't want to derail her, he didn't want to erode her confidence. She'd track the gene through his body, and they'd fight it. However it worked, whatever it did.

When the sun cleared the water there was no land in sight, though Prabir could see Teranesia's peak to their west through the binoculars. Straight ahead he saw nothing but sea. They wouldn't reach Yamdena till midnight.

Madhusree said, "First results. Are you ready?"

"Yeah."

"The São Paulo gene's been incorporated into spermato-genic stem cells, complete with the usual promoter."

Prabir nodded acceptingly. He'd been prepared for that, and however tainted it made him feel, a transplant could still rid him of the gene completely.

"But it's also present in dermal stem cells. With a different promoter."

"In my skin?" He stared at her, more baffled than alarmed. *"Why?"*

Madhusree shook her head. "I don't know."

Prabir looked down at his arms and hands; they appeared perfectly normal. He lifted his shirt above his waist. There was a glossy patch on his abdomen, a shiny purplish-black region the size of a large coin. He touched it warily. The surface of his skin felt the same as ever, but when he applied enough pressure to sense what lay beneath, instead of the usual springiness of muscle he met resistance from an object as hard as bone.

"It's solid. It's some kind of tumor." He was numb with revulsion. "Can you cut it out? Please?"

Madhusree said, "Stay calm."

Prabir removed his lifejacket and pulled off his shirt, almost dislodging the hypodermic in his haste; there were two more patches higher on his chest. He turned so Madhusree could see his back. "There are five," she announced. "About the same size."

"You could anesthetize me with the tranquilizer gun," he implored her. "They're not that deep. I won't lose much blood." The gene would still be in his body, but he didn't care. He wanted this visible, palpable sign of it removed.

"Are they causing you any pain? Any burning sensation? They could be completely benign."

"Benign?"

Madhusree held her hands up, pleading with him for cool-headedness. "If there's no pain or bleeding, they might only be replacing the normal dermis rather than invading other tissues. And if there's no inflammation, at least they're not provoking an autoimmune reaction."

Prabir took several deep breaths. He'd handled a peppering with shrapnel better than this. He said, "There's no pain, no inflammation."

"OK. I'll synthesize growth factor blockers tailored to the receptors the cells are expressing. That should at least stabilize them."

"You can do that?"

"Of course. It's a second-year lab project: Here's a cultured organ with an unknown tumor. Characterize the tumor, and stop it growing." Madhusree regarded him tenderly across the narrow channel of water. "You're going to be fine! We just have to be patient. We'll get to Yamdena, we'll get to Darwin, we'll get to Toronto. And then we'll fix you up for good."

As Madhusree worked on the growth factor blockers, the hard, shiny plaques beneath his skin grew thicker and larger. New ones blossomed, on his arms and legs and buttocks. The sensation of their presence when he moved was strange, but only rarely painful, and Prabir took some comfort from their uselessness; the São Paulo gene was behaving as stupidly and randomly as a virus blundering into a brand new host. Leprosy would have had about the same effect on his mating prospects. He'd hardly dared admit to the fear before, but as they'd left the island of the mangroves behind, he'd thought: *It could have the power to do anything. It could have the power to make me rape my own sister.*

It didn't. If the fishermen had been affected in the same way as him, they'd probably been hounded for their disfigurement by a superstitious mob, and merely tried to defend themselves. What had happened with Grant had just happened; he was tired of probing it for significance.

He lay back between the fuel cans and watched the blue water around them sparkling in the morning sun.

Just before eight o'clock, Madhusree threw him a plastic tube with a clear, oily preparation, still warm from the machine; the synthesizer, on request, had welded the tube closed. When Prabir placed it in the hypodermic's receptacle and hit the injection button, the various mating surfaces were sterilized by laser flash, then the tube was punctured at both ends and the contents driven into his vein.

He took another blood sample. Half an hour later, Madhusree had the results: the number of cells containing the gene had risen substantially, but that was hardly surprising given the visible evidence of his skin. If the blockers didn't work there'd be no hiding his condition by the time they hit Yamdena, but he'd given Madhusree his account details, so even if he was crippled she could summon enough money from the net to compensate for any squeamishness people might have about giving him a ride.

He watched her at the bow of their twin vessel, checking their position against her notepad's GPS to be sure that the motor was running true, scouring the horizon with the binoculars for landmarks, validating everything three different ways. He was not going to tell her: *You're carrying your parents' killer. You're saving a life that should not have been saved.* He couldn't pretend to untangle his own shame and cowardice at the thought of her knowing from his understanding of the effect the revelation would have had on her, but he didn't need to. He was not going to rob her of this feat. He was not going to corrupt it.

• • •

The data from his ten o'clock sample worried Madhusree. "Another line of dermal cells with different growth factors has taken over; I'll have to make new blockers. And there are traces—" She trailed off.

Prabir said, "Traces of what? No more tantrums, I promise." He joked lamely, "It's got me by the balls, how much worse can it get?"

"Traces of everything," Madhusree admitted. "Every cell type in your body that can be found in your bloodstream now has a small proportion bearing the São Paulo gene."

"Could that just be spillage? Whatever kind of cells the packaging around the gene is tailored for, mightn't it work inefficiently almost anywhere?" He was afraid, but he wasn't going to panic again. He was suffering from something like cancer. No one died of cancer in a day.

"I don't know." Madhusree's confidence was fraying. She was a nineteen-year-old biology student, and there was no reference site, no expert pathologist, no repository anywhere in the world with any real knowledge of what was happening to him. "I could synthesize antisense DNA," she said tentatively. "To bind to the transcripts from the São Paulo gene, maybe stop it being expressed."

Prabir's spirits soared. "OK! Let's try it!"

"I'll wrap it in lipids similar to the ones they use in gene therapy, but it won't get into every cell type."

"Some cells will get a dose, some won't. We'll have controls. What more can you ask for?"

Madhusree regarded him nervously. "It might have no effect. Sometimes the cell just chops up the oligonucleotides— the pieces of DNA—before they can interfere."

Prabir snorted, unimpressed. "They couldn't manage that with the São Paulo gene, could they? Will this have agonizing side effects?"

"I doubt it. But I can't be sure."

"No one can. This is all new."

"I'm out of my depth," she confessed.

He said, "It's my decision. Let's try it."

Madhusree synthesized and packaged the antisense DNA. Prabir injected it, followed by a new set of growth factor blockers. Then he sat back in the dinghy and waited.

The sun was high now, the heat was surreal. The boats see-sawed mechanically in the swell; it was like being strapped to some laboratory device for ensuring a thorough mixing of reagents. Prabir was amazed at the clarity of his senses, the sharpness to everything. It was the opposite of the suffocating blackness he'd felt when he'd willed himself toward death: in the bathtub in Toronto, in the swamp when he'd lost all hope against the snake, in the kampong as he'd strode toward the minefield. He thought savagely: *I am not going to die in front of her. It's not going to happen.*

His skin had begun to itch and chafe, so he'd removed his jeans; he was wearing nothing but shorts and his life jacket. As he tried to move his legs to shift position, he discovered that he couldn't. Where one ankle had rested on top of the other foot, the skin had glued itself together.

Prabir swore softly, and probed the weld with his hand. It seemed the plaques had broken through the skin above and merged, though he hadn't felt a thing. He almost didn't want to tell her, but he could hardly conceal it indefinitely. He called out, "Maddy!" When she turned, he smiled and raised his conjoined feet for inspection. "One of us might finally have to wield a knife, or I'm going to need crutches on Yamdena."

She leaned across the gap for a better look. Then her face contorted suddenly and she started weeping.

Prabir said, "*Hey!* Ssssh! Stop that!" He reached out a hand toward her face, not close enough to touch her, but the gesture alone made him feel as if they'd made contact.

He said, "You know what we're doing next year, to get away from Toronto? Now that we've joined the jet-setting class?"

"No."

"The IRA parade in Calcutta. You promised you'd help me pull the truck."

Madhusree looked away. "I don't remember that."

"You're a bad liar."

"Your skin grafts won't be healed."

Prabir shook his head, laughing. "You're not squirming out of this. I did the kebab skewer through my cheeks. You're helping me pull the truck!"

Prabir was unable to take the noon blood sample. The second set of growth factor blockers hadn't worked; the plaques had meshed and solidified across his shoulders, and though he could still bend his elbows, he didn't have enough movement overall for the task. Madhusree put on surgical gloves, stepped across between the boats, and pushed an empty tube into the hypodermic's receptacle.

She surveyed him unhappily. "It really doesn't hurt? It's beginning to look like acute psoriasis."

"It just itches a bit."

"Try to move as much as you can. I don't want you getting pressure sores from lying on one spot."

"I'll try. I don't think this stuff could form ulcers, though."

As she jumped back, Prabir said, "Hey! You know what we're missing? Radio Lausanne. The Furtado verdict."

Madhusree nodded unenthusiastically. She picked up her notepad and went to the Lausanne site.

Prabir couldn't read the screen, so he watched her face. Finally she admitted, "The synthetic chromosome came through randomized, like the test sequences. Not conserved, like the real one from the pigeon. So the theory hasn't been falsified." She regarded Prabir warily. "There might be something missing in the chemistry, though, something we can't characterize about the natural DNA. It took a long time to understand methylation tags. There could be another modification, even subtler than that."

Prabir said nothing, but he knew she was clutching at straws, the way he and Grant had when they'd first heard the theory and far too many things had fallen into place. Furtado was right: the gene could look sideways across a virtual family tree and quantify the usefulness of every potential change.

No treatment would ever destroy it. It couldn't literally foresee Madhusree's assault with the growth factor blockers and the antisense DNA, but it would always be prepared for whatever she injected, ready to make the best possible choice at the next replication.

It wouldn't kill him, though. His condition could not be an accident, a random side effect of the gene's naïveté in the body of a man. It had done this to him because it would benefit, somehow.

"How many tranquilizer darts do you have left?" he asked.

Madhusree was alarmed. "Why? Are you in pain?"

Prabir almost lied, but he said, "No."

He'd sworn he wouldn't die on the boat. How could he ask her to kill him, knowing what it would do to her?

But this would be different in every way. She would do it by choice, out of love. Not through stupidity and cowardice.

He explained calmly, "It wants to change me, Maddy. It wants to take me apart and build something new."

She stared at him, horrified. "I don't believe that."

"It's making a chrysalis. The covering is there to immobilize me, and it's started on all the other tissues now. It knows it's never going to have offspring if it leaves me unchanged, but all that's done is make it look further for ways to escape. It's found some kind of human cousin that undergoes metamorphosis. And I doubt there'll be anything left of me with the power of veto when I emerge as the reproductive stage."

Madhusree shook her head fiercely. "You're jumping to conclusions! You have a skin condition. An accidental product of the gene. *That's all.*"

Prabir said gently, "OK. Let's wait for the next results."

The fraction of infected cells had almost leveled off for his skin, but it had risen in every other tissue type. The antisense DNA had made no difference.

Madhusree added hurriedly, "I'll give you another dose. I'll change the lipid package."

Prabir agreed. "Give it one more try."

As she crouched over him with the vial, struggling to keep her balance on the swaying dinghy, Prabir said, "You know, if I'd been alone on the island when they died, I would never have left. I wouldn't have got away at all, without you to keep me going."

She said angrily, "Don't talk like that."

He laughed. "Like what?"

"You know exactly what I mean, you shit." Madhusree pulled the empty syringe away, refusing to look at him.

"You even hooked me up with Felix. I'd never have managed that alone."

"Don't, Prabir."

"If I ask you to do this, it'll be my responsibility. I can't stop it hurting you, but don't let it damage you."

Madhusree met his eyes; her face was burning with resentment.

He said, "No one in the world could have done more for me."

She spat back angrily, "How can you say that? You're already writing off everything I'm trying!"

He shook his head as far as he could; his neck was almost rigid now. "It might work, but if it doesn't, you have to be ready. You're going to have to be strong for more than this. The gene is going to try to take everything. All it cares about is reproducing. Everything that matters to *us*: love, honesty, intelligence, reflection . . . they're all just accidents. A few freak waves swept them up onto the beach. Now the tide's coming in, to wash them away again."

Prabir could see nothing but the cloudless sky. His sense of the heat of the sun was gone, and the motion of the boat had almost receded from consciousness. Fear and claustrophobia came in slower, deeper waves. He wanted more of everything. More knowledge, more friendship, more sex, more music. He wanted to see the revolution, he wanted to see the battle won. His sense of loss merged with the sense of confinement; he was buried alive and he could still see the sky. When the wave retreated he could almost laugh: he had nothing to fear from death now, he'd just been through the worst part of dying. A minute later, this observation was no comfort at all.

Madhusree moved into view. Prabir said, "At least it put the adult butterflies into diapause. You'd think it could cook up something for me."

"I'll tranquilize you now. Do you want that?" There wasn't much skin left where they could be sure of a dart penetrating, but the venous line was still open.

"Yeah. Then the rest of your supply. Then burn the body. Whatever fuel you can spare. Right?"

Madhusree nodded, almost imperceptibly.

Prabir said, "I'm sorry to put you through this, but there's no other way. Don't ever blame yourself."

She turned away. "Who'll pull the truck with me now?"

"What about Felix?"

She laughed. "Felix with hooks through his back?"

"He'd love it. He'd see fireworks with every step."

As she looked down at him, half-smiling, wiping away tears, something tore open behind his eyes and he was flooded with joy. It was everything he'd felt for Felix that was more than desire, everything he remembered inside himself as his father or mother had spun him in their arms, everything he'd seen on their faces, gazing up at him as they held him to the sky.

He didn't care anymore where it came from. He didn't care if he'd stolen it or not, earned it or not. If he loved her like this and she felt some part of it, it was not selfish, it was not evil, it was not dishonest. And however ancient it was, however mindless, he'd torn it out by its billion-year-old roots, dragged it into the full light of consciousness, and claimed it as his own.

He said, "Gather up the good things, and run."

As he heard the needle pierce the vial and felt the first cool touch of liquid in his vein, Prabir saw the sea from above. Madhusree leaned back, her hair flying in the wind, and cut the rope between them. She broke free and sped away, leaving the burning boat behind.

Chapter 15

Madhusree leaned over the side of the dinghy and vomited into the water. Her teeth wouldn't stop chattering. "I'm sorry, *bhai*, I'm sorry. I mess everything up. I fuck everything up." She checked again, but Prabir was still breathing. After six doses.

She fitted the last vial into the hypodermic. It was impossible. His brain should be flooded now, every tissue poisoned. Nothing could allow him to metabolize so much of it, so fast.

She hit the injection button then rocked back on her haunches, tearing at her hair. "I'm sorry, I'm sorry." She wiped mucus from her face onto her shoulder. She shouldn't touch herself with the gloves.

She waited, humming to herself, trying not to weep. Later. She'd mourn him later, when she'd done what he'd wanted.

She started sobbing. "Why did you follow me? Why did you come here? *You stupid shit!* I should have gone to the island. It should have been me."

She bent forward and touched the still human skin of his neck. Even through the gloves, she could feel its ordinary softness. His pulse had slowed, but it hadn't weakened. She lifted her hand to his nostrils, and felt the fine film of polymer quiver against her fingertips.

Nothing she pumped in would kill him. And even if that

wasn't true, she couldn't sit here trying poisons, dose after dose, until the thing metabolized the tranquilizer away so completely that Prabir woke, in agony from whatever she'd poured into his veins.

He couldn't be conscious, he couldn't be sensate. He was in the deepest of comas; he'd feel nothing. She tried to peel back one eyelid, but it was frozen in place. She turned away choking, her throat knotted. "I can't! I can't do it!"

She stared out across the sea, breathing deeply, trying to grow calm enough to finish this. If he lived through the metamorphosis, he would not be her brother. Worse, he'd not be anything he'd wanted to be. When the truth had become plain, she'd almost offered to follow him. *You don't have to do it alone. I'll inject some of your blood, we'll change together.* But then she'd realized that even if she'd meant it at the time, she would have backed out later. It was not impossible that the gene would give benefits to its host that they'd find worthwhile themselves, but she wasn't betting her soul on someone else's card game, however well it cheated for itself.

Not her own, and not Prabir's.

She turned without looking at him and picked up one of the fuel cans. She unscrewed the cap and tossed it into the sea. "OK, OK. He won't feel it."

She squatted down. He was still wearing the lifejacket; she couldn't stand the thought of the burning plastic clinging to him, even if the dinghy was made of almost the same thing. She undid the straps and pulled it off.

"OK. There now." She poured some diesel onto his chest.

Where the fuel touched the carapace, it blistered instantly, spitting a visible puff of vapor. Madhusree backed away, wailing with distress. "I'm sorry! I'm sorry!" She crouched at Prabir's feet, covering her head. "I can't do it! I've fucked up!" She drove the heels of her hands into her eyes, then started punching her forehead.

She waited to grow numb. Just for a few minutes, long enough to finish it. She hummed to herself. "You've gone into my head. You've gone into my memories."

That wasn't enough.

But it was more than the gene would leave of him.

She opened her eyes and stood up wearily. "OK. We'll do this together." She looked down; she could still recognize his face beneath the plaques. There was a blister full of gray fluid where the diesel had splashed his chest, but there was no blood in it. No Prabir. She didn't believe he'd felt any pain at all.

"Why did you take him? What do you want from us?"

Nothing at all. It had no purpose for anyone, no destiny. No journey in mind, no endpoint. It wanted nothing but itself. More of the same.

It didn't want him.

She'd been fighting it the wrong way.

She turned his frozen body over and searched his back. There had to be another blister, a boil, or a pustule, however tiny, in a place the fuel hadn't touched. Nothing was perfect, nothing. Some tiny fraction of the infected cells must have made the kind of mistake that let his body drag them to the surface in the hope of disposing of them.

Why hadn't the São Paulo gene hatched itself into a virus? Because a viral genome would be too remote to register as a cousin to any of its hosts, the changes required were too extreme. It thought it would lose by leaving his body; it thought it could only perish. All she had to do was prove otherwise—in a way that wouldn't give it the power to spread.

There. In a patch of real skin, a tiny boil.

Madhusree turned and leaped to the front dinghy, picked up

a fresh hypodermic and an empty culture flask, then jumped back. She squatted down and pierced the boil, then drew up a few milliliters of gray fluid. She squirted it into the culture flask, then leaped the gap again and filled the flask with growth medium.

"If you learn to come, I'll give you what you want. Just a couple of the right mutations, and you can surface like pus. My brother will do the work for you; you just have to surrender. I'll give you more of the same than you've ever dreamed of."

How much of his body weight did it actually have now? Five per cent? Three or four kilograms? She had enough medium to support about the same weight in tissue culture, for maybe half a day. Enough to distract it, enough to hold it in check.

If it was omniscient, she could never win: it would see beyond the lure and continue to reprogram his body for the greater long-term gain of reproduction. But any offspring it could produce that way were still hundreds of cellular generations into the future, a distant peak in a desolate landscape of extinction. It could see far enough to know that a burst of somatic cell division would simply kill its host: it had no choice but to find a way to make that host go forth and multiply. But once she offered it a path into a sheltered environment where it could feed and reproduce, cell by cell, without facing the same limits, a new feature would appear on the landscape of possibilities. A new peak, not as tall, but far closer.

She'd have to make that new peak as high as she could. High enough to draw the gene away from the route to freedom. High enough to hide Prabir's children.

She couldn't hope to do that with the supplies she had on board. But by midnight, she'd reach Yamdena. She could synthesize all the exotic peptides for the medium herself, the growth factors, the cell adhesion modulators. *What about the base, the matrix?* What could she make do with? Gelatin? Agar? She'd kick down the door of every shop in town until she found what she needed.

As they approached Darwin harbor, Prabir opened his eyes. He took in the sight of Madhusree, the culture flasks and pickle jars and other scavenged glassware spread all around her on the deck of the trawler, the needle drawing pus from his arm.

She asked him, "Are you in there? Is it still you?"

She watched his face. The skin was sagging and full of lymphatic fluid, where the cells of the carapace had stretched it before deserting his body for an easier life, but she believed she could read his expression in the tightening of the muscles below.

He drooled, "Calcutta. Next year. You're not getting out of it."

Madhusree wrapped her arms around him, shaking from exhaustion. "Welcome back."

She clung to him, selfish with joy, but she'd won back more than her brother. What had worked for him should work again, in the next infected human. They'd never be free of the gene, they could never hope to eradicate it. As long as they were made from DNA, as long as they were part of nature, they would remain vulnerable.

But they'd tricked it, this once.

They'd won the first battle.

Prabir said, "How? How did you do it, Maddy?"

She sat back and looked at him. He was grinning with amazement beneath the soggy mask, as if she were the one who'd risen from the dead.

"It was something you taught me. Something you learned from them." She reached down to stroke his forehead, then smiled.

"Life is meaningless."

Acknowledgments

Of the many sources I've drawn upon in writing this novel, I am particularly indebted to *The Malay Archipelago* by Alfred Russel Wallace (Oxford University Press), *The Spice Islands Voyage* by Tim Severin (Little, Brown), and the documentary *Guru Busters* (Channel 4), a portrait of the Indian Rationalists Association.